ANAGRAMS

Books by the author

Poetry

ANAGRAMS

A NOVEL BY DAVID R. SLAVITT

1971

DOUBLEDAY & COMPANY, INC., GARDEN CITY, NEW YORK

DRAWINGS BY RAYMOND DAVIDSON

Library of Congress Catalog Card Number 79–144299
Copyright © 1970 by David Slavitt
All Rights Reserved
Printed in the United States of America
First Edition in the United States of America

Let no man write my epigraph.

—George Garrett

to whom this book is dedicated

CHAPTER 1

Over the fear, the foolishness . . . Feeds? Too many 'f's. Foolishness!

He knew what he was doing. The prospect of the take-off made him nervous. Take-offs and landings both. He admired the calm of those travelers he had seen on other flights and the way they got onto planes, found seats, snapped open attaché cases, drew out vital papers or technical journals, snapped their cases and minds closed, and, with admirably sharp pencils, did calculations through the whole sickening business of the taxi-ing, the holding, and the rush forward, pausing only then, only when their heads were pushed back onto the headrests by the acceleration. And even then, for all he knew, they were still calculating. The probabilities of imminent death? Who knew?

His own attaché case was an old one, too thick to be stylish now, but good, given him when he had graduated six years ago (the initials near the handle fading now).

9

It lay on its side tucked underneath his seat. There were no technical journals for him, nor sales reports, nor lists of prospects, but only a copy of Aubrey's *Lives*, a copy of his own book, *The Double Agent*, and a sheaf of his new poems which he thought about now. He wondered why he had been so foolish as to take the only copies of the latest poems. There were the *brouillons*, of course, in his desk drawer at home, but he had made changes. The final versions were here, on the plane with him, and would be destroyed with him if the plane crashed into the bay, as so many seemed to be doing lately, or exploded in mid-air, or undershot the runway in Chicago. These 727's landed heavy, the reports had said. The casual grammar, like the expensive sports clothes of an executive out for an afternoon of golf, was a deliberate jauntiness intended to conceal only imperfectly the efficiency, the quiet competence—but what competence? The fuel lines of extruded something or other opened up on impact, spread gasoline all over, and whoosh! He thought with great regret of the loss of those poems. And of himself? Of course, but he would have to go sometime. The poems, had he not been so lazy, so stupid, could have survived.

Actually, he had deliberately refused to retype them, to leave them all in good order, safe in his Door-Store desk, because to have done so would have been to admit his fear and to tempt fate, the gods, God, to be as careful and precise as he and blow up the plane because he had made those preparations. It was like the life insurance machines into which he had never put a quarter for fear of collecting. He was lucky, had been lucky all his life. For lucky people to bet against themselves is ruinous.

Unable to read, unable to make more than the most perfunctory feints with his attention, unable to do anything but concentrate on the dangerous power of the plane, he fiddled with the line. *Over the fear, the foolishness sings like a bird* . . . Too damned many birds lately. They were becoming a positive tic, which he was too young to be able to afford. Still the idea of a bird, a jay, say, bright and annoying, scolding from a tree down at some blurred gray beast . . . Or silver? The wrecked plane. Morbid.

He looked out of the window, but the cruciform design of the plane did not leave much of a view. The transverse of the wing blocked everything but sky and a slice of the tired, windblown grass along the runway. He was in the middle seat of a row of three. He noticed the man between his own seat and the window. Brown suit, brown shoes. Shriner's scimitar in the lapel in diamonds and white gold. Or platinum? Ring. Flowered tie. Jerk.

Or, no, that was unfair. Snobbish and unfair. How did he know what this man was like? For all he knew, this brown blot might be a reader. The ideal reader. Gentle Reader of the old convention. They couldn't all be goddamned English professors, fluttery ladies, and crabbed graduate students. Somewhere, out in the heartland, drinking Seagram's Seven Crown and Seven Up, wearing brown suits and those shirt collars with metal spring stays, eating skinless franks, there had to be, here and there, readers.

He remembered the anagram game of the previous weekend. *Rare: reread: readers: dreamers.* Vicious game, he thought, but attractive. The fun of it was the way the words went through their permutations, changing, developing, as the players built them, stole them, and watched them get stolen back. The fortunes of the players varied, but the words only grew richer, fatter, more and more complicated. Something in that, somehow. A poem worked with anagrams in which the end words of all the verses were not rhymes but anagrams on earlier end words? No, stupid. Show off stuff. But why not? All poetry is. To dazzle, to amaze men in brown suits who, down at the lodge meetings, pound one another on the back and exclaim, "Judas Priest, but I read a goddamn fine villanelle this week! Really, A-number-one!"

"Izzat so?"

"The cat's very own pyjamas!"

All right, all right, so he was being snotty again. But, again, why not? Who had a better right to be snotty, having been more snotted, than the poet? As an act of contrition, however, he promised himself that he would speak to the brown suit, be friendly, at least offer friendliness . . . Motley to brownsuit, offering converse. He, Jerome Carpenter, had no personal complaint against the brown suit: he did not even resent the fact that the man was unlikely to have read his slender volume of verse. He assumed that. What bothered him was that the man read nothing—no poems, no prose, just scratched his ass and picked his nose.

But it was not so. Not at all true. The plane lumbered to the end of the runway, turned, graceless as a pelican, and then surged forward and struggled up. Jerome experienced a few moments of beautiful terror, during which the word *dentistry* flashed on his mind. The mental dentistry of something. And then the "No Smoking" stopped glowing, not only in his mind but on the little plaques throughout the plane. He took out a cigarette. So did brownsuit, who produced also a Zippo, and in front of Jerome's face, zipped it.

"Thanks, very much."

There, he had paid off his promise to himself. Had spoken. He was trying to imagine what else to say when brownsuit bent over, pulled his briefcase out from under his seat, and produced, improbably, a book. *The Web and the Rock.*

He saw Jerome looking at the title, and turned it to give him a better view. "You read Wolfe?" he asked.

"Oh, yes," Jerome said. It was partly true. He had read *Look Homeward Angel* years ago, in school, had started *Of Time and the River* a few years later, but had given up. Flabby. Prolix. And anyway, he hated Maxwell Perkins, inventor of writers, the editorial Stromboli, making his puppets perform. In England things are better arranged. The editor receives the manuscript and sends a note gratefully acknowledging receipt and diffidently inquiring about a comma on page 322.

"Great writer," said Brownsuit. "Last great American writer."

"Oh?"

"I thought Steinbeck would make it, once. But he pooped out. I don't care what the Finns say."

"The Finns?"

"They give the Novel Prize."

"Nobel?"

"Yes? Is that right?"

"Yes, and it's the Swedes."

"Makes no never mind to me."

The stewardess came down the aisle, inquiring about cocktails. Brownsuit offered to buy Jerome a drink.

"Scotch, please, with soda."

"One scotch, one bourbon, missy."

Missy! Well, maybe he was a Southern Finn.

"I'm reading my way through Wolfe all over again. Been at it for a year now. Since I retired. Used to be a chemical engineer . . ."

And on. He was a resident of Paradise, Kansas, and a graduate of Drexel Tech, which he now very much regretted, because he "had not had the liberal arts enough. And that's what it's by God all about. After all. Right?"

Jerome agreed. "Right," he said. He wondered whether he would be calling the stewardess Missy, when it came his turn to buy the next round.

"Mind if I ask what you do for a living?"

"Not at all. I'm . . . well, it's going to sound peculiar."

"No, never knock a man's livelihood, I always say."

"I'm a kind of a gambler."

"Never would have guessed. Cards?"

"Anagrams. I'm a professional anagrams player. I go around and get into the big games."

"Anagrams? Never knew there were any."

"In the colleges, mostly."

"Is that right?"

"Yup."

Jerome yawned. That way he could hide the grin. He didn't break, didn't crack up, which was pleasantly surprising, but he did have this idiotic grin on his face which

14

the yawn hid. What the hell had come over him? Of all the maniac things to have made up.

He made up more. It was not so difficult. The fooling around with words, but more than that, the sublime uselessness of the fooling around, the doing of it for its own sake only, with pride and ridiculousness, connected the vehicle with the tenor of the metaphor. To say that he was an anagrams player was to come closer to the truth than he ever could have done by invoking the faded gilt of the old, impossible claim, "I am a poet." One could as soon tell a man in the next seat in a plane, "I am a prophet."

"I've heard of the game," Brownsuit said, "but I don't recollect having played it. How does it work?"

Jerome explained, briefly, how one builds words from tiles in the middle of the table, and how one steals words. "I could take your 'anagrams', for instance, and turn it into 'grammarians' if I drew an R or an M or an I, and I could get the other letters from the table."

"Oh, well, okay then."

"I beg your pardon?"

"I mean, from what you tell me, it's a game of skill. And that's okay. You're a kind of a craftsman, really."

"You could say so."

Brownsuit was all right. It was not without some pleasure that Jerome called the stewardess and ordered another round of drinks, a bourbon for the Drexel Technician, and a scotch for himself.

"Well, to anagrams," the man said, raising his glass.

"And Tom Wolfe," Jerome returned.

He was all right. He was, after all, a reader, one of the

real readers a writer hopes for. A nut, of course, but what reader isn't? And the idea of finding a man, here and there, reading you after you were dead, thinking, for whatever fortuitous reasons, that you were the last of the great ones, and carrying your books around on planes, reading them in diners and cafeterias, and telling strangers about them and about you . . . What more could a writer hope for? Perhaps one day there would be some man in a brown suit reading Jerome Carpenter. And then, oh then, he would be a writer, would be able to think of himself as a writer, as a poet even. No, then he would be dead.

The trouble was that one is a writer only while sitting there at desk or table, lost in the manipulation of the words. And then it doesn't matter, for then the question does not come up. When one needs it, when a man asks, "Do you mind telling me what you do for a living?" when the time comes to fill in the blank for "occupation" when the world insists upon an identity, one is left with nothing. One has been a writer. One hopes to be a writer again. It is like the jumble of tiles, that was a word, and will be another, larger word, but is at the anagrammatic instant, nothing at all.

Still, it was truer at the moment than it usually was. He was on the plane, wasn't he, having been invited to Rockville College? With the invitation in his brief case, under the poems, they had conferred upon him the recognition that he wanted by inviting him to participate in the Festival of the Arts, hadn't they? It was a diploma, of a kind. Once it would have been something he could have waved in anyone's face, saying, "Here, see, here it is! That's what it says, and that's what I am. A poet!"

But it was too late for that. His book had been published and he no longer needed such cheap tricks. Besides, in an unexpected way, the invitation only made things worse. He was sure that at some point during the three day weekend someone would point a finger at him and cry out, "Fraud!" if only because he felt like one. All those girls, those eager, doe-eyed undergraduates, would be looking up at him, at the poet. He would laugh. Or they would. Maybe they would all laugh wonderfully together, dissolving into helpless, overheated waxworks, collapsing with the hysteria of it. Poet! Hahahaha! Hohohoho. Heeheeheeheeheeheeeee.

And the others? How did they do it? The other poets, novelists, short story writers who would be there had faced the same agonizingly trivial problem, and had found their solutions or their evasions. Most of them were safe and sound in colleges and universities, and in their niches in the physical and mental murings of their academies taught English or Creative Writing, or just sat "in residence," kept men and women, curiosities, like . . . like the capybara in the London Zoo, that huge rodent, a rat the size of a pig that lives in a dog house and eats whole lettuces. The American Men of Lettuce. But, wait, that was the beast! The fuzzy beast beneath the tree he'd put the jay on. *Over the fear, the foolishness, a jay . . .* scolding a capybara? Good God, all the animals were out now, roaming over Marianne's moor. Stop reading, he had told himself so many times. Stop reading poetry at least. At least until you have found your own voice, or have not found it but made it, bespoke speech. This

verse off the rack, this blarney from Barney's Boys' Town
. . . Well he was getting to be too old for it. Rimbaud
quit at nineteen. Went to Africa. To be a slave trader?
Or was that William Burroughs? Or Edgar Rice Burroughs? Better to go and be an anagrams player.

Quite inconsistently, he picked up his book, Aubrey's
Brief Lives, opened it at random, and started to read: "It
happened that G[eorge] W[ither] was taken prisoner, and
was in danger of his Life, having written severely against
the King, &c. Sir John Denham went to the King, and
desired his Majestie not to hang him, for that whilst G. W.
lived, he should not be the worst Poet in England."

He closed the book, keeping a finger in the place where
he had been reading. There would be that, too. Each of
them would be looking at one of the others and thinking,
"whilest he lives, I shall not be the worst Poet in English."
Terrible, the backbiting. Insecurity, that's what it was.
He stared at the cover of the book, and considered the
last word of the title. *Lives* could build to *silver* to *reviles*.
An ominous progression. It did not do to brood on the
meanings of the words. It was better just to let them be,
to let them lead their own lives as they would. He had
enough problems with his own.

He took the printed program of the three day festival
and tucked it into Aubrey, as a bookmark, but then took
it out again, and looked at it, running down the list of
names, carefully arranged in alphabetical order—except
for the last, Edmund Walter Hall. Who was Edmund
Hall? Jerome had never heard of him. Poet? He didn't
think so. Playwright? Librettist? *Peintre-graveur?* Scrim-
shaw whittler? He noticed that Edmund Walter Hall ap-

peared in a different type face from the other names, and then realized that he was a building. The chagrin dissipated almost instantly into vexation at the thoughtlessness of the typesetter, amusement at the error—his own and that which others would be sure to make—and regret for the brevity of the career of good old Ed Hall.

Over the loudspeaker system, the pilot, genial and reassuring, made his presence known. His welcome was a caricature of friendliness, but for all its deficiencies, good to hear. It was nice to know that there was in fact some human being up there in the front of the plane. "We'll be cruising at fifteen thousand feet," he said, and Jerome translated this, roughly, into miles, dividing by five thousand. Three miles, nearly. It did not bear thinking about. The pilot, Captain Angel, announced the temperature in Chicago, and the local time, and then admitted that there were fairly strong headwinds which would delay the ETA by as much as fifteen minutes, and he apologized. Jerome had been playing with the name, which sounded like a celestial rank. Captain Angel, General Angel, Throne, Power, Domination, and SUPREME COMMANDER. It was all peculiarly familiar. There was a movie, in which Claude Rains, or Cedric Hardwick had been some kind of angel. Or was it the other way around? Had it been a devil? Cary Grant had been an angel, once. And David Niven was the bishop. Absurd. But then he followed along, listening to the pilot's patter, and snagged on ETA, which took him a moment. It was an acrostic for . . . Yes, Estimated Time of Arrival. Lewis Carroll wrote acrostic poetry. And the psalmist. Again, show off stuff.

"Damn!"

"I beg your pardon?"

"We're going to be late. I'll miss my connection."

Brownsuit had been studying a slip of paper in his ticket folder, on which his flight numbers and flight times were listed. "I'll never make it."

"You've got half an hour, don't you?" Jerome asked. "Or more than that. There's some regulation about a minimal time between connecting flights, isn't there?"

"I don't know. Is there?"

"I think so," Jerome said. He wasn't at all sure.

"Here, look," Brownsuit showed him the slip of paper.

His connection for Paradise, Kansas, was supposed to leave Chicago at 5.30. He pulled back the brown cuff, and showed Jerome an impressive Rolex Oyster. It was already 5.15.

"You see? We'll never make it."

"That's New York time," Jerome said. "It's an hour earlier in Chicago. You'll make it."

"Hey, that's right, isn't it? I just didn't think. Forgot all about it. Jesus!"

But Jerome was not listening. He had gone back to the line which had started to twitch, encouragingly. Instead of *scolds* he would try *brays. Brays/jays. Prays? Church? Preys?* It was just thick enough for him to take out his ball-point pen and the invitation, on the back of which he began to write:

> *Over the fear, the foolishness brays. The jays*
> *should be still, the grove be like a church,*
> *solemn and grave . . .*

20

No, that was wrong. It sounded like Solomon Grave. Who was a cousin, perhaps, of Ed Hall. Solomon Grave, eminent writer of intellectual mysteries, connoisseur of wines, bon vivant, and prominent collector of medieval torture instruments . . .

He gave up, put the invitation back into his pocket, tried to recall what he had been doing before this little seizure, and remembered that Brownsuit had been talking to him. About what? He turned, ready to apologize, but Brownsuit had subsided from consciousness. He dozed. His head sagged at what looked to be a most uncomfortable angle. His jaw hung open. The flanges of his nostrils quivered slightly as he breathed, and while it was rather unattractive, it was so evidently helpless and vulnerable that Jerome did not allow himself the indulgence of distaste. He looked at the gentle reader, and then went back to his scribbling. He changed Solomon Grave to *grave and solemn*, then deleted *solemn*, and then restored it, but in a new syntactical position.

> *Over the fear, the foolishness brays. The jays*
> *should be still, the grove be like a church,*
> *grave as the solemn beasts of prey . . .*

Change *solemn* to *ceremonious*. Change *jays* to *jay*. And the rhyme for *church* . . . *Birch? March?* The month? As cruel as April, surely. Crueler. The equinox comes in March. Easter in either month. Easter/Nor'easter? Tantalizing. There was a vision of a whole poem, a savage Easter, acted out in the woods by the animals, death and resurrection. Pretentious? Yes, but with the right kind of tact, the right kind of subtlety . . . It was a possibility.

The plane was losing altitude. Jerome could tell, but he could not tell how he could tell. His ears had not started popping, and the altitude of the plane was still close enough to level so that, if he looked past Brownsuit and out of the window, the sense of falling diminished for a moment. But if he closed his eyes, and just sat there and trusted his own body, some sixth sense said quietly but confidently that they were going down. Sixth sense? Eighth. Or tenth. Sight, smell, sound, taste, touch. But hot and cold. They were separate. And pressure. And balance. The five senses were like the four elements, and the ends of the earth, and all the other conventions of ancient science which had persevered, embedded in the amber of literature. Touchstones. Were there still touchstones?

His body was falling and his mind was flying, higher than the plane. Cavorting like a dolphin in the ocean of air. Scan that! An iambic, a pyrrhic, an iambic, a pyrrhic, an iambic and an anapest? But there it was, over the damnable fear, the damnable foolishness. He thought of lighting a cigarette, decided against it because he wouldn't be able to finish it and would have to stub it out, wasting it. But then, considering that the plane might very well land heavy, and that he might himself be stubbed out and wasted, he decided to be profligate. He lit one. Brownsuit slept the sleep of the blessed. How did he do it? Did he believe the ads? Had he nestled into the cocoon of the image mongering those agencies had spun about him in which the pilot was no mere Angel but the Father Figure Himself, mature with graying hair, but still vigorous, comforting, stern but loving. Oh, God!

No, he was just sleeping. It was not belief but the body's obliviousness. They were falling, all of them, at a rate which could not be measured because there was nothing outside with which to compare. Jerome felt it in the pit of his stomach. He leaned again to look out of the window for a cloud, a bird, a glimpse of earth, but there was nothing but the streaming of thin air. And a stitch in his side from the leaning. He smoked his cigarette which tasted like straw. Worse than straw. It was dry, sour, bitter. He put it out, grinding it into the little metal shelf of the ash tray.

And still the No Smoking and Fasten Seat Belts signs had not been lit. There had been no announcement from the omnipotent pilot, who obviously had had a heart attack, who was up there balling the stewardess, who was reading his "How to Fly" book, still bogged down in Chapter I—How to Take Off—when he ought to be reading Chapter III—How to Land. Or maybe he had decided that the long way round was the shortest in the end and was doing the speed reading exercises from yet another correspondence school. It was very disturbing, all of it, and while Jerome invented more and more outrageous explanations for the inexcusable silence on the part of Captain Angel and the crew, hoping that extravagance itself would soothe him by implying the contrary, real world, he could no longer distinguish between the real and the imaginary, between the reasonable and the paranoid. He despaired and closed his eyes to wait for the crash. Yes, that was it. Brownsuit wasn't sleeping but only waiting with his eyes closed for what he, too, knew was coming.

But then there was a hospital-like *ping* and the signs lit up, and the Angel said fear not for they were approaching unto O'Hare International Airport. They would be landing in a few minutes.

The panic, the blind panic, subsided to mere fear. He clenched his fists as tight as he could and waited and waited, while the plane banked and turned, banked again, lost altitude, and then lit, with a screech of rubber on the paved runway. He sighed with relief and felt foolish, looking down at his palms where the fingernails had dug a row of moon-shaped stigmata into the flesh of his palms.

The curious thing was that he did not know Brownsuit's name. They had not exchanged names. He remembered their conversation, and its peculiar vacillation between reticence and candor. Had he given his own name? He didn't think so. And all he knew about Brownsuit—Drexel Tech, and Paradise, Kansas—might be as fanciful as his own profession of anagrammarian. Anagrammatist? Anagrammaticist? He did not for a moment believe that Brownsuit had lied to him. But he might have been speaking in an analogical or even anagogical way, as he, himself, had done. Lies like truth. But it was of no use now in a situation that required raw data, mere information. Jerome had to get the briefcase back.

The briefcase he had in his hand, Brownsuit's briefcase, held no clues. Oh, everything spoke clearly enough, but with the same combination of reticence and candor that had characterized their conversation before. Even in his absence, the style was continuing. There was no name, no address, no phone number. But there was a small Dopp-kit with Polident and Poligrip in it. So, Brownsuit had false teeth. There was a paperback of *Only the Dead Know Brooklyn,* with passages underlined. The Wolfe business was real. But the retirement? There was a mimeographed description of a plastic siding for prefabricated housing, and a printed brochure on trading in frozen hog belly futures. There was a playbill for *Hello, Dolly* a souvenir booklet from the Cloisters, and a package of Ramses condoms. Also a package of mentholated Tiparillos and two handkerchiefs. No monogram. Not even one of those little tags announcing that the handkerchiefs were "hand rolled in the Philippines"—which sounded like a wild sexual experience. Have you ever had it with a chest of drawers, two chinamen and a duck? No, but I've been hand rolled in the Philippines!

They had left the plane together, had walked through the long corridors to the luggage claim area, where the carousels turned, giving Val-packs and two-suiters a ride until their owners who watched intently for their little darlings to appear like parents at the other kind of carousel in an amusement park claimed them, with perhaps the same kind of relief. Samson Knight, Amelia Earhart, Mark Cross and Louis Vuitton, all rode around on that extravagant toy. Jerome and Brownsuit had been together and not together. They had been standing near each other, because to have done otherwise would have seemed unfriendly. But they had not spoken, nor had they said goodbye. That would have been too much. Their bags had appeared on the turntable at nearly the same moment, and each had gone forward to grab his suitcase. And what had happened in that moment Jerome could only surmise. Perhaps Brownsuit had moved his briefcase, transposing the two, so that when he, Jerome, had scooped up the one on the left it was not the one that had been on the left, but the other. The one on the right. The wrong. Or perhaps some third person had moved them out of his way, or had knocked one over, and in righting it, wronged it, changing the relative positions. And Brownsuit had grabbed the wrong bag.

It was no one's fault. Jerome could not blame Brownsuit or himself. The two cases resembled each other so very closely. They were both that reddish brown leather, both scuffed, both boxier than was now fashionable. It was only as he was boarding the Lake Central Airlines plane for the flight to Rockville that he realized that the switch had been made. There had been a moment of blind panic. But the trivial things were perfectly safe. The money was in his wallet, and the plane tickets in the inside breast pocket of his jacket. His suit was in the suitcase, now being loaded into the belly of the DC–3. All the expendable things were safe and sound. The poems were gone, however. The book, which could be replaced, and the typescript of the second, which could not.

Oh, there were some he could reconstruct from the manuscript pages, the leaves from legal pads on which the rich blue-black ink snaked over the yellow gloss of the paper, almost illegible after the corrections, the changes, the restorations, the doodlings. And there were others, a very few others, he could get from the magazines in which they had appeared. And six were out now, submitted to magazines, and would return. But for the moment, for the weekend, he was without his papers. "Papieren! Papers! Passport!" He would have nothing to show them, but Brownsuit's pamphlet on frozen hogbelly futures. His identity had left him in the O'Hare Airport. And what he had picked up was worthless. He could claim to have gone to Drexel Tech, pretend to have false teeth, admire Wolfe. But how tiresome. No, he would turn the briefcase in at the Rockville Airport, and hope that they could get his own briefcase back.

That would leave him with nothing. He would have no poems. The poems, in Brownsuit's maniacal care, would have no author. A putative author, only, like Homer, or Shakespeare. They would be better off that way. And he would make it up, somehow. He would get up there, in front of all those students, and read his poems. Any poems. "In my craft or sullen art . . ." Well, maybe not that one, but damned near anything else. "Strange fits of madness I have known . . ." "Venus take my votive glass . . ." "As some brave Admiral in former war . . ." Who would know? And of those two or three who might catch one of the poems, who would dare to speak out, cry "Fraud!" point the accusing finger, make a stink.

He was in the DC–3, in a seat beside the window. The plane was fairly empty. Jerome checked the time, calculated that they would be landing in twenty minutes or so, and thought about John Royle, who would be waiting for him at the airport. It would all depend on John, and what John thought. He was not going to do anything that would hurt John Royle. But for the rest of it, for the solemnity of the teachers, the pretentiousness of their degrees, the stupid eagerness of the students, the lousy lawns and the Georgian buildings, with their nostalgic charm built in as by Brownsuit's plastic prefab sidings, he had nothing but contempt. After five doctoral dissertations and a dozen Masters' essays, he saw it all for the fakery and trumpery that it was. He had gotten all the good out of those dissertations and essays. Eight thousand for each dissertation and four thousand for each of the essays. And all kinds of information about the poetry of Frederick Tuckerman, the novels of Ronald Firbank, the bookplates of the Pre-Raphaelites, the shamanism of Moby Dick, and the imagery of the letters of Thomas More. All the clients of the Ariel Editorial Service had got out of the deal had been degrees, jobs, and a sense of guilt. A swindle, a gross swindle, but ultimately just and fair. The system was stupid and deserved what it produced. And how fine to appear now at Rockville College, in the guise of a poet, and fool them yet again, with more intellectual thievery! If John didn't mind, he might do it. It would be amusing, anyway. Otherwise, he could get his book. John had one. He could read from it. And this new poem, perhaps, could be ripped untimely from the jacket pocket. He pulled it out and looked at it.

> Over the fear, the foolishness brays. The jay
> should be still, the grove be like a church,
> grave as the ceremonious beast of prey
>
> March

What could he do with that? March is a lion/lamb month.
Could he get them to lie down together? Lamb. Of God.
Qui tollis peccata mundi.

The lamb of March. *That crouches, watches, blah, the
lamb of March. That crouches down to watch the lamb
of March?* It wasn't right. The repetition of the "ch" sound
was annoying, and the syntax was flabby. A subordinate
verb that slid listlessly to an infinitive, and then feebly
indicated the lamb of March was not good enough. And
he wanted the idea of adoration in there more. It was
better before. No, *before* was better. *That crouches down
before the lamb of March.* So.

He put it away, amazed to have got that far with it.
It was crazy, trying to compose in a plane. What was
Warren's line? "At 38,000 feet you had better/Try to remember something specific . . ." Tough to do. But having
done this much, and this well, he did not want to risk
ruining it. If it went wrong it might take him months
before he could find out where the mistake was, if he
ever found it at all, and then whether he could go on,
picking up from this beginning again, starting with the
same freshness and the same puzzled, expectant and yet
rather detached hope would be doubtful indeed. It was
almost always easier to start a new poem than to go back
to a botched beginning.

He looked at the invitation with the four lines scribbled on it, considering the ways it could go. He did not
intend to go there now, but having put his pen away—a
ball-point he didn't much care for—it was interesting to
examine the possibilities, and pleasantly professional. It
was like the evening conference in the tent of the general
when he reviews the results of the day's fighting and

considers the moves he might make in the morning. It was not the most intense involvement, but it was the only one which allowed for any self-awareness. It was the one moment at which he felt like a poet, competent, responsive, professional. There was no posturing. It was as if the old Welsh bards or the medieval makars were still going, in the old way, as craftsmen, just like carpenters, wheelwrights, joiners, coopers, or any other craftsmen. It was even physical, the way those other manual crafts were physical, with the same sweet fatigue, the same prickle of sweat.

The end of a poem was different. If the poem worked, he was either elated, wildly elated, or distrustful, depending on the poem, or maybe upon his own metabolism. And either way, the feeling faded. The elation gave way, as all elation does. Or the suspicion lulled itself, or jogged him back to more tinkering. But here, pausing, at the end of a stanza he felt alert and alive, riding the thing and able to feel himself riding.

A series of quatrains? A series of ten-line stanzas each of which was two quatrains with a couplet thrown in somewhere? Or a sonnet? He could see a sonnet-shaped poem, with the way it ought to be set out in the octave, and the way it actually is slapping back in the sestet, which would get back to the jay, the foolishness, the irrelevant people in all the northern renaissance painters who are not listening to the sermon of the saint, but are eating a pear, or scratching themselves, or suckling a baby. The up and down of it. The rhythm of breathing. The double beat of the heart: Lubdupp, octave and sestet. Maybe. It was a tight form.

He lit a cigarette. He looked ahead at the front of the cabin where there was a board in which small plaques announced the names of the pilot, the co-pilot and the stewardess. The pilot's name was listed as C. O. Jones. Balls to you! He turned away and looked down at the plaid countryside, reddened by the late afternoon sunlight. It was stupid about the briefcase, and annoying, but not so bothersome as he had expected it would be. The thing was to stay loose. Poets were such anal bastards, hoarding their little sheaves until they got thick enough to send out as a book. Actors were looser, admirably so, playing it and then forgetting it. *Actors.* Could build to *carrots.* Or, if the letters broke right, *Socratic.* He remembered that he was a professional anagrams player and smiled. He might just keep that.

The plane started its descent. Jerome felt the pressure on his eardrums, yawned, felt the popping as his eustachian tubes opened, yawned again and felt sleepy. Idly he watched the ground come up to the plane, watched the growing of apparent seedlings to saplings, to tall, old, twisted trees. Odd. An illusory demonstration of relativity. He wondered if it would be worth it to study physics for ten or fifteen years and redo *De Rerum Natura.* Who'd read it except C. P. Snow? Lucretius was the Snow *d'antan.* He felt the bump as the plane touched down, reached for Brownsuit's briefcase, and prepared to de-plane. The stewardess said, "Bye, now," and smiled, as if they were old friends. Lovers. Well, why not? They had risked death together. Not the little death either, but the big one. He remembered that lousy Dickey poem about the stewardess falling out of the plane and stripping naked as she fell. Stupid. No, just badly done. There was something sexual about stewardesses—in a very sexless, intellectual way. His (heh-heh) meat, exactly. J. D. would suggest Jimmy Dorsey a lot longer than James Dickey. Or Juvenile Delinquency. Or Salinger. He wondered why Salinger never used his "Jerome". Not a bad name. "Bearing a holy name."

He walked across the asphalt. Nowhere. It was not the airport, but not the plane, either. You were on land, but couldn't smoke. It was better done in London, where bus-driving Charons whisked you across to the land of the living.

CHAPTER 2

The color of whiskey. A very satisfying color. Rich, soothing, reassuring. Quite lovely. Ink should be in that color. Could it be got in that brown? Who wrote with brown ink? Roethke? Brown ink. Elizabeth Barrett and Bobby.

John Royle raised the glass, looked at the sunlight as it shone through the Crown Royal, and took a sip. Only a sip, a gesture, as if to show that he didn't really need it, could get along without it perfectly well, was only posing for a possible candid photographer from the Calvert people who might be looking for some drunk of distinction . . . Show us your Lark! Show us your bird! Is it a silly millimeter longer? He took another sip, not posing this time.

And, in order to prove to himself that he was not posing, he glanced into the mirror, to see the same old wreck, the puffiness, the pallor. Or was he imagining it? Was not this too a pose? Young poets are romantics, Stevens said, and old poets are bums. Selah! He would live up to

35

it. He would live it up to live up to it. Another little old
taste, there. Ah. Allez. Alley-oop. I'll lay up. For a while,
anyway.

And he did. Lie down, on the bed, prying his shoes
off, the heel of one with the toe of the other, and then
the heel of the second with the bare toe, peeping out of
the sock of the first. Show us your toe! He needed the
rest. Not because he was tired, but because he wasn't.
This kind of word play, this kind of energy, this kind of
manic-kind, man un-kind, inhumanic . . . It had happened before. Boded no good. The whiskey could dull it
for a while, and the rest, the pretense at rest, the lying
still for a while, postpone it. To pretend to sleep, as
Nijinsky had done. Same problem, same solution. Diag-
nosis: Ziss mann iss out from his fucking mindt! And the
joke, of course was no joke.

He lay there on the bed with his eyes closed. He allowed himself small fancies, little crazinesses, harmless
departures from sanity, as, for instance, the merging of his
body not with tree under which Nijinsky pretended to
fall asleep, but with the hotel. The entire building became
an extension of his body, and he could feel the ivy growing on him, slowly up his legs. He scratched his calves.
The support hose were not ivy, but his recognition of that
rational explanation was not comforting. Rational explanations were misleading. Only in a rational universe are
rational explanations relevant. Floods, earthquakes, ty-
phoons, volcanic eruptions, all have rational explanations and all such explanations are beside the point. It is
the rage of nature, the fury of an offended God, the punishment for sins, the blind extravagance of the waste of

the world's workings. Thank you, thank you, you are too kind.

He acknowledged the roar of applause from the amphitheater, smiled, bowed, and waved at the bouquets of flowers that the young women of the audience threw at him. He could really hear the applause—which, by his theory, might be said by the ignorant to be the hum of the air conditioner (but what the hell did they know?)—and feel it as it shook the ivy that crept up toward his groin. It would reach the apex of the arch, there, in forty or fifty years, he guessed. Well, he could wait. Would have to wait. But that was one of the risks of business, as the landscape architect said. You lay out one of these gardens, and it doesn't get to look the way it is supposed to look for ten or twenty years. And at fifty, it looks better than it is supposed to, sometimes, assuming, of course that the development of taste proceeds in the same way as the development of the bushes and trees—which, ideally, is precisely what ought to happen don't you see?

Another long satisfying wave of adulatory applause. No, not another, but the same wave, continuous. A splendid idea, he had to admit, this wiring system here in the amphitheater, from his microphone on the dais to the earphones, so that the audience could applause continuously during the entire speech, and yet not miss a syllable. Very thoughtful of the administration. Most considerate. Should be the rule everywhere.

The door opened, and Marty came in with the shaving cream.

"You asleep?" she asked.

37

"Yes," he answered, "as a matter of fact I am. Sound asleep."

"All right, so it was a dumb question."

"No, no. I didn't mean it that way at all. I was just playing with it. I mean, wouldn't it be marvelous in the middle of a conversation, to stop, interrupt yourself, and ask, 'Are you asleep?' and then go right on?"

"What?"

"Wouldn't that be marvelous?"

"I don't think it would be very marvelous, no. I think it would be pretty insulting."

"Yes, but marvelously insulting?"

"Oh, all right. Anyway, here's your shaving cream."

"Thanks. Thank you very much. Thank you. Thank you, one and all. Thank you."

"What's the matter with you?"

"Nothing much. I'm just going crazy, that's all."

"Why? What's the matter?"

It was just fine, the way she asked, in that matter-of-fact way, planting her ass in the chair, and looking at him with forbearance and admiration and that lovely docility. But how to tell her? How to rupture that more difficult innocence, that mental cherry, that beaming optimism, out of which the long, straight hair grew like wheat from the scalp of the Great Plains.

"Just that. That I'm going crazy."

"Crazy people never say they're going crazy."

"Ah, but they do, Marty, they do. One of the manifestations of my kind of paranoia is that the patient frequently insists that his disturbance is self-induced, voluntarily assumed, deliberate. It is a way of insisting that even though he has lost control he is still in control."

"Well, are you? In control, I mean?"

"No. Or not quite. Not absolutely. I just don't know. I get this way sometimes. Sometimes it gets worse, and then sometimes it doesn't. Sometimes it just goes away."

"You want to take a nap?"

"I've been pretending to."

She looked at him, hesitated, and then did not pick it up. So it was up to him whether he was going to go on and explain all about Nijinsky or not. He decided not. Marty's great gifts to him were care, order, admiration, beauty, lust, and typing—possibly in that order. Deep understanding he shied away from. When a clock is working, you don't take it apart. And when it isn't working? You kick it! And the machinery might get jogged into life again, start clacking and groaning its way on to the coo-coo of the hour. Show us your bird!

He looked over at Marty, sprawled on the chair as she had always sprawled in front of him in class, not even knowing how those long, slender legs could affect him, wholly unaware . . .

And he had no doubt whatever that she had been unaware. That ingenuousness was the rock upon which they had built together. She was so restful, so easy for him. And how often do such girls come along? Intelligent, but not knowing anything, and yet incapable of being really surprised by anything. Her long, delicate face, Modigliani in its shape but Manet in its coloring, and her long, blonde hair, and the green eyes that gazed so steadily . . . She was like a nude in a painting over a bar in one of those old saloons.

He closed his eyes again, and listened to the hum of the air conditioner, which now was only an air conditioner. And that was a good sign, he supposed. Perhaps that moment had just been a passing incident, the result of some micrograms of chemical that he had secreted, touching the nerve endings somewhere and speeding up the associative process. And the alcohol had countered it. Could that be? Why not? Whine not, the angel said.

He had been in love with the angel. She had stood on a box, with glitter all over her hair, and the glitter in the blue spotlight had caught his eye, his heart, his tongue, so that he had forgotten his lines. And now, he could not remember the angel's name, the little girl with whom he had been so desperately in love. The first one. He had been in the fifth grade. Miss Seabranch he could remember, but not the girl's name. Terrible. And he had always been bad with names.

"Would you freshen this, puss?" he asked, holding out the empty bathroom tumbler.

Marty took the glass and the weight of it left his hand. He had not even opened his eyes. Deliberately, he did so, and she changed, literally in the twinkling of an eye, from the abstract "Puss" to the specific, the particular, to Marty —Martha. In theory at least an improvement, for the particular was always supposed to be preferable to the general, the specific, the concrete, the demonstrative adjective better than the indefinite article, the real better than the theoretical. In theory. Generalities are to be avoided—was the general rule. But then, by the particular rule, they might be admitted. And the general notion of Puss, endearing, affectionate, purring, nonintrusive, slightly independent and genital, certainly had its charms. Pussy hath charms to soothe the savage beast. If Pussy be the food of love, eat on . . .

She brought the tumbler, now half full, back to him, and held it out with an almost oriental submissiveness. And she sat down, on the bed this time, gazing at him . . .

"I have these episodes," he began.

"Episodes?"

"I go crazy every now and then. It's happened before. I get high, manic, and I just fly off. I guess I should have told you about them before. But each time I get over them, I have the idea—or maybe it's just a hope—that that was the last of them, and that I'll be okay. But a couple of months or a couple of years can go by, and I'm fine, and then it comes back."

"Is it very bad?"

"No. It hasn't been. I mean, I don't get violent, or anything. I just get very happy, and strenuous. I lose touch with things."

"Is it crazy to be happy?"

"Too much of anything is crazy."

He took a sip of the whiskey and felt the warmth of it as it went down his gullet. The thing was to stay half sozzled, tranquil, subdued, until the stability of a slightly depressive sanity returned. It would be a long haul, getting through the three days. The company of other writers, the adulation of audiences and students, the excitement of good talk, the feeling of being connected to the great fraternity of writers—or, to hell with that, of being better than most of them—would all buoy him up, dangerously high. Silly, of course. Stupid, actually. The same old windbag writers, and the same old innocent look on the young, new faces of the students, and the same show-and-tell, and drink-and-yak . . . What the hell did any of it mean, but the five hundred dollars for the three days? And what did that mean, really? He'd never even see the money. Numbers, into the checking account balance and out.

But even though he tried to take the gloomiest view of it, he could feel his breathing, his heart beat, his mind race, his hair and fingernails grow. And Marty, sitting on the bed down near his knees, looking at him, dumb with affection, accepting the news that he was going out of his mind, accepting anything at all, because after all he was a *writer* and that, she thought, made him special. Well, it did. Not the way she thought, perhaps, or not even any way that he could explain to himself. But somehow, still, special. Or was that just a habit of mind, a sloppy habit he'd acquired years ago when he'd been young and never broken?

The vines were climbing up his legs now like Jack's beanstalk, growing at so many feet per second per second (whatever that meant) that he felt half inclined to open his eyes and actually look down to watch them grow. The tendrils were clutching around his calves and knees, moving, holding him with their delicate little fingers. Jesus, he really was wacking out. He could feel it!

He opened his eyes and found that the tendrils were fingers, Marty's fingers. She was stroking his leg, offering herself if that was what he wanted. Did he want her? He

42

was touched by the gesture, but did he want her now? He had to shave, and they had to get to the airport to pick up Jerome. He wondered what time it was. It was a nuisance to have to think of things like that. There might just be time, but what would be the good of it if all the time he had to think about finishing up on the dot, getting dressed, shaving, and getting out to the airport. Better wait until later. Of course, he might be drunk by then, too drunk to take advantage of the offer. But the offer was what counted. The thought . . . The situation. The old crazy bum, the poet, taking comfort from the sweet young thing, she giving it for her crazy reasons, and he taking it for his. Let me not to the marriage of true impediment mind admit . . .

He put his hand on the back of her head, touching the fine, straight hair, and stroking her with minuscule gestures of two fingertips.

"I ought to shave," he said, at last.

"Yes," she said, dreamily.

"Really, I ought to . . ."

"Yes."

"And we ought to go to the airport."

"Yes."

"You're a love, you know that?"

She put her head down on his thigh. It was a gesture of affection, of submission, of adoration even, but it caught the wrong way, for her jaw bone cut across some nerve, and the pain startled him. Still, he did not move, and although he felt the numbness replacing the stab of protest of the pinched nerve, he endured it, for the sake of the picture that they made in his mind's gallery. And hers.

43

Only after what seemed to be an appropriate time had passed did he move, disengage himself from her, kiss her on the forehead and on the tip of the nose, and then, with a sigh, heave himself off the bed. He sat on the edge of the bed, swinging his legs, trying to restore the feeling to the numbed limb. The tingling sensation came back, and it felt rather the way the brick wall would have felt had the ivy been ripped off it. He reached for his shoes which were, he noticed, perhaps for the twentieth time, in need of new heels. He had to attend to that. Or have Marty do it for him. But was she ready to be sent on errands of such unmitigated homeliness? Typing his poems, making his meals, sharing his bed—that's what she wanted to do, and what they all wanted to do. The vague dream they seemed to have of a life as a handmaiden to literature remained constant no matter what young brain it inhabited. But taking shoes to the cobbler was a dreariness. Or perhaps not. He wondered about her shoes.

In the chair, she was putting the Capezios back on. They seemed scarcely worn. New. Everything about her was new. What business did she have in one of those gloomy shops with the smell of leather and rubber and wax, and the dejection of all those unclaimed hats on the shelf over the old, hand-operated cash register which was covered with vine leaves (signifying abundance and prosperity) and the racks of shoelaces and boot polish? The very air was old and sad in those places, the light itself always pallid and depressing. Temples to the gods of deterioration and decay, they were. He would take his shoes in to be fixed, himself. When he had time.

"You ready?" he asked.

"Aren't you going to shave?"

"Shave?" he asked. He put his hand to his face and touched the stubble. "Oh, yes. Of course."

A bubbling up of laughter at his vagueness, his fuzziness both of mind and of cheek, and, he hoped, at his conformity to that idea she had of absent minded professors and poets. He suspected that to her he was some intellectual and artistic version of the Raggedy Andy doll of which she had been unwisely deprived by her otherwise doting parents not so very long ago. But it did not do to dwell too much on these thoughts. The main thing was to enjoy her, to enjoy himself.

And, in order to do that, he went to shave, imagining as he looked at his face in the mirror, the casual, affable smile he would wear when presenting Marty to Jerome. Jerome would be impressed, shocked just a little. Envious? Glad for the sake of his old friend and mentor? All of those things. And the smile he would wear would have to be appropriate for any mixture of those qualities. He peered into the mirror and, despite all the finesse he had hoped to bring to bear, watched his image grin like a Greek comedy mask, like the Joker in Batman, like the old sign for E. M. Tillyou's Steeplechase at Coney Island. Well, that would serve too. Onto the grinning countenance he spread the lime scented lather which covered the face but not the lips. He looked rather like Marcel Marceau. He thought of covering his forehead with the lather, too, and going out to mime for Marty, to make her laugh. But there wasn't time. The plane would be getting in soon. Shaving is the difference between washing and laving. Crazy.

45

He picked up the razor and began.

And, whoops, he cut himself. It was a new blade in the razor, and he felt nothing. In fact, the first he noticed of the cut was the drop of blood dissolved into the lather, the red fading to pink. He dabbed at the cut with a finger and flicked the foam into the basin. *Stand from the fosse, leave me my bloody bever for soothsay* . . . something, something, something. *Then Anticlea came.* Auntie Clea?

He reached for the Dopp-kit, found the styptic pencil, and dabbed at the cut, curing as with a magic wand, by its touch.

The girl behind the counter of Lake Central Airlines was trying, presumably, but what, after all, had Jerome expected? A miracle? Intelligence? Competence? She held the card in front of him, showing pictures of all the usual kinds of luggage, while he explained, proud of his patience, that his briefcase was exactly like the one he held in his hand, the similarity being the very reason for the mix-up in Chicago. And had he continued in this basic English, he might have had some chance of success. But when he had the irresistible impulse to allude to the missing briefcase as a "duffelganger" he lost the Lake Central girl, who looked at him, pen poised over her printed form and asked, "How do you spell that, sir?"

"No, no," he said, trying to smile, "it was a little joke, not a very good joke."

"I don't understand," she said.

"That's why it wasn't very good," he said, and began again. "There was a man. He was sitting next to me on the

United flight to Chicago. He took mine and I took his. Briefcase." He held it up for her to see.

"Oh," she said, as if humoring a lunatic, and trying to keep calm while waiting for the men in the white coats for whom she had rung, pressing the concealed buzzer under the counter. "And his name?"

"I don't know his name. All I know is that he was going to Paradise."

"I beg your pardon?"

"Paradise. In Kansas."

"Oh, that Paradise," she said.

A wave of hysteria hit him in the pit of the stomach. It felt not unlike nausea.

"What other Paradise is there?" he asked.

"There's one in Pennsylvania, I think."

"Oh, yes!"

And on and on. She took his name, and his local address and his home address. She accepted Brownsuit's briefcase and handed him a form to sign. He scribbled his name. Why had there never been a song about Paradise, Pennsylvania? It had the same rhythm as Kokomo, Indiana. Or you could do it with a triplet and a break: Paradise (beat) P.A.

And then he went to the baggage claim area to retrieve his suitcase. He claimed it, and was in turn claimed by John Royle.

"Hey, how are you? Good flight?"

" . . ." He had been about to speak, but Royle continued, and introduced Marty, "Have you met Marty Green?"

"How do you do?" she asked.

"How do you do?" he asked back. Apparently there was no point to answers any more. A new style? A new literary form, even, in which the old works could be redone in the interrogative: Should you call me Ishmael? and so on all the way to the end. At which you could put a simple *No*. The anti-novel.

"Marty came down for the readings," Royle said.

"Oh, did she?" Jerome asked, clinging to the interrogative.

Marty looked away, not bothering to blush or be embarrassed.

Jerome realized that his fooling around had not been entirely pointless, felt a twinge of remorse for having been so thoughtless, and then, immediately, a warmth of relief at the way Royle had responded, and the way she had floated over it all. And gratitude for that relief. And admiration. She was very pretty, but that was to be expected. And she was apparently very sure of herself, sophisticated, poised . . . Bully for her!

"Is that it?" Royle asked, indicating the rather tired Val-Pack.

"That's all I've got left," Jerome said, and he explained about the mix-up of the briefcases. Not all, of course. Not the business about the duffelganger, of the momentary notion of *poésie trouvée*, in which as a substitute for the lost book and manuscript pages he had imagined himself breaking up Brownsuit's hogbelly pamphlet into *vers libre* lines. It had seemed jolly enough up in the plane, but down on the practical and unyielding ground only silly and stupid. *Poésie oubliée?*

Royle was reassuring. He was certain the airline

would get the briefcase back eventually. And, meanwhile, he was confident that a copy of *The Double Agent* could be had from the Rockville College library.

"I hope so," Jerome said, feeling better already. Royle had been the agent for *The Double Agent.* Or had been the double agent, for he had also served as the reader for the publishing house. And even in this absurd crisis, Jerome was inclined to rely on Royle's judgment. If as remote and improbable a prediction as "Oh, sure, they'll do the book," could come true, then the prediction about Lake Central's retrieving the briefcase might come true, too.

"Come on, we'll go to the hotel and call the library from there," Royle suggested, and the three of them began to move which also felt good. There was a plan now, and they had started to do something, even if it was only to walk out of the airport, get into the big, red convertible—rented? or Marty's?—and drive into the traffic.

Royle was at the wheel with Marty beside him. Jerome was over at the right. It was difficult for Royle and Jerome to talk across Marty. But, recognizing this, she played hostess.

"Do you teach, too?" she asked.

"No, not really."

"Jerome, actually, is an anti-teacher," Royle said, smiling.

"A what?" she asked.

"I write dissertations. Theses. Papers. For money."

"You're kidding."

"No."

"I don't believe you," she said. She glanced at Royle for

49

some hint, some look, but the grin was inscrutable, fitting perfectly well either way.

"All right, then," Jerome said, "I sell dark glasses whenever there's a total eclipse."

"Coronation programs."

"I am a professional anagrams player."

"He's a producer of blue movies."

"I paint 'Souvenir of Baltimore', on those hand-painted souvenir ashtrays."

"Why Baltimore?" Marty asked.

"That's the only city where there was an opening."

"A tough game," Royle said, shaking his head, sagely. "Terrific competition."

"And the exams," Jerome said. "Brutal. Three hundred candidates for two positions: Ashtray painter and S&P man."

"S&P?" Marty asked, relaxed now that she had decided it had to be a game.

"Salt and Pepper."

"Of course."

The car veered left as Royle made a turn off the highway and into the Rockville College drive, between the two stone gates and under the wrought iron archway.

"Levavi Oculos," Royle intoned, reading from the inscription on the arch. "Abandon hope all ye who enter here."

"I thought it meant Levy, the Oculist." Jerome said.

She was smiling now, the audience for their Smith and Dale act, which was fine. The two of them needed an audience, deserved one . . . and if she performed certain other services for Royle in the dark of the night, well, he was entitled.

The car moved slowly up the serpentine asphalt drive, as if in a film. On the rolling greensward attractive girls posed according to the whim of a rather old fashioned director, some sitting on the grass, others lolling prone, pretending, not very convincingly, to be reading, and still others walking slowly, according to some stylized plan. Jerome gazed out at the scene with considerable satisfaction, but still half expecting that each curve would give the whole thing away, revealing those impressive buildings as nothing more than facades, behind which Mongol warriors, crusaders, Apaches, and Transylvanian peasants mingled cheerfully as they made their way to their low calorie lunches in the commissary. But the whole shot held all the way past the administration build-ing to the portico—a frugal borrowing from the Civil War sets—of the Collegiate Arms Inn. (Surely the scriptwriter should have been able to improve on that. Or was that one of his private jokes? Or a mistake, as in the thesis on the family constellation in the plays of Noel Coward, in which the foolish client had not taken the instructions but had merely typed them, incorporating them into the text: "The views of Erik Erikson, on the contrary, are TO BE LOOKED UP AND INSERTED HERE.")

Jerome got out of the car, gave his bag to the doorman, and went inside to register while Royle drove around to the parking area. At the desk Jerome was given a card, one of the blanks of which called for his firm. He hesi-tated, wondering whether he ought to write in Ariel Edi-torial Service, or leave it blank. Or scrawl something illegible? Or enter something absurd: Venezuelan Secret Police, or American Beauty Merkin Mfg. Co., Inc. In the end, he just left it blank. The man at the desk glanced at the card, said nothing, rang the bell, and gave the bellman the key. Jerome followed him to the elevator.

In the car, as it made its slow ascent, the bellman, a man of about forty, with gray hair and a rather distinguished look—he wore his green, gold-braided uniform quite well—asked Jerome, "You here for the Literary Arts Festival?"

"Yes."

"Thought so. I can tell about people."

"Oh?"

"Sure! I'm a writer, myself."

"Oh? You publish any of it?"

"Nah!"

"Oh?"

"Hell, I don't even write most of it down. But in here," he said, tapping his temple with an extended forefinger, "in here, I'm a writer. I think like one."

"I see."

Mercifully, the elevator stopped, and the bellman led the way down a carpeted corridor to Jerome's room. Jerome stood there watching as he opened the window, opened the bathroom door and turned on the light, took the luggage rack from the closet and put the Val-Pack on it, and went through his little routine. The question was how to gauge the effect of the conversation in the elevator. Was it a pitch for a larger tip? One writer to another, or, more pertinent, a less successful writer to a more successful? To hell with that! Or was it less calculated, merely intended to be cordial and affable, one human being to another (we're all writers under the skin)? That, too, was annoying, but the bellman's effort was not finally reprehensible. Jerome decided to let chance decide, reached in his pocket, felt his silver, discovered that there was only a small amount (it turned out later to be thirty seven cents, but that wasn't enough), and went for his wallet. But if it was to be a bill, at least it could be a tired bill, a tattered, limp bill. He withdrew a dollar so world-weary as to be virtually a kind of naturalized Italian currency—with Giorgio Vacciontone, *il padrone della republica*, looking out, rather grumpily, at the neapolitan curlicues of his elaborate frame.

"Thank you, sir," the bellman said, with enough enthusiasm to make Jerome sure that he'd overtipped.

"*Prego.*"

"Beg pardon?"

"You're welcome."

"Yes, sir. Thank you."

The bellman left, gloating no doubt at the success of his elementary stratagem, and leaving Jerome to take the case from the rack, open it up and hang it from the closet pole. He was annoyed at himself for not having asked the bellman to do that. But then, he reflected, with these mental writers you can't be too careful. You never know when they might be writing. And it would be a shame to intrude!

He unzipped the Val-Pack and watched it relax like a tired old woman shedding her girdle. He thought of taking the suits out of it and hanging them separately on the closet pole where they could unwrinkle, but suddenly it seemed more important for him to unwrinkle. He lay down on the bed. Oh that my briefcase were in my arms, and I in my bed again!

He looked at the hunting prints on the walls, the lean horses and the black and tan hounds, and the red coated gentlemen of the chase. Odd getups, those. Like the Venezuelan secret police, or the Lake Central Airlines Lost and Found crew, as they cantered over the Kansas cornfields, in pursuit of briefcases, crying, "Yoiks! Tally-ho!" and "View-haloo!"

The notion of the chase caught at something, as if there had been a piece of mental cuticle that he had developed and that snagged now as he thought of . . . Of what? The Venezuelans? The briefcase? The duffel-ganger? The fox in the print, or, if not in the print, then hiding, behind one of the cabbage roses on the wallpaper, out of the frame of the pictures, heart beating, hackles up, eyes bright and burning, listening for the baying of those black and tans. He lay there, trying to think, listening to his own breath, his own heartbeat, and then remembering, pulled the piece of paper out of his pocket.

grave as the cremonious beast of prey
that crouches down before the lamb of March

he added:

. . . sound of the heart's beating
the blood's pulse in the vein, the vain . . .

Something.

The phone rang. It was Royle, announcing that the car was parked and inviting Jerome to come to room 317 for a drink.

"Yes, thanks, I'll be right there," Jerome answered.

"See you."

"Right."

Regretfully, he put the paper back in his pocket, glanced with a certain sad affection at the cheap horse-and-hound prints, and went into the bathroom to splash cold water onto his face. He looked into the mirror, smoothed his hair down with his hands, and, after he had grabbed his key, he closed the door, feeling the click of the lock as if it had come from his own viscera. There would be time later, he told himself. Or tomorrow. The thing about poetry was that it was never urgent. He had once received a letter from a publishing house, a letter intended to be gentle and encouraging in which the editor-in-chief had described the poems as graceful, charming, accomplished—but lacking in urgency. He was, he said, returning the poems under separate cover, and he did so—at the appropriately leisurely book-rate postage. It wasn't yet the elaborate and total reversal that Jerome would have liked, but there were now some first inklings of urgency to the book. What the hell was he going to do unless a copy could be found? Finish that poem and write another dozen or so? In two hours?

He knocked on the door and it opened. Marty greeted him in hushed tones. "Come on in. He's on the phone."

Jerome entered the room, a mirror image of his own. Or, no, not quite. Instead of fox-hunting prints this room had bullfighting prints. All the local sports of the

Mid-West, he supposed, graced the rooms: alligator wrestling, jailai, bocce, Russian face slapping, mountain climbing, deep sea diving, and ostrich riding. Were they out of their minds? Or had the decorator simply indicated to some assistant that each room was to sport some different sport, so that the assistant, being something of a sport himself (herself? itself?) had gone to some encyclopaedia and listed eighty sports. Kangaroo boxing. Knife throwing. Cliff diving.

"I see," Royle said into the phone, having been listening for the few moments in which Jerome had been standing there. "But still, there must be some way of finding out who has them. They must be charged out to someone . . ."

He subsided into listening, and indicated by a gesture that Jerome was to fix himself a drink.

"Jerome Carpenter," Royle said.

"Yes?" Jerome asked.

He pointed to the phone. "That's right. *The Double Agent.*"

Suddenly Jerome knew. He knew that John Royle was talking to the library, that the book was out, that it could not be found, would not be found, and that now it was urgent. What was he going to read?

"Well, I'd certainly appreciate it," Royle said. "Yes, either here at the hotel, or at Edmund Walter Hall. Yes, thanks. Thanks, very much."

He hung up. Jerome didn't even have to ask.

"Well," Royle said, after a beat, "there are two copies. You can't be unhappy that they're out. Your fans await you."

"Two of them do."

"Don't be gloomy. For ten the Lord would have spared Sodom and Gomorrah."

"Thanks a lot," Jerome said, putting the ice in his drink. "But in the meantime, I'm standing there like a pillar of saltines."

"Don't sweat it. Have another drink!"

"I haven't finished this one yet."

"Well, get to it. That may be your only way out."

"You mean, just . . . get drunk? Do a Dylan Thomas?"

"You could. Or a Hungerford."

"What did Hungerford do?"

"Ah, a lovely performance. A performance worthy of any poet. I can't think why it hasn't happened more often. I expect it has, but was hushed up. Maiden speeches in Parliament, and that sort of thing. Hungerford came out to read for the very first time onto the platform of the Women's Club of Decatur, Georgia. He looked out at the audience, a sea of hats and a wilderness of cotton prints, and was abruptly seized by an attack of nausea. He wasn't just queasy, but sick. Desperately sick. And he looked around, trying to find something in which to be sick. And there it was, behind him and off to one side. An eight foot Steinway, to which he ran, the lid of which he opened, and the belly of which he filled with the contents of his own. Then he wiped his mouth with his pocket handkerchief—real style there, I think—and left the platform. Antonin Artaud never reached such heights. Le Pétomane never did better."

"Le Pétomane?"

"He farted—that was his act—at the Moulin Rouge. Could put out a candle from a foot and a half."

"Really, John," Marty said, chastisingly.

Royle laughed, a loud, long, hooting laugh, as of some tropical long-legged bird. Was the laughter at her prissiness or her presumption, or at the absurdity of his own remarks which had succeeded in getting a rise out of the delicate girl? It was, at any rate, a weird, high laugh, and Jerome found it uncomfortable. The apprehension he felt was puzzling. Royle was all right, wasn't he? But this was odd for him, a departure from his usual style. And of no help.

"That's all fine," he said, "but what am I going to do?"

"Appear to be unstable. Pretend to have lost not just your briefcase but your mind. That'll get 'em!" With his thumb and forefinger, Royle made the conventional child's representation of a gun, and, bending the thumb at the joint, fired at Jerome, who clutched his chest and sagged in his chair. "See?" Royle went on. "It's not difficult. You're at least as crazy as I am."

"Thanks." Jerome sipped at his whiskey, wondering briefly whether drunkenness might not be a solution, however desperate. Or, perhaps, somewhere on the road towards that drunkenness, there might be some way-station where a lesser remedy might present itself, something genial and crazy and charming. "I was thinking on the plane that I might just read other people's poems. Steal things out of the library."

"Or borrow from the rest of us. There are six of us reading tonight. If five of us kick in with a couple of poems apiece, you'd have ten things to read."

"No, that's no good. Stone? Hartshorne? What would they be able to give me?" Sam Stone was a novelist, and Agnes Hartshorne was a short story writer.

"Hoo!" the long-legged bird cried again. "And what would they have that you'd want?"

"Have you called the bookstore?" Marty asked.

They hadn't. And the bird sounded again, a long, triumphant peal, as though to announce that it had found a tasty morsel, a silvery fish or a whole school of fish.

"Hey, thanks! That's the first sensible idea I've heard all day," Jerome said, and he went to the phone. He picked it up, then put it down and pulled the directory out of the shelf of the night table. He rummaged through the yellow pages, nervous and clumsy. Marty took the book from him, found the number, picked up the phone, gave the number to the hotel switchboard, and then handed the phone to Jerome. "Thank you," he said, and she flashed a small smile. She was okay, Jerome thought. Really okay.

He got through to the bookstore, and asked if there were any copies of *The Double Agent* by Jerome Carpenter, feeling like an impostor because he was not accustomed to asking for himself. It was like having oneself paged in a hotel, mildly funny or desperate and insane. The woman had gone to check. She returned to the phone. No, there were no more left. There were ten copies on order, and she would be happy to reserve one if she could have the name.

"No," he said, "I need it right away. It can't wait. It's . . . urgent."

She was sorry she could not help. He hung up.

"Well, we're down to the bottom line, aren't we?" Royle said, lying on the bed, and balancing his drink on his chest. "Down to the old nitty-gritty."

"Aren't we now?"

"Well, my boy, it is time for you to show us what kind of stuff you're made of. The old pirate of academe, hoisting his jolly roger one more time."

"What do you mean? What are you talking about?"

"To the library! Go! With my blessings! And with your yellow pad! And steal!"

"I can't do that!"

"Why not? Poetry is a part of life, isn't it? You write fake dissertations? You can write fake poems. It isn't healthy for the poetry to be kept on a shelf like that, as if it were something sacred and apart. Wheel and deal! Crib like a thief! Improvise! Who knows, but something good might come out of it. How many poets ever even have the chance to work against a deadline like this. What have you got, three hours?"

"If I skip dinner?"

"Make it an hour and a half, then. Cyrano made up a ballade while duelling, didn't he? You've got an hour and a half!"

"But I've got to do more than a ballade! I need about twenty minutes."

"Fifteen will do. The word, said George Fenamin, falling out of the sky in the shape of a duck, is 'eclectic.' And Groucho answered, 'You bet your ass!'"

"You're raving!"

"All of us soothsayers and oracles hear that every day. It's divine madness, old sock! It's the gift of tongues."

Royle stuck out his tongue, and did a plausible imitation of the act of Le Pétomane.

"All right, I'll go and see what I can do," Jerome said.

"I'm sure you'll do splendidly. You are, as they used to say in the *dix-huitième,* a man of parts. And who knows what evil lurks in the parts of men? Or what good?"

"Who knows, indeed," Jerome replied, and, feeling not a little embarrassed by the situation, by Royle's weird mood, by Marty's wide-eyed silence, by the task ahead of him and its imitation of his grubby existence as a part of Ariel Editorial Services, he drained his glass, put it down on the dresser, gave a sloppy military salute, and left to plunder the treasures of the library and devise, somehow, a third of an hour of impromptu art. In my crafty, sudden art . . .

Well, why not. Why in hell not? And what a fine thing, Royle thought, if Jerome could bring it off! To go off to the library and sit down and whip together a series of poems, or, even better, one long poem . . . *Un Moment en Enfer.* The air of having been dashed off, of having been poured out in passionate instantaneousness, that was what so much poetry tried for. The fakery might work out to be legitimate. Or to be a legitimate comment. A legitimate zotz. He sighed not so much out of fatigue, as out of a desire to emulate fatigue, to court it, to keep low and calm. But the idea of Jerome, going off that way to plant another patch of rhubarb in the gardens of academe was too much to endure calmly. It made his breathing shallower, his pulse faster, as the adrenalin trickled out and into his bloodstream. How gorgeous to thumb the nose that way, with Ariel, with the ever increasing colony of impostors and frauds that Ariel settled into one college after another. Being a poet was not insult enough any more. They had found out that even poets will meet classes, come to department meetings, serve on committees, and get grades in on time. Royle did all those things. But Jerome didn't. He was the wild dog that sets all the little Pekingeses and dachshunds and toy fox terriers baying and howling in their little boxes and dog-beds and runs, all up and down the suburban block.

"Aaawoooo!" he howled.

"John! What's the matter with you?" Marty asked. "You almost made me spill my drink."

"You hang around with lunatics, that's one of the risks of business," he said cheerfully.

"But what was it? I mean, what were you thinking about?"

"I was practicing my bird calls puss."

"That was a bird call?"

"The mute swan."

"Mute?"

"At the end, just before they die, they make noise. All the things they've been saving up to say, maybe. Or maybe not. Maybe they're just late bloomers."

"Sure," she said, "That must be it."

"You're humoring me, aren't you?"

"Yes," she said.

"Good. You just keep it up. And as long as you're up, freshen this, would you, puss?"

He held out the glass.

"Don't you think you've had enough of that stuff, maybe?"

"That's not humoring. Or humorous. That's just humus."

She looked at him, taking readings, he supposed, from all the gauges that she could read, as if he were some sort of huge machine, covered with little dials and meters, and she the engineer. She got up and got the bottle. Well, she was not such a bad engineer after all. And if he was going to take on apprentices for these little cruises, he had to put up with something less than perfect efficiency and competence. What the hell had he expected? She was not Jill, and that was the whole point. Had he wanted to, he could have taken Jill along. Hell, he could have worked it so that Marty stayed home to babysit, and he could have come with Jill. And probably should have. But how do you know when one of these episodes is going to happen? And for how long do you put up with that perfect competence, that unrufflable understanding, that serene forbearance? Jack and Jill went up the hill and fetched the pail of water. Okay, and Jack fell down, which was bad enough. He felt like a fool, a clumsy clown. But when Jill took the tumble, too, just to make him feel less lonely, less hopeless, what good did that do? No good at all. Made him feel worse. The idea of Jill tumbling after, deliberately, out of charity . . . Well, who needs it? And he answered himself, with perfect clarity, *I do*. Which only made it worse.

"Thanks, puss," he said.

"You're welcome."

So, she wasn't going to push him any more. She would

forbear too. He was pretty lucky, he supposed. But it was depressing. And funny. Hilarious, even. Absurd and ridiculous that he should think of it as a problem. How many men wouldn't give a testicle to be able to use the other one as frequently and in such delightful and varied company as he had been doing? He sipped the whiskey, disappointed, for he had not been able to feel the least bit drunk. Not even groggy. He continued to burn brightly, despite all the extinguishers. Like one of those coal field fires that burn on for years. I burn my coal field at both ends. It lasts a hundred years. So all my foes and all my friends, let's have a round of beers. He wondered whether it was worth repeating aloud, for Marty's benefit. They had been very quiet with each other. More forbearance? To hell with it. It wasn't all that good, anyway. Nothing was, any more. Or, to be more sanguine about it, his critical faculties had outstripped his creative abilities. Or whatever. Nothing in seven months. If he had any sense, he told himself, he'd use this episode to some good purpose, cut out, take off, hole up in some cheap cabin, and write poems while in the other cabins on all sides ordinary people shacked up, committed suicide, divided loot, plotted the overthrow of governments, and did all the things that people do in cabins. They were always called Whispering Pines or Dun Roamin'. But he would not go. He would stay here and drink, and eat, and act like a poet, and arouse suspicion and envy from faculty members and admiration and envy from undergraduates. Act like a poet. It was easier to do that than to be one.

He thought of Jerome, in the library, wondered how

64

he was doing, and wished him well. As by an act of will, to add that in with the other wishes—for the cold sweat, the fear, the bowel tightening panic.

Marty was sitting on the bed. He noticed her sitting there, waiting for him to take notice of her. Like a dog. He stroked her neck and touched her ears. Dogs like that. She stroked his leg and started to stroke higher, as if her hand were iron and his genitals were magnetic.

There was some better machine. A generator, of course. He considered his genitals as a generator, as a car radio with the hydraulic, automatic aerial, as a radio transmitter sending out its beep-beeps into the ether. *Le machine de ma Chine.* The machine of my China? What else could you do with that? What had been done? There was Stevens' *Le mononcle de mon oncle.* And Whittemore's *Le masseur de ma soeur.* But what else? He thought for a while, going over 'm' words, and smiling at the notion that to Marty it would have to seem like satisfied purrings. *Le mamelon de ma melon.* The nipple of my melon? Well, why not? Da-da. Or Ma-ma. He looked down at Marty, and watched her hand move over him, very domestic, in a motion much like that of a woman at an ironing board.

He thought again of the cabin to which he ought to be going, in an old rusted Hudson Terraplane, with no identification in his wallet, no laundry marks in his clothing, and a couple of hundred dollars in small, used bills. And a yellow pad and an Estabrook fountain pen. Green. It was all terribly clear. And if only he could imagine it with microscopic detail, sneak into the imaginary cabin, and look over his shoulder, he might be able to read the words on the pad, steal his own poems, plagiarize from his own imagination . . . But he would not go. He would stay here, dissipate, enjoy, wallow like a child in the feather-bed of young minds. And young flesh.

Through half closed eyes, he looked at Marty, grave as she could be, distractedly playing with him, looking like a little girl with her toy, staying inside on a gray day, inside her room, inside her head. She was not really a beautiful girl, Royle observed, but pretty. Very pretty—which is sadder and more delicate, like the delicate wild flowers that fade, after their moments of trivial splendor. Sad and delicate, and sad because of the delicacy.

"What are you thinking?" she asked.

"About you," he answered.

"No, don't lie."

"But I was."

"You're nice to say so."

He tried to remember something of his thoughts that he could tell her, but there wasn't anything. She would not want to hear that he had decided she was pretty rather than beautiful. She would not want to hear that she was going to fade and was all the more delicious be-cause of that. She would want to hear . . . What? Some nonsense. That he was composing a poem. For her. Could he? He thought for a moment, and decided that the poem had already been done, many times before. 'Blue Girls' and 'Gather ye Rosebuds' and God knows how many others. It had been a legitimate emotional moment, a real combination of feeling and perception, but it was already expropriated by those swarms of poets who buzzed around in his mind, encapsulated in the amber of

66

their craft, his thoughts caught in their words, tamed by
their rhymes. Nothing was real except her hand on him,
the blonde down alive with the afternoon light as it
slanted across her wrist . . . The bracelet of bright hair
about the bone. Jesus, there was nothing left: Me Tarzan,
you Jane, we fuck!

Well, why not? That was the ultimate art form, the only
real one, the one in which one's sense of rhythm, one's
vocabulary, one's creative intuitions came into play, always new, unhampered by tradition, unfouled by publi-
cation, untrammeled by fellowships and grants, and
untouched by prizes and awards. The only legit art form
left.

He touched her arm, running his fingers along the
down of her forearm, which would last, and then up to
her upper arm which would not. Jill worried a lot about
her upper arms, the give-aways of age even in well-
preserved women. They had gone to hear Dietrich, and
all Jill had been able to talk about had been those incredible upper arms. Men noticed these things less than
women did . . . until women taught them how to notice.
What women could never understand was that there was
a coziness, a richness to those very flaws that they worried about so much. The beginnings of flab in Jill's upper
arms were comfortable, were soft as babies' thighs, were
evocative. It came back to gardens, and the appeal of
aging trees with dead branches and intricate gnarls.
Marty was a new dogwood, all spindly and upthrust,
with a scattering of flowers. And dogwood was fine in
its season. Springy, and all. But an elm was majestic. An

oak. A beech tree. He thought of Graves' alphabet of trees, and decided to hell with it.

He moved his hand to the back of Marty's neck, pulled her to him and kissed her. Because he wanted to. But also because the idea had crossed his mind that a little piece of her ass, just a snack, a tid-bit, might be exactly what he needed to calm down, to counteract the zooming, the high, the increasing spin of the fly wheel. He could use a little of that post-coital tristesse. *Bonjour, tristesse. Bonjour, monsieur. Voici le mamelon de ma melon.* No, it didn't work. *Melon* was masculine. *De mon melon.* Come to think of it, *mamelon* was masculine, too. Insane language.

And then the static began to let up. It was like a radio left on, tuned to a station that had signed off, and picking up only the sputter of spark plugs of a truck idling a block away. The truck drove off, and the sputter diminished leaving only a memory in the ear, like an after image—or was that the same truck, now half a mile away?—and then, finally, silence. The softness and wetness of her mouth, the touching compliance, the willingness to be taken as lightly as a cashew or a potato chip one munches while reading, the smoothness . . .

The phone rang. He picked it up.

"Mr. Royle?"

"Yes," he asked.

"This is the banquet manager. We're ready with the thousand shrimp cocktails you ordered."

"You're what?" he asked, and then, with his attention now switched back to the telephone, "What thousand shrimp cocktails?"

68

"You didn't order a thousand shrimp cocktails?"

"No, I did not!"

"Oh dear. How distressing. Would you be interested in a couple of hundred?"

"No!"

"Fifty?"

"Absolutely not!"

"A couple of dozen? We'll give you a very good price!"

"What the hell would I do with . . ." And then he stopped. "Sam?" he asked. "Is that you?"

"No, sir, my name is Horace Fenstermacher, and I am the banquet manager of this hotel."

"Oh, come off it!"

"But the shrimp cocktails, sir!"

"Double the order. Make it two thousand! And put it all on Sam Stone's bill, would you?"

"Yes, sir," the voice said, eagerly. "And thank you, sir. You've helped us out of a very awkward situation indeed. They were starting to spoil, you know. Our refrigerators aren't geared for that kind of an order . . ."

And then the voice broke into shards of laughter, in all different keys, low guffaws punctuated with high yips.

"All right, Sam, come up. I'm in 317."

"I'll be right there," Stone said.

Royle hung up. "That was Sam Stone," he told Marty. "One of his crazy bits. He wanted to know if I wanted the thousand shrimp cocktails now."

"Yes," she said, smiling. "I heard."

"Well, I . . . I had to ask him up. I couldn't have put him off. I'm sorry."

A brave smile, as from a child who is used to being put

off, and suddenly he felt a wave of tenderness for her, a pang of regret that there was so little he could give her, a tremor of guilt, even, because her claims on him were all the more legitimate for her refusal to make any claims. Her silence was unanswerable.

But there was nothing he could do about it now. Stone was on his way up, with his jokes, his heartiness, his mock machismo, and his arrogance. And his talent. Down underneath all the elaborate wrappings, a good mind. Royle sighed. He kissed Marty lightly on the lips.

"Later, puss," he said. "We'll have time later."

"Sure," she said. She jumped up and went to the mirror to adjust wisps of hair and to straighten her skirt. She, too, was forbearing. If only one of them were to show some selfishness, make some demands, be difficult. Even malicious. Delicious malicious Alice, asked Sacher-Masoch to her palace . . . Malice? *La malice de ma lice!* The malice of my bitch! He thought about that.

There was a knock at the door.

Jerome crossed the trim lawns that were sporting one of those pointless, intricate effects of Mama nature, the dabbling aesthete: the brightness of the new green of early spring washed over by the dullness of a leaden dusk. It looked artificial. Or perhaps that was the spill-over from the architect's drawing board, the neat quadrangles of his plan making the grass look artificed and deliberate. And, of course, it was. But the hour and the quality of the light conspired to make the reality look like the model, an architect's office toy grown huge. Even the two students at the opposite end of the quadrangle from Jerome looked as though they had been sketched in by the draughtsman's pen to give an idea of the scale of the buildings, and had been carefully built by a too literal contractor. The first prize in the competition: a full size globe.

He turned a corner, made his way between two of the neat Georgian buildings, and onto another page of the architect's sketch book, where there was a long mall leading up to the steps of the library. It was all very neat, the wash of color merely a suggestion, an attempt to counter the harshness of the black and white of the pen drawing. Neat, and delicate. And vulnerable. Frangible. He felt the pity for it that an anarchist must feel, detonator in hand, looking with sweet, profound sadness at the railroad bridge below him, susceptible to his whim, and therefore his creature. Not that Jerome had any detonator. He was, himself, a living bomb. Like that fellow in the Auden poem. "Clutching a little case . . . He walks out [something something] to infect a city." Damn! It wasn't so bad that he couldn't remember his own poetry, but not to remember Auden's was a nuisance. He didn't have it right, except about clutching the little case. And he had mislaid his little case, anyway. Which would be a funny version of the Auden poem, he decided.

He climbed the steps to the library, and went inside. It was a hot one. Libraries are either too hot or too cool. This was one of the former, with students, teachers, researchers, librarians, and guards, all heavy lidded fighting off drowsiness. A few more shovelfulls of coal, and they'd all drop off, succumbing to the spell of the evil magician

71

in the basement who had cleverly disguised himself in a maintenance uniform, the cap and coveralls of which hid his horns and forked tail. And into this enchanted land, a prince in a tropical worsted suit would come some day, to wake them all up, take out a book, and free the enslaved peasants in the valley. Would it be he? Hell, no! Let the peasants fend for themselves! Let 'em eat Toast-ems!

He wandered around, not wanting to bother anyone, not wanting to have to explain himself. He found a reading room, a sort of library within the library. He wandered along the shelves, looking for poetry. And found it, all together, 811 and 821, in the old Dewey Decimal System. The second and third Dewey numbers he'd ever learned. The first had been 599—for animal stories.

But to business! He would be shrewd about it, clever and bold. A journeyman poet, not too flashy, respectable but not memorable, whose poems nobody in the world would know by heart. That was what he wanted. He looked. Merrill Moore? Too idiosyncratic, too identifiable. And not Marianne Moore. Howard Moss? Howard Moss! Perfect! There couldn't be five people in the world who knew a Howard Moss poem by heart, or could even recognise one if they heard it. He opened a brown book and read a first line or two: "In Pusseyville, where pussies live . . ." What? He had to be kidding! Another: "Last summer's weed sprang from my window box,/a perseverant marvel . . ." Was it *perse*verant or perse*ve*rant? Ugly, either way. A perseverant marvel, indeed, Howard Moss! And you ought to know! Your career is a perseverant marvel! He who steals my wallet or my good name is a shrewd cookie, but he who steals trash is a lunatic. I will not steal from you.

He put the book back, and then just stood there, feeling the hopelessness of his situation growing about him, like the numbing cold that puts arctic explorers to sleep. Somewhere over there in the 599 section, there was a book about explorers who had eaten the last of their sled dogs, and, in the last chapter, succumbed to the drowsy comfort of the cold. He had been horrified at the idea of eating dogs, and had been rather pleased about the death of the explorers. Sentimental, he supposed now, but calling the emotion didn't make it go away. Maybe God is sentimental, a hopeless devotee of pulp fiction and B movies.

He went to sit down in one of the big, green leather chairs, afraid, even as he did so, that he would fall asleep like that undergraduate across the room in his beige shetland sweater and khakis and buff desert boots. He looked like a chameleon who had finally given up and was waiting to be picked off the green rock by some bird. The room was overheated. That was why the beige boy had fallen asleep, and that was why Jerome knew it was risky for him to sit down. But what was the risk? That he would sleep through the reading? Wonderful! He sank into the chair like one of those explorers had sunk into some soft snowbank, and let the fatigue swirl around him like warm water, washing away the will. Those clothes on that boy, he supposed, might have been vivid cranberry, turquoise and daffodil yellow when he'd come in, but utter relaxation had faded even the fabrics to those earth tones.

He adjusted his head to a position of greater comfort,

and, as he did so, he noticed on the table beside the deep chair a magazine. It was an undergraduate thing called *Spectrum,* which was banal, but not so bad as it could have been, not so bad as some of them that come on to shock and stayed to bore—*Afterbirth* or *Pismire.* He picked it up to pretend to read, as the bums pretend to read in the New York City Public Libraries on rainy days.

He let the magazine fall open in his lap, and as it did the idea fell open in his mind. He could take a poem out of an undergraduate magazine, steal something from one of the kids in the audience. Just for the sheer danger of it. He thought with disproportionate and melodramatic pleasure of the youngster in the audience hearing his own poem from the mouth of one of the big shots up there on the stage, and the puzzled rage, and the sudden doubt that the shock would produce—the poor thing would wonder whether he had really written the poem after all, or had read it somewhere, forgotten that he'd read it, and, in one of those monumental slips, scrawled it out as his own. Gorgeous!

He flipped through the magazine, and found a likely candidate:

LEDA IN THE RR STATION

By D. Martyn Vattlis

Long, along the rails, the spurt of light from its O
eye kept coming and coming and coming and coming.
Papers white as petticoats fluttered and upped.
Silver white on top, it was all the fiends'
below: pistons and cogs and wheels in a whirl.

leda stands with a portmanteau
her hat is fixed with a pin
she won't lose her bonnet when the gusts are upon it
as the 6:42 pulls in
perhaps her pretty new slip will show
(there are rosebuds stitched on the hem)
The Olympian to Chicago hit 80 over the bridge
and left the trembling trestle. Leda
leaned over to look for the local,
put one foot onto the track and fell . . .

(You guessed it.)

And suddenly she was a damned fool
or on the rail bed there for the love of God
or the train (an ex-swan, if you please) dead,
or alive in a brand new way. And she went
to Zeus, or Christ, or Utica, Buffalo, and on
to Chicago.

(It all depends on how
you think of
these things, I suppose.)

Well, that was urgent. Inept, but not without some flashes of something. He read it over a second time, trying to decide whether it was fixable. That was the way to do it, of course—to take some poem by an undergraduate, improve it, but leave it recognisable, and give something in exchange for that moment of anger and fear that the kid would go through. An educational experience! It would be amusing for a pirate from Ariel actually to deliver something of value for the money the college was paying, something more than a diversion, a bid for prestige, and a break in the social routine for the faculty. Fine, but what to do about this poem by this Vattlis person. (What kind of name was D. Martyn Vattlis, anyway? Anglo-Latvian?)

He took out his ball point pen and a piece of Collegiate Arms stationery he had brought with him, and set to work. What was there worth keeping? The attitude, nearly bored, rather indifferent, oddly distracted, with those throw away lines in parentheses (barely stifled yawns) was original. Clumsy but authentic. The kid was trying to work out a voice, an attitude toward the material. He wasn't just copying gestures of other poets. Or not much. The indented, uncapitalised section was neo-cummings, rather. But still, there was a voice, brash, wise-ass, and too strident, but a voice. And that was worth something. Worth attention.

What could he do with it? How could he best sidle up to the reality, stalk it, catch it, unawares? Were poems like unicorns? He wondered. Real innocence could just go out there and wait and the poem would come cantering up, gentle and affectionate, to lay its horned head in the chaste lap. But nobody stays a virgin for long. Not even an intellectual virgin. And the professional must learn to outwit the timidity of the beast, contrive snares, know the habits of the animal, play it. This Vattlis, like most undergraduates, was no longer that perfect innocent. English courses, no doubt. A dreary way to pop a cherry—by eroding it.

But the poem. Back to the poem. What was there underneath the construction that one could play on? Something physical and indisputable and yummy. The bait.

He thought about trains, trains in movies, real trains, subways, elevated trains, Disneyland monorails. The phallic business of a train roaring into—or out of—a tunnel was too intellectualised, too conceptual. It had been too much worked. But still, he remembered standing on the subway platform at 116th St, and feeling the vertiginous tug, the seductive, suicidal allure of the speed and noise of the thing. Its size.

He started to scribble, writing as quickly as he could, forming the letters so hurriedly that nobody else could have read them, and not even he, in six months, would be able to read them. But for the time being, this would do:

> The Olympian to Chicago hit 80
> over the bridge. The trestle trembled. Leda
> leaned, looked, The light from its O
> eye hypnotised, coming, coming . . .

That was a little better. Tighter. And lower down, the end was workable. But the middle was muddled, still.

> And Oh, God! But how else do you explain
> the way she fell for it? The white line
> runs along the platform, cautions: "Keep
> Back". And nobody's said that she was insane.
> But there was that passionate purr along the rail bed
> and the way that little locomotive loomed.
> She's dead, or alive in a brand new way, transported
> to Zeus or Christ or Buffalo and Chicago.

Not too bad, that. He counted the lines. Twelve. What the

hell! Two more, and it could be a kind of Merrill Moore
sonnet.

> Beware, you Ledas. Read your timetable notes.
> The train will make no stop to take on baggage.

He read it over, mostly to check it, to make sure that it
was good enough. Not great, but acceptable. Minimally
competent. That was what he wanted. But also, he was
trying to decide what it was—because it was neither this
nor that, neither his own poem nor Vattlis's poem any
more. It hung out there, illegitimate, brash, peculiar. Or,
actually, it was like one of those old communal produc-
tions, cathedrals and the like, that may have been important in themselves, but were never signed or claimed
or narrowed that way. They dedicated it all to God, and so
it didn't make any difference who had carved what, or
who had set which stone upon which. A not at all unattractive way to be. And he supposed that if he believed
in ART that way, he should be satisfied to have the poem
improved, to see it better than it was. And he was satisfied. Not as a career, perhaps, not for all time. But this
time. This poem. He felt very good about it indeed. Too
good to try to work up the rest of the portfolio. Something else would have to happen. He could fake a heart
attack or a coughing fit.

But he could not sit in the library any longer. He would
go back, join John for another drink, and then meet
the others and have dinner. And then into the lion's den.
To bell the cat.

CHAPTER 3

The name of the restaurant was The Bird and Bottle, alliterative, redolent of hearty old Englishness, boring. There was, Sam Stone said, a museum attached to the morgue in New York City where curiosities of death were on display. One of the more remarkable exhibits, he said, was the charred penis of a man who had urinated in a subway station. His stream had touched the third rail, and the current had run up the stream to electrocute the fellow. His bird was displayed in a bottle.

They all laughed, but in differing ways and with different tones. John Royle and Jerome Carpenter laughed simply because it was funny. Agnes Hartshorne laughed at Stone rather than at his joke. Maybe she thought the joke was funny, but she was not going to let down her guard on that account. Genteel, southern, perhaps a touch dikey, rather refined—she published in the *New Yorker*, which was something nobody else at the table did—she was not the sort of person to whom one told such stories.

Unwilling to go as far as not laughing, she settled on a strange eruption that was something between a giggle and a snort, all the while keeping the expression on her face quite severe. Elaine Dinsmore was a trifle embarrassed. And Professor Burton, at the head of the table, their host for the evening, at the dinner and at the reading afterwards, laughed to find himself in such company. How splendid to hear such droll things first hand, and not just read them in footnotes or discover them in correspondence in those uniform, marbled cardboard boxes in libraries.

"That smarts, eh?" Stone said, pushing his success.

"I don't know," Royle said. "Never tried it. Maybe it's the ultimate thrill."

A waitress came up to take the order for drinks, Jerome looked around the table and considered ordering a triple anything. The elation of forty minutes before had faded, and the feeling of soundness and wholeness that had come from doing the work on the poem had dissolved as it always does, but faster this time because of the impending reading, the presence of the other writers, the presence of Professor Burton who would not, Jerome was sure, be amused. He felt the absolute agony he remembered from his childhood of having to wait for the disaster of his performance at Mrs. Rutherford's annual recital, the terrible time of waiting with the other children, the meanness of rejoicing at their mistakes which would make his own playing less obtrusive and relatively—though not absolutely—less terrible.

He settled at last on a double scotch, and was displeased with himself not because he had really wanted a triple but because he had been unwilling to let the others hear him order it. The waitress took the rest of the orders and went off to the bar to get the drinks.

"How did you make out?" Royle asked, quietly.

"I didn't."

"No?"

"I couldn't find anything I liked enough to steal. It was pretty depressing."

"Everyone feels that way," Royle said. "Maybe that's why we write. I think it was Disraeli, or somebody around then, who said, 'When I feel like reading a novel, I write one.'"

"But that doesn't do me much good for this evening. I mean, what the hell am I going to do?"

"Tell funny stories, maybe. Lecture."

"Oh, sure."

"You could stutter. If nobody understood a word you were saying, it wouldn't make any difference what you said. Camp it up."

It was not likely. He had not had the nerve to order a triple scotch in front of a handful of people. How could he be perfectly outrageous in front of a whole roomful? He thought of leaving the table, leaving the room, going back to the Inn, or the library, and scribbling frantically to see if he could come up with something before the reading. But, no, he would wait for the whiskey. He'd need that either way, whether he stayed or ran. And all this banter . . . made him think of that phrase in the other pocket. *Over the fear, the foolishness.* Damn, but that was right. He didn't remember the rest, and would not, at the table in this company, take the paper out of his pocket to look at it. But whatever else was good or not good, that phrase was okay. It was sound and right. And there was a poem in it, bumbling toward Bethlehem to be born.

Meanwhile, he was sitting there, uncomfortable, foolish, living out the line of his poem.

"Look at it this way," Royle said, "and take some cheer in the fact that it could be worse. I mean, where's Hungerford?"

"I don't understand. What has that to do with it?"

"He's supposed to he here. But he isn't. He's probably off puking somewhere, terrified. Or maybe he's just avoiding dinner so that there won't be any damage to the Steinway later on."

There was a rustle behind Jerome and he turned, expecting to see Hungerford make his entrance. In a play, the mention of a name would be enough to bring the character onstage. But instead of Hungerford, there were two men, townies, who had come into the room. They went toward another table, and Jerome, having nothing better to think about, watched them. They approached the table at which two other men sat—were they salesmen?—and were greeted.

"How a' ya?" one of the seated men asked.

Jerome turned back to Royle who was listening to Sam Stone tell a story, the beginning of which Jerome had missed. And it was impossible to pick up because he kept using pronouns, the antecedents of which were beyond all guessing. Jerome looked back at the salesmen, and remembered that odd greeting, that Dixieland-Bronx pronunciation of the name of the fiftieth state. And how was that for spinning flax into straw, old Rumplesnitz? How a' ya, indeed!

"I'm Aggie Hartshorne," Aggie Hartshorne said. She was sitting on Jerome's right, and, being polite, she was reminding him of her name so that he wouldn't have to go "Uh . . ." while talking with her.

"How a' ya?" he said, and instantly felt like a jerk. "I'm Jerome Carpenter."

"I'm fine," she said, humoring the lunatic. "And you?"

"All right. A little nervous, I guess."

With some kindness she reassured him, talking about readings and how they could affect writers. Her theory was that it was partly the strangeness of a direct encounter with an audience and partly the meeting with other writers both of which groups were inevitably disappointing. "One always imagines an ideal audience, and no audience ever is. And writers are never what we imagine either, never so witty, so warm, so elegant nor so wise. Never George Sanders. Never Katherine Hepburn."

"No?" he asked. She was trying to be nice, and he was trying to be nice back. But she didn't know about the man from Paradise, and the belly futures, and the briefcase, or Vattlis. She was comforting him the way she would have comforted Hungerford.

"I'm not boring you, am I?" she asked, abruptly.

"No, no. I'm sorry. I was thinking."

"Never think at table. It's bad form. Observation is permitted, but not thinking."

"Oh?" His interest was engaged now. "But poets don't observe much. You write fiction and you have to observe things. But we only mumble to ourselves, and occasionally notice that what we have been mumbling makes a kind of sense."

"Now that's better. If you could only keep to that style and go on saying clever things, it would not be a bad weekend."

"You expect it to be bad?"

"Don't you?"

"Oh, yes. But all my poems have been lost."

"Lost?" she asked. And then she smiled, and the smile erupted into laughter. "Oh, that's rich! That's very good! That's marvellous!" punctuated by peals of laughter, in which Jerome joined because her taking it as a joke was, in itself, a joke.

"I left them," he said, "in T. E. Lawrence's taxicab."

"Delicious!" Miss Hartshorne exclaimed. "Beautiful!"

Jerome raised his nearly empty glass to her and then drained it. He had decided on the instant to order another drink. There was no discernible difference, anyway, between drunkenness and sobriety, between lunacy and sanity, between sense and nonsense. Not here, at any rate. He looked up for the waitress, and saw not the waitress but the gaunt, pale figure of Hungerford. Jerome tried to remember Hungerford's first name—Not John. Bob? Chuck? (Up, Chuck, Speak for Gaines!)

"Ed!" John called. "We were worried about you."

"Car trouble," Hungerford explained.

Royle introduced Hungerford to Professor Burton who introduced him in turn to the others around the table. Jerome, when it came his turn to utter some word of greeting, fell back on "How a' ya?" and immediately felt stupid again. Why was that dumb phrase still thrashing around in the scuppers of his mind like some fish that refused to gasp its last and die? What did it want to become? What could he do with it? The Honolulu relief roles as the Hawaiian Dole? The Hawaiian language with all those liquids and vowels? But all he knew of that was the vague residue of having heard the Hawaiian War Chant and the Aloha song. Which was all anybody knew of it.

Which was the opportunity! He could translate—or claim to be translating—into Hawaiian. Anything. Rilke, Dryden, Hofmannsthal. Into Hawaiian? Why not? *Ikehà manùha òha ìnee wà eelà!*

Hungerford had sat down and the waitress had come over to get his drink order—and to take orders for refills around the table. Jerome asked for another scotch, hoping that the waitress would merely duplicate his last one.

"Single or double?" she asked.

There were people looking at him, listening to him. John, Sam Stone, Agnes Hartshorne and Professor Burton up there at the head of the table. He tried, but failed. He couldn't bring himself to do it.

"A single this time," he said.

She nodded and turned to Sam Stone. Jerome turned inwards and fumed at himself. He would not be able to do it, after all. He could not get up there and spout fake Hawaiian. And he was disappointed! Which meant he had begun to look forward to it, had actually taken a few steps down that road. Two roads diverged in a yellow wood. I took the one less traveled by. That has made all the difference.

Could you be a *poète maudit manqué?* A poet *comme-maudit?* (*Comme-maudit Francaise!*) *Anahà ha àneh ùnu hàmala.*

"Who is your favorite poet?" Agnes asked him.

"Hm? Oh, I don't know. Pope, I should think."

"How boring."

"Pope?"

"No, not Pope. But I'd expected you to have an eccentric answer."

"Sorry," he said. "Who is your favorite short story writer?"

"I am."

"Oh, well. All right."

"Did you really lose them?"

He considered what to say. He wanted to make up something even more improbable. That he had traded them all for some magic beans.

"That's right," Royle said. "He did."

"But . . . but that's terrible."

"Yes, isn't it?" Jerome said, rather vaguely, smiling at what he suddenly fancied as the romantic negligence of it all.

"And there were no copies to be had from the library?" she asked.

"They were out," Royle said.

"Oh, well! Then you have nothing to worry about. They'll be at the reading, won't they?"

It was at the same time a new gleam of hope and the end of all the stratagems of which Jerome had become rather fond. The sirens, singing their Hawaiian translation of Homer receded into the foggy horizon. *Akàhooey là! Eea nà'eenà! Aloha!* He would miss them.

The waitress came to take the food orders. Jerome chose a ham steak with pineapple rings, even though it was not one of his particularly favorite dishes.

Edmund Walter Hall—dear, old Ed—was in front of them. Car doors were thunking about them as they pulled into one of the Reserved slots in the parking area. Stone's laugh floated across the air from one of the adjoining slots. Jerome had lost confidence in Agnes Hartshorne's reassurances that one of the copies of *The Double Agent* would show up at the reading. The reasonable probability was all on her side, but there is a point beyond which reason and probability had little influence either on one's own expectations or on the behavior of the world. The attorney's assurance that the governor must come through with a stay of execution is merely another torment for the condemned man in Death Row. And they had left the coziness of the cell block and were making their way now, across the courtyard to the gallows shed, the great difference being that instead of the civilised gallows Jerome could look forward to a horde of people who would by their laughter embarrass him to death. And instead of the taciturn guards and the sympathetic priest, he had only writers about him. Trivial scribblers! He supposed that he ought to compose himself, and work up some witty piece of gallows humor. He ought, at least, to write down some of the Hawaiian. *Hoowa tà'a oli'ày.* The glottal stop. Where you catch the *Streetcar Named De-*

*sire. Traveling Through the Dark. At the End of the Open
Road.* In a *Country Without Maps.* What else was there
like that? The metaphor of the journey, man. He was
skittish. He would lay his head on the big black block,
await the cheap and chippy chopper, and merely giggle.

Professor Burton led the writers across a corridor tiled
in black and white marble and into a small lounge where
they could wait until the program was about to begin. As
they crossed the corridor Jerome saw through an open
door the undergraduates sitting on couches and on the
floor in a large meeting room. There seemed to be an
awful lot of people in there. He wondered if he would
have come, had he been an undergraduate. Perhaps. To
see Stone. To see John Royle, he liked to think. And perhaps to see, if only to reassure himself that she was a
flash in the pan, the product of luck and puffing, and a
symptom more than a writer, Elaine Dinsmore. He would,
himself, not have been worth his going to see. But what,
then, did he have to worry about. *Àka hooey là!* That's
what!

But there was nothing else for it. He certainly wasn't
going to juggle, or balance pencils on the end of his nose.
He knew how to hold his nose, wail, hit himself in the
larynx, and perform a passable imitation of a bagpipe,
but he didn't think he would do that. He would do better
to compose something in Hawaiian. He took out a piece of
paper from his pocket, his ball point pen, and . . . But it
was the invitation he pulled out. He forgot about the Hawaiian and looked down at the sketch of the stanza he
had done on the plane, not that he intended to finish the
thing on the spot and on demand, but only hoping that

by sneaking up on it this way and looking at it freshly he might be able to tell if it was as good as he had been hoping.

> *Over the fear, the foolishness brays. The jay*
> *should be still, the grove be like a church . . .*

He stopped. Unless one stressed the second *be*, the second line was a foot short. He beat it out and thought of Arnold Stein or whoever it was who kept publishing articles on metrics in the PMLA. He had imagined Stein's office to be full of spoons, the bowls of which had beaten furrows into the wood of his work table as he pounded out his living. Jerome did it again. No, there were only four feet there.

"Is everyone ready? Is there anyone who wants to wash his hands?" It was Burton, announcing piss call. There was a bustling. Jerome had time to play a little more. There were only nine syllables. *Whole.* In front of *grove. Whole grove be like a church.* Padding? But the vowels were nice that way. He ignored the consonants and tried just the vowels. Ou-ē-ı̂-ə-ō-ō-ē-ī-ə-ur. The two long o sounds in the middle were a nice peak. Just the vowels that way, and it sounded rather Hawaiian.

He wrote in the change.

"Relax," Royle's voice said. "Professor Burton found one. It's his own copy, actually. One of his students had borrowed it."

Jerome looked up. Royle handed him a copy of *The Double Agent.*

"Oh. Thanks. I mean . . . Thanks."

"I'm as relieved as you are." Royle said. "I was . . ."

"Yeah." Jerome cut him off. What was there to say? He smiled, grateful, sheepish.

"Don't lose this one!" Royle said.

"No. I won't."

"Is everyone ready, then?" Burton asked, and they filed out to the reading.

The audience was sitting there, scattered around in the leather (or were they Naugahyde?) chairs and sofas, and packed in on the floor, all of them looking toward the seven chairs at one end of the room on which the six writers and Professor Burton sat. Jerome could feel their gaze, as if those seventeenth century physicists had been right and there were actually eye beams that went out from the eyes and bounced back like radar. It was not any hostility or animosity he felt, but only the weight of the attention of so many.

He was to go first. They were to read in alphabetical order, which was nicely egalitarian, but which worked out, nevertheless, to a reasonable order. Himself, as the throwaway, the animal act or the Zouaves that led off the Ed Sullivan show, and then Elaine Dinsmore, the first big attraction, the walking wound. And then Agnes Hartshorne, whose short story would be a change of pace from two poets. And Hungerford, the entremets. And Royle, and Sam Stone, bringing up the climax of the evening. Jerome was to read for ten or fifteen minutes. Make it ten, and let the others take up the slack. They had not come to hear him. He could be modest. And relax. He opened his book to look for something appealing, something just a little showy, but still solid. Something at the same time simple enough to be accessible to the ear. And then he noticed the notes. Written in, around the printed lines of his poems, there were notes, in a small, delicate hand. Professor Burton's? Or the student's? No, it would have to be Burton. No student would borrow a book and write in it. Even in pencil? To impress the professor? Or, worse, had the professor written in the book to impress the student? It was like that graffito—"Fuck the third grade"—which was more and more depressing the more one thought about it.

Worst of all, and most depressing, was the fact that his poems had been expropriated that way, had been subjected to these annotations. It was as if he were dead and the carrion birds had already landed to feed on the remains. The notes were not stupid. That wouldn't have been so bad, would have been, anyway, tolerable, he supposed. But, worse, they were insane. Erudite madness. The keenings of a Kinbote, the botchings of a Botkin.

As, for instance, the gloss on "Who lay in the grass, gorging on green fruit . . ." a more or less direct line. The green fruit was greengage plums, and they were green because the grass was green and because of the Lorca line, "*Verde, verde, yo te quiero verde.*" But Burton had looked it up somewhere and written in, beside the line, "Dionysius—cf. Frazer, 387, 'he of the green fruit.'" What was there to do? How to evict Dionysius from the poem? How to foreclose?

Again, another note from the dotty *dottore*: "St. Jude—martyred with a club." St. Jude had nothing to do with it! It was just a club. "Like a sword hanging over your head, but crude, rude/as a club . . ." Why did it have to be so obscure as Jude's club?

He wondered whether, if he'd known about it, he would have used it. But the thing was that he hadn't known about it, and that it didn't belong in the poem. Or did it? Was every reader's poem a part of the poem? Even this Balmy Botkin? And from Botkin he went to Bodkin, Maude, and from her to the other Maude, and what a pair of lethal ladies they were, Bodkin and Gonne.

Professor Burton was welcoming the audience, welcoming the writers, saying the grand, gracious things he had worked out to say as the Duke of Bedlam who had come to open the fair. And in a moment, he, Jerome Carpenter, fugitive from Ariel Editorial Service, writer of cribbed masters' essay and fake doctoral dissertations would get up, pretend to be a poet, walk three or four steps to the lectern, and tell them . . . What? What was there to tell them? They were all sitting there, waiting to have the secrets of the universe unlocked by some ray of wisdom that would converge on their foreheads like that ray in the ad for the Rosicrucians (AMORC) (Not a religious organisation) . . . Horse shit, he said to himself, clearly, making the final s separate and distinct from the digraph that followed it. It sounded rather delicate and refined that way, wonderfully sharp. It had the precision of wasp's sting, when every letter is articulated. "Horse shit," he said again.

Professor Burton glared at him. Had he heard? He had. He was not pleased. Had he taken it as a comment on his nut notes? Good. Let him. Anyway, Jerome was sure he was off to a great beginning. Or, perhaps, right there, in one of those accidental moments of divine inspiration, he had given that secret of the universe, right there, and had said all there was to say. All else was commentary. What did Burton want? "Life is a fountain?" Horse shit!

Professor Burton sat down. Jerome sat for a moment until he realized that it was his turn, now, now he had to get up, now he had to walk the three steps and . . . do what? At the lectern, he opened the book at random, in the manner of a bibliomancer who hopes for a sign from the book itself. He looked down and saw his poem, a kind of answer to Frost's poem about birches. He looked up.

"I'm afraid that this first poem requires a word or two of explanation. I mean, not the poem, but one of the terms in it which may be unfamiliar to some of you. The birch miner, or birch leaf miner as it is sometimes called, is a pest that . . . uh . . . attacks birch trees. It's a larva, actually. You have to spray for it three or four times during the summer. And if you've got a large birch tree, the spraying can be a big job. You've got to get one of those big ones that can throw the lindane—or whatever you're using—twenty-five or thirty feet up into the air to get to the top of the tree."

He paused, looked down, cleared his throat, was about to begin to read, but then he had another thought he thought he ought to share. "Oh, and the birch miner makes the leaves of the birch tree turn brown and fall off. The trees look pretty awful."

He looked out to see how they had taken all this agricultural agent's lecture. Was it Henny Youngman who asked at the start of his act, "How do you like me so far?" This would be a good time for that. Or, better, he could just go on talking about garden pests for two or three hours, show a few slides, and sit down. Would anybody notice? They were so receptive, so passive. He had the delicious idea of turning the page to another poem altogether, one that had nothing at all to do with birch trees. They practically begged to be gulled, to be conned, to be utterly confused and mystified. But the poem was there, in front of him. He looked up and smiled, and hoped that the smile would pass for charm. It would have to do. He looked down at the book again, cleared his throat and started to read.

It only took him a couple of lines, maybe three, to get into the poem. And then he didn't care about them any more, or about Professor Burton behind him, or about anything but the cadences, the music of the lines, the dialogue between rhythm and meter, the volley of the vowels and the conspiracy of the consonants. It was a good poem. Felt good, tasted good in the mouth, still. And if it took off from Frost, it took off far enough and high enough, describing the ailments of a birch tree with grace and precision, and bringing the nastiness of nature into it so very casually. It wasn't the Frost poem, so much, as the idea of the Frost poem, the anti-poem in the heads of damn near everybody who turned what Frost had said into the dreariest kind of Currier and Ives crap. Really, what Frost had been talking about was human limitation, swinging up toward heaven and down again, and still affirming, but in a great, tough-minded way that the earth was preferable, in some ways, to heaven, and that "One could do worse than be a swinger of birches." And he had picked that line up, bending it a little, in "Lest they get worse, to be a sprayer of birches . . ." in the middle, there. It was a nice thing, and, while he was reading it, for that couple of minutes, satisfying. He looked up at the end, happy with the poem, and not particularly caring whether they had shared his happiness or not. But they applauded. He felt very good.

He turned to another poem and continued reading. He read four before he began to wonder how long he had been up there, and how much time he had left. He had no idea whatever of how much time had gone by. It felt like a minute or two, but he knew that it had to be more than that.

"Do I have time for one more?" he asked Professor Burton.

The professor nodded, yes, and Jerome reached into his pocket for the Leda poem, his flashy conclusion, the silly virtuoso performance. He did not want to miss the chance to play with that one. He wondered whether Vladimir Horowitz used to worry, off stage, after a concert, that the applause would die down before he had the chance to go out one more time, for the last encore, and do that flashy arrangement of "Stars and Stripes Forever." Musical nonsense, but impressive. And the only way of expressing the wonderfully manic feeling that came from having performed well, to dazzle because you felt, for the moment anyway, dazzling.

He looked up from the paper and said, "I have a new one, one that isn't in the book. And it's always interesting to try out one of the recent things." And then he read it.

It went well enough. For that matter, it went as well as any of the other, real poems had gone. There was a lightness in his voice, a tone that communicated to them out there that it was, somehow or other, a joke, and they took it that way—as an extravagance, as a tour de force, which he supposed it was. But the applause that followed it, identical with the applause that had followed the other poems, or even louder than that, depressed him. He tried to explain to himself that this final round was not just for that final poem, but for him, for his *oevre*, or, at least, for the whole group of poems that he had read, and for the reading. But there was still the nagging worry that nothing made any difference, and that if this spurious, foolish put-on could please them, then their pleasure didn't mean a thing. He acknowledged their clapping, nodding his head, bowing, as it were, from the neck, and saying, softly, inaudibly in the noise of the clapping, over and over, "*Àka hooey là! Àka hooey là! Oàhu!*"

He sat down. Professor Burton got up, thanked him with a great show of warmth, and began to introduce Miss Elaine Dinsmore, girl wonder. The introduction was hardly necessary. Everyone knew who she was, had come to hear her, and to see her, and to sympathise with her, the poor dear. Who was there, in the room now, who didn't know her touching story, hadn't read in *Time* or *Newsweek* or *The New York Times* of her incredible recovery from the most severe mental illness through the healing wonder of art? Human interest? She was as good as a baby girl caught in a well on her birthday, with the rescuers drilling away in a race against death, while the mother, up above, wept over the icing of the birthday cake. That, and the sponsorship of Richard Lovell, had made her Miss Poetry of the year. Not since Sylvia Plath

had put her head into an oven and twirled the little
Magic Chef dial up above Broil past Death and all the
way to Fame had there been anything like her. Jerome
had sat at the other end of the table from her at dinner
not so much because he had been avoiding her as because
he was recoiling from her. He watched as Professor Burton concluded his introduction, turned, bowed slightly,
and Elaine Dinsmore ambled up to the lectern, walking
with that slight stoop that tall girls often affect. It didn't
do any good, and only made her look worse. And yet,
because of the poetry and the aura of the poetry, it was
perhaps a philosophical stoop, as if the griefs of the ages
were piled on her frail shoulders for all the world to see
if only it had eyes. And if it didn't have eyes, ears would
do, because she was ready to tell all.

He was not being at all charitable towards her. He
wondered whether it was envy, raw green envy, that
prevented him from offering that sympathetic fellow-
feeling for which she asked. Or was it the insistence with
which she asked? He listened to her for a moment:

> I have discarded hair and fingernails
> have felt my teeth come loose, dangle, fall
> out, leaving the space tender. Boils
> I've observed growing to their ripeness, growing . . .

It was her abortion poem. Or maybe it was only a mis-
carriage. He hadn't been sure, or cared enough to puzzle
it out. But he remembered it, and remembered his discomfort at it. Her work was not his cup of tears.

She stood there, reading her lines about her loins with

the most improbable calm and a rather attractive precision of diction, and Jerome tried to leap from the reading and the poem to the experience itself. But there was
not much left of it. It was like one of those shrunken
heads in the museum at Harvard, all wizened and diminished. It could hardly relate in his mind to the tall, big-
boned, broad-beamed girl before him. There was a kind
of delicacy at the neck and jawbone. Concentrating on
those features, he tried to think of her in a sexual way.
But the drone of her voice interfered. And the ridiculousness of knowing so much about her, even though they
had just been introduced. Why was she telling him—and
the whole room—these terribly private things? What
could he say to her afterwards, at the party at Professor
Burton's house? All the forms of normal discourse were
violated.

He looked out at the audience, trying to gauge their
reaction to La Dinsmore, and as his eyes swept over the
attentive faces out there, he began to wonder if perhaps
he was crazy and they—and Elaine Dinsmore—were right.
He looked at the eyes out there, riveted on the speaker,
and . . . But then he noticed Marty. Where had she been
all this time? And suddenly he realised that she could
not have come to the dinner, that her presence there
would have been inappropriate and too public a flaunting,
and that she had had to go off by herself and eat
. . . Where? In the dining room of the Collegiate Arms?
In some hamburger joint of the cheerlessly cheerful kind that always sprouted on the fringes of campuses?
In her room? Each tableau appeared in his mind, and
each was more depressing than the last. The mawkish-

ness of it did not bother him. There was something poignant about solitary meals in strange towns, just as there was something pathetic about small sums of money. The ruinous cost of Gogol's overcoat! But to hell with that. To hell, for the moment, with literature and the metered complaints of Elaine Dinsmore. Jerome's attention was fixed upon the oval face and the long blonde hair of that girl. Into his brooding, Miss Dinsmore intruded.

> And into the marsh comes the tide
> to hide all that breeding, the
> salt tang of it, like tears . . .

Still? Still on the same old thing? Was that all she wrote about? She had as much range as one of those Chatty Cathy dolls! It was depressing. And, even worse, it was wrong! The great heartbreaking moments about sex were not the biological ones after all, but the social ones of the kind that Jane Austen and George Eliot described. Or of Marty's kind, eating alone in a hotel room during the official dinner party.

They were applauding. Startled by the noise, and hoping that nobody had noticed how he had been drifting and that he had been late in joining in, Jerome took his hands from his lap and beat them together. They stung. He felt like a trained seal that had just performed "Going Home" on the bicycle horns. (My Antonin.) It was the fact that he was one of the performers that made him feel odd about clapping. They were watching him. And clapping was really a dumb thing to do. Strange way to show approval. He wondered how many others in the room had been embarrassed and were clapping now because they didn't want anyone else to know that they had been embarrassed.

Or was it possible that the private retreats into which her confessions forced an audience were the object of the game? That was where one was supposed to go? Her poetry would not be anything more, then, than an occasion for feeling. But no, if that was art, what he did was not. Simple as that.

He stopped clapping. He was virtually the last to do so.

Professor Burton rose to introduce Agnes, who announced that she would read a new story entitled, "The Peacock's Tail." She cleared her throat and began. It was a story about a middle aged woman on a plantation in the Delta who was convinced that her children were trying to poison her, and who tried to protect herself against them by getting a flock of peacocks because she believed in what was, apparently, an old piece of folk lore about peacocks ruffling their tails in the presence of poison. It was a dark, gloomy story, rich with details, and yet pushing toward the dreaminess of insanity. And the turn of the story was that the children were in fact poisoning her, peacocks or no, but that she had, in those last weeks, enjoyed the birds and loved them.

It was easier to listen to a story than to a barrage of poems. Or, at least, it was easier for Jerome. He supposed that he was probably able to listen more intently, more openly, to fiction if only because he was not in that racket, was not competing, was just another consumer. But that was perhaps too harsh. It was a good story. And he liked

Agnes. And it was a nice thing about those peacocks. He wondered where she'd found that out. That peacocks fan their tails in the sight of poison was a good thing to know, even if it wasn't true. The illusion of control over the world, the persistence of that kind of witchcraft was, he felt sure, very close to the heart of whatever it was that they were all doing. Any child who has ever walked the pavement, avoiding the cracks and the lines in the cement out of solicitude for his mother's backbone was a potential poet. Or a reader of poetry. It was a shame that so many lost it.

He was sorry, now, that he had been so preoccupied at dinner. He had dined with her, but they had hardly talked. And he remembered, now that the thought had struck him independently, how John Royle had mentioned in a letter that Agnes Hartshorne would be there, and had added a laconic parenthesis, "(she's okay)" which was high praise. He promised himself that he'd ask Royle about her, at the party afterwards. And immediately he found himself comparing her with Elaine Dinsmore, about whom there was nothing left to ask. This was far better. "What I miss," one of the editors had written about his new volume, rejecting it, "is your own voice, your confession, your person . . ." Shit on that!

Agnes Hartshorne finished her story. Applause. Professor Burton, carnie barker of the high-brow mid-way, ringmaster of the animula acts, raconteur, wife-beater, child-molester, philanthropist, and department chairman, was introducing Hungerford. Old Chuck.

There were metaphysical poets, but he was the emetiphysical. Or meta-emetical. Rometic? Vorticist and vomiticist. A book of verses underneath a bough. A loaf of bread, a bottle of ipecac, a Steinway grand piano and thou. He was being less than kind. A little more than kin and less than kind. Because he admired, in a way, the physical honesty of the guy. It was, this standing up before the mob, nauseating. Artaud would have admired it. The theater of cruelty. The theater of indigestion. My Antonin, again, eh?

Hungerford looked pale, but not green nor ashen grey. He walked to the lectern very steadily, if rather too carefully, like a drunk who is trying to walk that straight line, fool the cops, and avoid a charge of drunken driving. He put the book on the lectern and, from the back, Jerome could see him wiping his sweaty palms on the cloth of his trousers. It was impossible not to feel for him and with him. Beyond the jokes Jerome had made, beyond all that camouflage of the mind, there was the real object. If only the fellow didn't have to look out and see all those people looking back. Blindness could be a blessing. Homer had been lucky, after all. What could he have seen in the faces of those Smyrna merchants worth looking at? Izmir, it was now. All those guys in the marketplace, in brown togas, selling rugs, and speculating in frozen camel bellies. He began to read. Jerome did not listen. He was deaf in his left ear. Having had a chronic middle ear infection as a small boy, he had no ear drum left. It was a nuisance, sometimes, but there were compensations. He could fall asleep in any noisy place simply by putting his right ear on the pillow. He saved a considerable amount of money on phonograph records, not being equipped, himself, to receive stereo. And, at moments like this, he was able to lean upon his right fist, slouching in his chair just a little bit to do so, and closing off his right ear with the fist upon which he leaned. He would not intrude, would not add his own weight to the burden of scrutiny under which Hungerford labored. The book he held in his hand betrayed the slight trembling of his hands, of his stretched nerves, vibrating under the tension. The torment was as eloquent as any poem could be, and Jerome realised that he was blocking his ear partly out of sympathy, but also because he was afraid that the poems would be less than the poet, and would demean and diminish that touching terror.

Oh, it was agony to see him, to stare at the barely perceptible flutter of the pages of Hungerford's book. Was it true, then, that all poets were like this? Jerome could remember no particular moment at which he had decided to become a poet, or realised that that was what he was. But there was a mood, a general impression he could retrieve, a memory of a lonely childhood, of long, quiet afternoons in his room, and how that room was a refuge from the boulders of Central Park in which no picturesque trolls or malevolent spirits dwelled, but savage boys, his own age, of whom he had been terrified. The thought of it, even now, in the safety of maturity, and the security of this civilised room, made him start to perspire, not so much with the old fear which was gone, but with the shame of it. To have been beaten, to have had to hide as he had done, caused him still to feel the heat and dryness of his breath, the shallowness of his breathing. He put his left hand to his jaw, to touch the scar, the small L-shaped scar from a snowball that had a piece of ice in it.

But like the deaf ear, he supposed, there were advantages in terror, too. He had not been able to see it in himself, but looking at Hungerford, he was able at least to speculate on the possibility that fear, raw, physical fear, had a kind of gift to give, too. Who but the terrified has heard his own heart pounding, listened to his own stertorous breathing, wishing that heart and lungs would be more quiet, and yet learning in their pulsation the lessons of rhythm and metrics? It was animal fear, of the kind that animals have, and who knows nature as well as the animals? Over the fear, the foolishness, of course, but first the fear. Life, at its most intense, is aware of death. Or is it that the fear of death makes us aware of life? The trouble was that all these formulations were too heavy, too dignified in their tone. Too heroic. But a scared kid, who invented new and ever more circuitous routes home from school, was as scared as any hero. More. Was as scared as any coward. The meek he knew about. He wondered whether the cowards were going to inherit the earth. If they were, he knew he stood a good chance for a piece of the legacy. As did Hungerford, there. And Royle? And Stone? He had no idea. And the women?

But women were always frightened. Timid, cautious, they were unanimous in their meekness. Maybe it was the fact of childbirth and the dread of that? No! And yet they seemed to live in their own bodies more than men.

He was finished. They were clapping. Jerome clapped too, more sincerely, more enthusiastically than for anyone else. And he had not heard a word of Hungerford's recitation. So, he had joined the others, was part of the audience, now, and that worst part, the part he had feared and despised because it came not to hear the work but to see the man. The work and its quality were irrelevant—absolutely irrelevant. He was beating his hands together so that the palms stung, and he had not heard a syllable. And this was what he had feared for himself, and had been so reluctant to receive. It was depressing. The mindless adoration, the lack of discrimination and judgment, the easy fervor all contradicted what he was about in his writing. And yet he had gone over. Hysteria and the madness of crowds was what it was. Terrifying. And yet familiar enough. In all those Italian churches, the deplorable inconsistency of the artistic performance, and worse than that, the utter indifference to artistic performance, had been irksome and distressing. In one lunette, a Michelangelo, and in the next, a perfectly dreadful nineteenth century Jesus with eyes that followed you as you moved. Absolute Woolworth. Woolworthlessness. But the believers, for whom the walls were decorated, did not care. They looked through the differences in composition and brushwork, through the facility or ineptitude of the handling of light and shadow, through the tough-mindedness or the sentimentality, as if these things hardly existed, and saw only the portrayed figure, the Jesus of their own mind's eye, to whom they could pray. And the truth of it was that, in all probability, the excellence of aesthetic judgment had nothing to do with faith. Or varied inversely with the faith. To the real believer, it was all the same. And here he was, believing. In what? Ah, but the believer does not ask questions.

When John Royle had taken his place at the lectern,

Jerome felt himself relaxing. He knew John's poems, knew John, felt as close to John as to any writer in the world, and looked forward to hearing the familiar poems read with the familiar inflections, and the idiosyncratic lilt of his meters. He could, at last, suspend his critical faculties, and enjoy, directly and entirely what he heard. And yet, he thought, that was not the ideal way, either. Oh, of course, it was fine for him, nice and cozy, the way it would be for a child hearing a favorite bedtime story from Daddy, in his own room, in his own bed. But it was not fair to the poems, which deserved better than that easy acceptance. The poems were fine, tough, carefully wrought pieces, and to use them in this way would be to abuse them. It would be like using a tempered Damascus blade to spread margarine. The virtue was in the strength, and the strength ought to be used, to be tried against the best steel one's mind could produce. That was the critical apparatus which the enormous strength would conquer, which the sharp edge would cleave, and it would be in that triumph over legitimate resistance that the poems would show their worth and their honor.

Out of loyalty to John Royle, then, and out of friendship, he roused himself from that nursery's truckle bed and forcibly brought himself back to Edmund Hall, sat up straighter in his chair, and listened with his guard high, parrying, trying to ward off the thrusts of imagery, the feints of wit, the fancy footwork of the prosody, and the sudden saber slash of vision. But it was almost impossible to do. He felt a hit, a palpable hit, and then another, and then . . . But it was so much better to yield to the poems. He was cheering for Royle anyway. As they were, all of them out there. And in an odd glancing way, as out of the corner of his eye, but still with perfect clarity, he saw an explanation, a perfectly possible explanation for Royle's silence, for that long dry spell. The honors, the success, the invitations to do think-pieces for *The New York Times*, the prizes, all of these desirable things were conspiring to confuse the man. It was hard for him to know when he had done well if there was no resistance. Or it was hard for him to feel the need to do well if anything at all met with approval. What kind of bullfighter could continue to work close to the bull if the aficionados shouted Ole! whenever he smiled at them, whenever he adjusted his hat, whenever he farted? It would all seem pointless, wouldn't it?

Once more he roused himself to attention, listened hard, fought against the poems, but again he collapsed. It was like reading a history. He could admire small things, but the large patterns were already clear, the results known, the battle having been fought and won long ago. A poem yields itself that way only once. Often it is not at the first reading, but the second or third. But that is the time, the one time. The poem opens itself up, and the mind of the reader opens itself, and there is a meeting. And after that there is only the reenactment, which is less vivid, less sharp. After a long time, of course, when the poem has faded sufficiently, there can be a new reading, but even that will lack the sudden shock, the astringency, the prickly immediacy of that first full encounter. If it were otherwise, Jerome thought, we could each find our perfect poem, and stop, marry that one and remain faithful to it. As readers and as writers, too. Hav-

ing written the one finally satisfying poem, we could stop.
And there was something appealing about those obscure
names in anthologies, the authors of those single poems,
who appeared to have done exactly that. It was not true.
Henry King, for instance, continued to write after "The
Exequy" but he might as well have stopped there. And
maybe that was it with John. Maybe he had decided
what King ought to have decided, that the uttermost
poem was already there. No, it didn't seem right. It was a
nice construction, but false. Still, there was something to
play with, some connection between Royle and King.
King's blood—Royle? Ridiculous.

Why was he not listening to his friend? He felt guilty,
traitorous and stupid. But it is impossible to absorb more
than two or three lyrics. The first one wounds, and the
second, perhaps. And the third kills. And then the others
are simply bullets in a hunk of insensate meat. At the
most there is a twitch when some moribund ganglion is
bruised or severed. That Damascus blade was just another butcher knife now. For him. For the others out
there in the audience? Perhaps there were a few still
alive, only wounded. Or not even touched. The idea of
the audience as targets in a shooting gallery. Two ducks
and a candle still up. And Royle, the sharpshooter, ping-
ing away at the few remaining difficult marks. Jerome
had been lucky, he thought, to go first.

Having settled that question, even though he had
hardly been aware before that it was a question, he felt
that he had accomplished something. He had decided
something. He had been lucky to go first. Good. And
God saw the light that it was good. And if He had not?

If He had changed His mind right then? And God saw the light and asked, who needs it? And He blew it out. The end. There was a whole genre. "Call me Ishmael. No, actually, my name is Herman. Oh, to hell with it. Call me . . . In fact, don't call me, I'll call you. The end." What other great first lines were there? "Of man's first disobedience and the . . . Fruit? Would you care for a piece of fruit? The pears are very nice. Here, let me get you one." Whereupon Mr. Milton went out to the kitchen, and, being blind, fell upon the coal scuttle, hitting his head on the corner of the stove and expired. His countrymen feigned grief but were secretly pleased at the news. As one poet admitted at the funeral, "So long as J. M. was alive, I was not the greatest poet in England."

He gave it up and returned to John Royle's poems, listening as he had been listening at the start, uncritically, for the pure pleasure of it, with the familiarity framing the poems in irrelevant but not displeasing arabesques and curlicues.

John finished and there was applause, and then Professor Burton, Anatomist of Melancholy, introduced the man who, he was sure, needed no introduction—Mr. Samuel Stone. Burton sat down and Stone took his place. Took Royle's place, really, for Burton scarcely counted. And the difference between the two men struck Jerome as the difference between a boxer and a wrestler. It was their physical presences, the shapes of their bodies that suggested the comparisons. Royle was rangier, and looser in his movements and gestures. And he had that odd trick of moving his head at the neck like a Balinese dancer—or like a boxer. Stone was chunkier, barrel

chested, stolid, and his beard was at the same time menacing and comical, as were the get-ups of villains of the
wrestling ring. (Whatever happened to Gorgeous George
and The Masked Marvel?) But the difference between
boxer and wrestler seemed for a moment a reasonable
way of thinking about the two men as practitioners of
their different art forms. The poetry was like boxing,
faster, flashier, and more satisfying to watch, even if it
was more demanding upon the knowledge and perception of its audience. The wrestling of prose, the sweaty
grappling with the world in long hammerlock paragraphs,
the vulgar plotting, the temptation to cheap showman-
ship, to pandering to ignorance, and to easy moral pos-
turings were all the business of fiction writers. *Proseurs.*
Still, there was something impressive about the beefy
strength, the thickness of the volumes, the canvas thump
of meaning and the groan of characterisation that came
out of it. Stone looked, indeed, like a wrestler. Especially
from the back.

He was still clearing his throat, and rearranging papers
on the lectern. And now he was taking a drink of water.
Would he then sneeze, which would authenticate the
truth of his tales, as in the folklore of whatever country?
What country? Did "Til Eulenspiegel" begin with a
sneeze, Jerome wondered. Some record liner had explained about the myth of the sneeze. And he had heard
—from John?—that the stories were true, that Stone wrote
only true stories, reciting, over and over again, the same
story which was re-enacted between writings, to refresh
the truth he liked to tell. The stories were of seductions
he had effected, and were themselves the penances for

the seductions. They were handy penances, because they were wonderfully sincere and self-abasing—Stone was always the villain—and yet effective in furthering his career. And even profitable. What was it that *Playboy* had paid for that last one? $2,000? $2,500? A lot.

And yet, and yet . . . Jerome had to admit that he was interested in hearing this story Stone had started to read, that seemed as though it would be true to form and recount some seduction or other. Or some combination of seductions. If, indeed, he was ever that profligate with his material. There was an altogether deplorable but still undeniable feeling of being on the inside of things, of knowing the secret. Scholars made a great deal out of identifying fictional characters. Squire Allworthy was so-and-so, who financed a lot of the buildings in the City of Bath. That kind of knowledge. But it was the same kind of knowledge as the Woolworth girls enjoyed, as they moved their lips (from which they had just blotted the last traces of a chocolate malt) along the lines of the latest bestseller. *The Adventurers* was Rubirosa, and the *Valley of the Dolls* was Judy Garland, and . . . And so what? But one could say, "I know!" and smile, content. Or was it that the truth of fiction was no longer enough, and that there had to be some external referent to authenticate all those long descriptions, all that dialogue, all that plot?

He listened to Stone's confession, spotted the Stone surrogate in the story, and contemplated the stripping away of modesty and of privacy which was not only the subject of the story, but which the writing and public reading of the story repeated. Stone was very good, he noticed, on smells. He was good at all kinds of tawdriness, describing vividly the dandruff on a collar, the battered bristles of a hair-brush, the frayed edges of the world. The attempt, Jerome supposed, was to be prickly, as if to imitate the artichoke, so that the soft heart would be all the more appreciated when one finally got to it. The artichoke theory of art was the optimistic one. The onion was a better vegetable. More homely, and with nothing in it at the middle but smaller, more tightly coiled rings of the same stuff. And tears all the way. He was coming to his climax—his hero's and the story's. And maybe his own. And all those undergraduates, the young men and women out there, were gazing at him, as if he were some kind of Salome. But no, at the end he switched roles, and suddenly there he was, bringing his own head in on a plate, and the head was smiling, hoping for approval. Ludicrous. As in *The Mikado:* "Now though you'd have said that head was dead, for its owner dead was he . . . Though lifeless yet, it couldn't forget the deference due to me." Jerome had left out a line, but it didn't seem to make any difference.

It was curious about Stone. There was no accounting for taste, said the old saw, and yet, even so, it was hard to see how so many wives of faculty members went for him. He was hardly attractive in any conventional way. Stocky, and with that peculiar little beard, he looked like a cartoon character. And yet, according to his stories and according to the gossip Jerome had heard from John, he did seem to find many willing partners in his researches for further fiction. But maybe that was it. Maybe those women wanted to be immortalised in prose. Maybe it was the charisma they wanted to take to bed, and if they regretted the package, they were still willing to put up with it. It made no sense. He wondered what he would do, how he could expect himself to react, if he were to find out that Stone had been telling the truth, and that these colleges were actually full of sexual possibilities. What would he do if there were girls lined up back at his room at the Collegiate Arms? He could not answer because he could not bring himself to believe in the question. It was one of those fake questions, like the one in freshman ethics about pushing the button that would provide a million dollars, but would kill a Chinese. Sure, he'd push the button. So solly, please. But if there really were such a button? Really really! It's impossible to tell. Maybe Truman ordered them to drop the bomb because he just didn't believe in the bomb. Couldn't imagine it. Well, probably he couldn't. Not really.

But now, after the coupling, after making the beast with two backs, Stone was putting his character through all kinds of hell. From the woman. From the woman's husband. From himself. It was a goddamned True Confession. But so was *Madame Bovary*. He had misjudged Stone and the story. It was truer and better and more honest than anything that Jerome had been able to imagine. Brash, really, in its honesty. For the ending was another trip to another college, for another reason, six weeks after the incidents of the main part of the piece. And there was another wife—this time of the department chairman. And the hero—protagonist, rather, for he was anything but heroic—was feeling the same quiver in the loins, sending out the same tentative feelers, and getting the same answers. He had learned nothing, had accomplished nothing, had changed not at all. The whole period of remorse and anguish had been nothing more than another kind of self-indulgence, no more admirable or significant or noteworthy than the lechery which had given rise to it, and would again. Was it the circularity that made it go, the shape, the sense of form? Was it nothing but a clumsy sestina in prose? He had no idea. But it was, at least momentarily, effective. And funny, too. It was, Jerome imagined, a general public invitation for all the girls and all the women in Edmund Walter Hall to meet with Stone later, back at the Collegiate Arms. The line would form outside of Stone's room. Well, maybe it would. Maybe, Jerome thought, he should put up a sign —two barbarians, no waiting—and pick up some of the overflow.

Professor Burton again, thanking them, the writers, for coming, and the audience for coming, and at last sitting down which was the sign for everyone to get up, writers and members of the audience both. Their revels now were ended.

"Do you write with music? I mean, with the phonograph playing. I always write with the phonograph playing, and I was wondering if that's right."

The girl was pert, a blonde with a little turned up nose and a page boy, and the anxiety with which she asked the question, the eagerness for reassurance that, yes, she was a writer, was all the more touching for her Breck-ad prettiness. Deep down inside there might be a tall, stooped, anguished Elaine Dinsmore. But that was sentimental and romantic, wasn't it? And, worse, it was a sign that Miss Dinsmore had won at least a skirmish on the darkling plain of his mind. Nonsense!

He was tempted, then, to turn the question aside with some silly answer, an answer that could be no more silly than the question, but he looked around, pretending to be considering what to say, but in fact panning over the room. There were other young men and women clustered around Jerome, who had their own questions to ask. And they might hesitate if he failed to take this first question seriously. Why had they come to him? It was a question better left unanswered. But there the answer was, in the larger crowds around Stone and Dinsmore and John. These had shrewdly decided that the Carpenter line was shorter, and that, for their purpose, one writer was nearly as good as another. Which was probably true.

"No," he said, "I don't. But that doesn't mean you shouldn't. It's a personal thing. Rilke used to write with a bag of rotten apples in his drawer because he liked the smell, but I don't do that either." He wasn't sure, now that he'd said it, whether it was Rilke or Heine, but it seemed ridiculous to go back and correct himself. It was all ridiculous. "Solomon Grave writes with a goose quill," he continued, "and Eliot wrote directly on a typewriter, which I don't do. If you write better with a phonograph, then it's right for you."

"Thank you," she said. "Thanks very much. I've worried about that a lot."

"How do you get your ideas for your poems," a tall, redheaded boy asked. His red hair and light blue eyes gave his face an interesting look, slightly whimsical and at the same time possibly insane. He was the kind of fellow, Jerome decided—on no evidence at all—who goes berserk and shoots people from the tops of bell towers. The question was not very interesting, and that was disappointing. Lunatics ought to ask original questions.

"I don't," he said. "You don't write poems from ideas. Or I don't, anyway." He explained, not so much for the redheaded questioner as for the others around him how he began with a cadence, or a phrase, or sometimes an image, and allowed that original grain of language to collect other phrases, other cadences, other images around it. He explained how, as Frost said, a poem begins in delight and ends in wisdom, and how, at the beginning, one is often fooling around, in a child-like or even childish way, babbling like a three year old to whom language is fresh and bright.

"But what about that last poem you read?" He looked up to study the dark haired, slightly pudgy girl who had asked the question.

"The one about Leda?"

"Yes," she said. "You must have had some idea . . ."

"That was an exception."

"How do you mean, sir?"

Sir! It was lovely! What victim refers to the bandit as sir? Or was it a put-on? Even lovelier!

"Actually, I stole that one," he said.

"You did? I mean, I wondered . . . I was afraid . . . I wrote . . . I mean . . ."

"Miss Vattlis?"

"Yes," she said, embarrassed. For herself? For him?

"I stole it from you this afternoon. It was the best poem I could find to steal."

"But why?"

"For the fun of it!"

"Fun? But that's . . . Plagiarism."

"Sue me," he said, smiling.

"But . . ."

"Then don't sue. Learn. I mean, you know, you're supposed to be here to learn. That's why they charge you, isn't it? So learn. Forget the changes I've made, but try to figure out why I made the changes."

"But can you do that?"

"Sure, I did, didn't I?"

He handed her the poem, scribbled out on the Collegiate Arms stationery. She took it, then hesitated.

"Would you sign it for me?"

"Me? But it's your poem."

"Would you sign it anyway?"

"All right."

He took the poem back and wrote over the top of it, "To D. Martyn Vattlis, from Jerome Carpenter, with kind regards and thanks."

She took it, read it, and looked up. "Thank *you*," she said.

"But it was plagiarism, wasn't it?" the redhead asked.

"No, it was collaboration. It was teaching. It was, if you really want to know, fun."

"I see," the redhead said, and he walked away. So did the others.

Puzzled? Angry? Pleased? Jerome didn't much care.

Left alone he felt . . . He tried to decide how he felt. Good. *Epater les élèves!* Shake 'em up.

He went over to Professor Burton to return the copy of *The Double Agent.* Would it have fared any worse, he wondered, in Brownsuit's briefcase?

CHAPTER 4

A descent. Surely, Royle thought, it was a descent. However fragmentary, however imperfect the worlds of the reading had been, still the positions of their creators had been absolute and authoritative. Any one of them could, by a stroke of a pen, revise, retract, extend or obliterate his creation. But now, instead of that awesome and lofty power, they were going to Burton's party where they would be merely characters in somebody else's novel. For the giver of a party is a kind of novelist, Royle thought, a kind of little god. And that, he supposed, was the reason for the appearance of so many parties as set pieces in novels. Tricky, though, because to make it work right the novelist had to work through the host. Or one of the guests.

He rubbed his hand across his forehead, partly because of the warmth of the room in Burton's basement, but just as much as a way of wiping away these giddy and silly speculations. It made no sense, had no weight. The idea of himself as a character in a novel did not seem impressive. Who would want to write about him? And why? Well, there were reasons, he supposed. Not good ones, but reasons. It was a shame that novelists did not have to issue invitations to their characters which the characters could accept or decline as they liked. He smiled at that, barely noticeably. The idea of Count Tolstoy having to make apologies to his readers for the sudden indisposition of Mr. Karenin, who had decided after all not to attend . . .

But after all, who would refuse an invitation from Tolstoy? Lesser novelists, minor novelists, those were the ones who had to scramble and maneuver to get their characters to attend. The lions had merely to drop a hint, and the silver trays in their foyers were instantly dripping with calling cards, folded in those meaningful ways. Or, better yet, unfolded, so that the old lion could take them all into his study, spread them out on his huge and yet elegant regency desk and proceed to shuffle them and deal them as in a game of patience, watching them all as they joined or refused to join, met or failed to meet, and smiling a small smile at the inferences of passion, purpose, love and enmity that he could draw from the situations in which the cards found themselves.

But it could be better even than that. For the furthest extension of the fantasy—and Royle was pleased and somewhat relieved to find that he knew it to be a fantasy —was the situation of Burton's party, the room in which he sat, the people among whom he found himself. They were all writers, and each of them could be imagined at a desk, dealing out his cards, shuffling and dealing again.

And there would be as many novels arising out of the party—or novelist's descriptions—as there were characters at the party. Like *Rashomon,* or *The Ring and the Book.*

It was probably a poet's conception of what a novelist did, Royle supposed. A novelist, a real novelist, would not be so elaborate about it but would plunge in . . . Dull fellows. Literally, they were dull. Poets could be crazy or nervous or odd, but they were sparkling, most of them. At parties. Novelists sat there like sponges, soaking up. Or not like sponges so much as like great wooly beasts, for down under all that osmotic fibre, there had to be some sort of creature, large, slow, like some enormous shaggy sloth blinking its yellow eyes. Yes, they would be yellow, and somehow improbably delicate, with beautifully articulated lashes under all that outer shag. So, if he was going to play the game, he ought to play it properly. Starting with Stone, not so much because of Stone's eminence—Royle did not believe in reputations, his own or anyone else's—as because of Stone's resemblance to the animal he had conjured up as the novelist's totem.

Stone would see the room. They all saw rooms, described locations, labored with furniture and fabrics. The room, then, in Stone's view. He would see it as Burton's work, not only in conception but in execution as well, and read in those long hours of weekend labor down here Burton's dissatisfaction with intellectual endeavor. That the chairman of an English department should devote his time to the installation of prefab panelling, should invest himself into his investment, "Because, surely, dear, the house will be worth more with a finished basement, should we ever have to sell it . . ." he would have Burton saying. A nice, thick soup, for Burton would be concerned not with the necessity of selling the house, but with the hope of selling it one day when that invitation should come through from Harvard, the land of the respectable, the happy hunting ground where all good academics go. Or all lucky academics. But he would be fooling himself there, too, because the reason for doing the basement playroom would be simpler and more honorable than that. Or, in Stone's view, less honorable. The love of the manual work of finishing the walls and laying the floor, and putting in the lighting. He had done it well, too. It looked nearly professional. Naturally he was proud of it, and therefore the parties for visiting lecturers, poets, novelists and the rest of those cerebral tennis bums would be down in the cellar. In the basement? Basement where kings grow base,/To come at teachers' calls and do them grace.

But that would be beneath—or beyond—Stone. Royle felt good thinking of the one-sidedness of the *bouts rimés* or *bouts romanés*. He could get Stone, but Stone could not get him. Novelists couldn't think like poets. Or could they? Well, some could. Nabokov, for one, but he was a poet. Anthony Burgess or Elliot Baker. Neither of them had got it right. Joyce, of course.

It didn't have to be done that way, though, with perfect verisimilitude. Stone would get it in somehow that some of the visitors would notice that the party was not in the living-room but downstairs, where there was asphalt tile instead of carpeting to spill drinks on and grind cigarette butts into. The idea of the academic critic who considered the actual writer as somewhat gross and unseemly. As ants probably consider aphids. As dairymen consider their grazing Guernseys. Stupid unnecessary things. That would be the easy part of it, though. The unresolved question, the unresolved question in Royle's mind was whether Stone would get the other part of it, too—Burton's pride in his handiwork, his answer, however modest, to the accomplishments of his guests, his own making, his poesis of plank and panel, his imposition of order and form, however conventional, on what must have been an ordinary dark cellar of the twenties when the house had been built. An unpleasant question, because its answer would depend upon Royle's final estimate of Stone's worth—as a novelist and as a man, too. Would Stone be able to transcend himself, feel some imaginative identity with a character, or not even a character but another living man? Stone, that hulk of arrogance and ability surrounded by crude defenses! He was an intellectual in a way that only Jews can manage to be. It was something that they had brought over from Eastern Europe, or perhaps something they had always carried with them. And it was always there, ready for use as an excuse in childhood when Stone brought back his bulky, handstitched wallet and his mess of a leather bookmark from arts and crafts. If, that is, he had gone to camp. Or there it was to fall back upon for answer to that affront of a C— in shop, and the idea that an academic grade should have anything whatever to do with the despicable manufacture of bookends. These, of course, would have been Stone's projects. Bookmarks, bookends. And he would have made a mess of them, too, not so much carving and joining the wood as chewing it into shape. And there would be, then, a certain envy he would have to feel of Burton's commonplace competence.

He declined to venture an answer, mostly out of reluctance to condemn Stone. Let him who lives in a glass house without sin first blast the Stone. Igneous, metamorphic, and sedimentary. He would be the last kind—sedimentary. With that funny little beard that so far missed the patriarchal and prophetic as to demand some ineffectual gesture in that direction, Royle decided that Stone's name in this novel version of what was really happening ought to be something like Micah Shist. He smiled at that, because it would have been good enough to use if he were actually going to do such a thing, not just thinking about it, but writing it down, making it happen.

So, he had the room and the point of view. What he needed now was some action. Was there any? There couldn't be anything interesting in a whole gang of people standing around and drinking and talking, could there? Well, of course there could. At the very least, there was a kaleidoscopic amusement that the right kind of lens-and-mirror arrangement could reflect and refract into patterns, each of the guests at the party turning conveniently into one of those colored pebbles. But that was more his own kind of playing, a poet's kind. Stone would see it all in terms of motive and countermotive. He'd make it into some kind of sexual stock exchange. Whether it was or not. He saw the world that way. Could Royle? It was a great many balls to keep up in the air at once.

"Are you all right?" Marty asked, having come over to him, and whispering either out of concern or out of concern lest anyone else notice her concern (for her own part, or for his?).

"I'm fine," he said.

"You're sure? You just . . . sit there."

"Yes, fine. Thanks. I just want to sit for a bit."

"Can I freshen your drink?"

"Thanks, yes."

Why, he wondered, had she offered that? She was worried about his drinking too much. But she was worried, too, lest anyone else notice her worry. Or, perhaps, if he were going to sit there like a catatonic, she'd rather have it thought that he was drunk. Better drunk than crazy. He'd drink to that.

"What are you thinking about?" she asked. She had returned, with a fresh whiskey-soda, proffered to bwana.

"Balls in the air," he answered, laconically.

"What?"

"As a title."

"For a poem?"

"For a poem. Or for a pawnbroker's trade paper. Or a homosexual nudist magazine."

"An astronomers' newsletter?"

"Very good, very good," he said, imitating W. C. Fields for no reason at all. "How about a society page headline just before the debutantes come out?"

"Okay," she said. And then, after a pause, "You're sure you're all right?"

Royle nodded. Marty stood there for a moment, looking at him, and then, pursing her lips—in thought? or forming for him a surreptitious kiss?—she turned away and returned to the party.

And that, of course, was precisely the kind of thing for which to look. Those little signals, all the more delicious for their ambiguity and their subtlety of delivery. How many pursing of lips, pressing of arms, intertwining of gazes had he missed? Perhaps Stone was right after all. Perhaps the invention, wild and at random, of all these twiddlings of antennae was right. Not that Stone was able, actually, to observe them. But his invention of them approximated reality closely enough. That would be just fine, certainly, for a premise: that art neither followed nor led life, but danced with it, in one of those contemporary dances where the partners gyrated close to each other, but without actually ever touching. Why not?

Anyway, he had a title. *Balls in the Air* by Samuel Stone. 354 pp. Holt and Heath. (a shame those houses never merged; their colophon could have been the tendre croppes with the yonge sonne shining above) $5.95.

He looked around the room for his first chapter. Burton was talking to Stone, and Carpenter was talking to that Vattlis girl. Okay, the situation is clear enough. Stone is standing there, getting lionized, which is not so unpleasant, but what he really wants to do is move in on Carpenter and take the Vattlis girl. Can he make it? That's what he'd be wondering, figuring the odds on that business at the reading where Carpenter had borrowed the girl's poem. Would that make them closer or would that put an obstacle between them? Hard to say. But then, as a novelist, you don't have to know, only to say. Say anything. Say it makes it easier. We've already shared a poem, so why not go the whole way with it and hop into the kip. Stupid, but so were most plays of that kind. And they worked just as well, stupid or not. Even the great ones, the famous literary ones. Marvell's suggestion that we're all going to die soon, so let's fuck, was that stupid? Or Donne's business with the flea having bitten both of us and married our blood in his body. Ridiculous. "Mark but this flea . . ." "Your flea is worth about a C—, Jack." "But sir, I've had personal problems . . ." "Oh, then A—," "Thank you, sir." "Any time, Jack."

Ah, these windy divigations. Where was that from, he wondered. Eliot? Tate? Pound? He couldn't remember. It was one of these phrases that had etched itself into his head, popping up on the scanner every couple of months or so. He had grown accustomed to it, had incorporated it into his mental furniture so completely that he could no longer trace it back to its source. Good thing or bad? Bad, he supposed.

He looked up, sorting out his characters. They had all moved about, and were in different configurations now. Carpenter was no longer with Vattlis, but with Agnes Hartshorne. And Stone had escaped from Burton's admiration to Elaine Dinsmore to try to win hers. Hungerford had taken Stone's place beside Professor Burton. It was easy enough to interpret. Vattlis and Carpenter had not been getting on. The aggressor, whichever that had been, had given up. But not in time, for Burton had kept Stone on too loose or too tight a tether. Or maybe Stone had decided that Dinsmore would be an easier point to make. And Hungerford had moved in to try to get some material benefit—a job, or a recommendation, or an MLA invitation to read a paper. Or maybe not. Maybe they were all talking about football or something. Royle had no idea. He could hardly bring himself to care. The interesting thing was the configurations themselves, like the lovers in the second circle, blown by the winds, *di qua, di là, di giù, di su* . . . The image, Royle decided, had arisen from a moment like this, at some Florentine cocktail party in which Dante had been sitting in some corner watching the ebb and flow of people, streaming like the motes that float on the tears on the cornea. Ah, but then he had settled, had picked out a pair of lovers, had brought them to life . . . Royle was not up to it, not now. Hadn't been for some months.

Nor, to be honest, was he up to this elaborate game he had invented for himself. If he was going to bring a couple of characters to life, it would have to be directly and not through Stone's eyes, after all. What the hell did he really know about Stone's mental astigmatism? And that was the point of it, after all. With that rare writer who could look at things without any distortion whatever—George Eliot or Anton Chekhov—there would be no point to the game at all.

He took a slug of his whiskey, consoling himself that the elaborate machinery wasn't going to help. He was thrown back on his own resources, which were damned meager. Or, no, not entirely. He could imagine Carpenter and Vattlis, easily enough. Vattlis, after all, had disappeared. There were, no doubt, reasonable and boring explanations of her absence. She was in the bathroom, probably, or . . . But why not play it a little. She had gone out to the lawn, having explained—if there had been any occasion to explain—that a headache had come on, and that she needed air. But this was obvious stagecraft of the kind one finds in second rate playwrights and most lives. The point of going outside was to wait for Carpenter, the poet/thief, the wily picaro, the gay dog! And of course Carpenter would hang back for a while, not wanting anyone noticing the coincidence of the two disappearances. He would hang around, not to protect his own reputation, for he had nothing at all at stake, but hers. He would talk with Agnes, sweet, menopausal Aggie with the improbable red hair, and then he would discreetly steal away to Miss Vattlis outside, and the shelter of one of the back seats of all those parked automobiles. With luck, one of those old Nashes with the reclining seats. *Où sont les Nashes d'antan?* All in the junk heaps. They've hauled our Nashes for the last time, padnuh!

But screw all that. It wouldn't be a Nash, anyway, but a homelier Chevrolet. Shove your lay in a Chevrolet. He could see the car out there in the darkness. She would have had the sense to pick one in the darkness, screened from the light of the street lamps by the foliage of some obliging tree. Through the window of the car one would be able to make out the glow of her cigarette coal, a poignant parody of the ancient symbol of the red light. She would be there, waiting, smoking, having second and third thoughts, but committed now. And there was Jerome, breaking away from Agnes Hartshorne to go outside and do his duty to God and his country and to obey the Scout law. The Scout Law is: If they's big enough, they's old enough, and help yourself to the hintermost!

But he was still slogging hip deep in the big muddy of

Stone's mind. There was, after all, nothing at all to lead him to suppose that Jerome was going off—had gone off— to some tryst with the girl. It was all supposition. Supposititious. You could have a supposititious child, as James II had proved. But could you have a supposititious screw? Why not. Especially with Stone doing the supposing. Stone? Himself! It was his own supposing. And why flinch from it? Wasn't he here with his own chicksie-babe? With Marty in tow what cause could he have for recoiling from the idea of Jerome having his jollies? With a shake of his head and a smile that he supposed would look quite idiotic to anyone who noticed it, he reflected on his peculiar position and sipped his drink. Sex wasn't the problem at all, but only the way in which the problem presented itself. Now and always. It was really a kind of prelapsarian yearning for a cold bare room in a prep school dormitory, a scarred wooden desk, a sheet of yellow legal pad paper and ambition burning at the heat of dedication so that it felt like the real thing. That old, hard, gem-like flame, yessir. After that, it was all fall, *La Chute*, and not even with that kind of dignity but ridiculous, like Alice down the rabbit hole, down to the bottom where a whole bunch of dirty old men smoked and drank and stood around as at a cocktail party, wearing little buttons that said, "Eat Me."

Hell, he didn't even have to go back that far, to some dream of an Eden-like prep school life of volunteer Abelards. He could allow, even, for maturity, for a certain amount of sag in the flesh and flabbiness in the tissues and in the head. He could admit Jill and the children into it. And a drink before dinner. All the normal things.

But to have become a sodden lump at a cocktail party sitting in a corner, smiling, giggling sometimes (not aloud, he hoped, but even there he had doubts), trying to get hold of himself by slowing the self down, shooting the beast full of booze the way the bring-'em-back-alive hunters did it now, hitting their rhinos with tranquilizers. And he could see Jerome as a younger version of himself, a second carbon, maybe, of that page of which he was the last throwaway onionskin. The boy shouldn't be smudging himself up that way.

It was, he knew, sentimental nonsense. Utter blather. But recognising that sentimentality did nothing to diminish the force of what he had felt. For some reason, some obscure, foolish, entirely unreasonable reason, he disliked the idea of Jerome out there, in the back seat of somebody's car, fumbling around in the dark and sweaty silence. And it would be silent, too. What the hell was there to talk about when you were screwing a stranger? Nothing. He knew. Oh, yes, he knew. So what was he getting himself all worked up about?

But he was. And slowly, carefully, as if in a dream in which he was watching himself from the outside, he put his glass down on the table next to his chair, and with effort and deliberation leaned his torso forward, engaging the leverage of first his calves and the balls of his feet, and then, in a second stage, his thighs. He hung there for a moment, like a plane at full power on the runway—one of those Fairchild-Hiller jobs where you can look out of the window and actually see the wheels—and then took off, feeling the seat of the chair peel away from the seat of his pants from back to front. He could imagine a full

whine of jet power as he felt the muscles of his legs take
the strain, and then, there he was, up. Standing up and
walking. He wondered whether he should have taken
his drink with him. A shame to waste good whiskey. And
he doubted that the glass would be there when he returned. But, no, he wasn't going to take it with him. If
God meant for us to drink while we are walking, he rea-
soned. He would have given us stewardesses.

It was very interesting to walk. He felt rather fragile.
Calmly he considered that. It could be the booze, or the
hysteria that he had been using the booze to fight.
And being aware of the fragility was odd—not frightening or even alarming, but curious. It flashed across his
mind, like a footnote to his primary thought, that
Tchaikowsky had conducted with one hand at the back
of his neck in order to prevent his head from rolling off
and out into the audience. Tchaikowsky or someone else.
Royle wondered whether it was fear for his own head, or
fear lest the gaucherie of the thing distract the audience
and the musicians from the music. A fine way to conduct,
Piotr, with your head tucked underneath your arm!

He shook his own and was pleased to find it more or
less firmly affixed. A slight creak when he turned to the
left, but that was okay. A little oil. For the necks of China!

He left the room, that monument to Burton's handi-
ness, and started up the stairs. He had, of course, no idea
of what he would actually say to them out there. Playing
dirty doctor, eh? Naughty, naughty! Come inside for
cookies and milk and behave yourselves! Mustn't make
too much of these episodes or the children's attitudes can
be terribly warped. Oh, yes, by all means, calm and mat-

ter of fact. With that wonderful authority that kindergarten teachers have.

The stairs seemed endless. Interesting invention, stairs.
Which came first, he wondered, second floors or stairs?
Silly to build second floors without any way of getting
up to them. But silly to build stairs if they didn't go anywhere. Amazing, the advances of technology. Quirky
minds those fellows have. Under Newton's tree, Royle
was sure he would have invented apple-sauce. And faced
with Gutenberg's tray of type, he'd have invented alphabet soup. Peculiarly oral, that strand. He wondered if he
was hungry. No, probably not. Up, up. To the top of the
stairs. And through the hallway to the front door.

What the hell was he going to say out there?

Hallelujah, sinners! I am come to confess my wicked
ways and to set your feet on the paths of righteousness
and virtue. I have lifted up mine eyes, and I have seen
Levy the Oculist, looking down at you.

He paused at that, poking at the idea. He could see the
sign, a grotesque pair of eyes behind a pair of huge spec-
tacles. Looking out over an ash heap. It was from *The
Great Gatsby*, the oculist's sign. But he could *see* the sign.
From the movie version? With Alan Ladd, he remembered. And the name of the oculist was over or under
the disembodied eyes on the sign. B. F. Menkleberg, or
something like that. And later on, there was a car crash
under that sign. He promised himself that he would reread
Gatsby, find that image, see what Old Fitz had done with
it. It'd be funny if the movie turned out to have been
better.

But this was no use now, at the moment, and with the

task at hand. He must be crazy to go out there like this. It was none of his fucking business, anyway. Crazy.

But that was it, that was precisely what he needed. Some sort of an excuse, immediate, unanswerable, overpowering. He could simply say, in as calm a way as he could manage—that would be even more menacing, as Piotr Lorre had proved—that he was losing his grip, going out of his mind, and in need of help. With an immediate soft-on, Jerome would bound from the car and take him back to the hotel. No sweat, no problems. And it was even true enough to be convincing! He was not right. Not crazy, maybe, but not right.

He closed the door behind him and was surprised to discover that it had begun to drizzle. Or was it mist? No, thicker than that. And downward. It was, indeed, a drizzle. Not that rain was, in itself, remarkable, but it had not been like that in his projection, his scenario downstairs. And it took some adjustment on his part to run through the whole thing again, here in the rain, to see if it still worked, but it did. And he felt rather clever to find that the rain had not washed away his entire construction—like one of those heroes of caper movies who, having lost knife and gun in the swamp, removes a shoelace, deftly garrotes the hostile guards, and then, with thrilling sangfroid, relaces the shoe with the weapon.

He walked down the steps and stood on the lawn, waiting for his eyes to get used to the darkness. A trick he had picked up from those caper books. But his adjustment was better than any that those strenuous protagonists achieved. The coolness, the wetness, the fresh air all combined to clear his head. The whiskey, all that fine whiskey he had been so assiduously lapping up to dull himself, leaked away. It was as if he had taken his sodden mind and squeezed it like a sponge. It was still a little damp, maybe, but working. Racing, even. And while he feared that, it would be generally useful for the time being, while he was actually engaged in doing something.

He looked off toward the darkness between the houses and could make out the shapes of trees. He started across the lawn, toward the street.

"John," a voice called.

"What? Who's that?" he asked.

He turned around to see Marty. It made no sense at all. She wasn't supposed to be here. What the hell did she think she was doing out here like this?

"What are you doing?" she asked him. She had read the last line properly: puzzlement, disapproval, concern, and a touch of hurt all nicely blended. But it was his line!

"What are you doing out here?" he answered back, ad libbing. Oh, *sang pur, sang-froid.*

"I came out to ask if you were all right. I followed you."

"Oh," he answered. That was reasonable, wasn't it? The rain had done it, had blurred everything.

"So?" she asked.

"I came out for some fresh air," he said. And that was Carpenter's line. That's what Jerome was going to say, assuming that Royle had come out in time to catch him before he nestled into that back seat. The only difficulty was that, had Jerome actually delivered the line, he, Royle, would not have believed it. That would have been all right, but now with him delivering the line to Marty it was more important that she believe it. He didn't want her to think that he had come out here for some assignation. (Ass signation? Ass ignition!)

She did not look skeptical. She certainly did not say anything. There was no "I'm dubious./Hello, Mr. Dubious, I'm Kronkheit!" But she could not afford any such show of doubt. Her own position was not strong enough. Poor thing.

"Actually, I came out here to see what old Carpenter was up to," he said.

"What?"

"Sure, why not? Practice, you know. You think it's easy to be a dirty old man? You think you just wake up one morning, take your teeth out of the glass of Poli-dent, and discover you've made it? It takes years of practice. Dedication. Perseverance. It's practically an art form, puss."

"What is? Being a dirty old man?"

"Yup," he said, and smiled his best men's room attendant smile.

She laughed. He had no idea what the laughter meant, precisely, but didn't care. The laughter itself was a good thing. Always go for the jocular. He whispered in her ear, "Want to come along? Feelthy tableaux vivants?"

"All right," she said.

He put his hand up and with the index finger against the lips commanded silence. He felt fine. He had managed it beautifully, having adapted himself not only to the rain, but to Marty's unexpected appearance. How intricate it all was! He was off on his original errand with Marty's company. She was practically an accomplice. And she would certainly endorse his pleas for help and his claim that he was verging on hysteria. What normal person would sneak around peering into car windows this way? Well, to be honest, most normal persons, if they had a chance. But it was eccentric enough to pass. He glanced at Marty and saw her look away from him. Great! Perfect. She was worried about him. Of course she was almost always worried about him. But she was really worried now, and he could use that. It would all work out. And Jerome could have no choice but to drive him back to the hotel, where he would recover. Not so quickly as to be suspicious, but soon enough so that the weekend would not be spoiled.

He led the way across the lawn and toward the row of cars parked along the curb. Marty followed. Silent and stealthy as one of James Fenimore Cooper's Indian guides. She would be okay. It was himself that he worried about. He felt on the verge of a wild wave of hysterical laughter, rich, triumphant peals of it, warming as wine, wonderful . . .

It was not unreasonable for her to be there, Jerome decided. On the contrary, it was entirely normal and sensible. In theory at least, the whole purpose of the literary festival was to amuse and to instruct Miss Vattlis and her kind. It was all for the students, wasn't it? So of course she would have been invited to the party afterwards, her presence being Burton's excuse to put in for the whole thing, and to get the English department to foot the bills for the Wild Turkey and the Chivas. Still, Jerome was not especially pleased to see Miss Vattlis. He'd done that, finished that bit, and was ready to move on to something else. He had nothing against the girl, but the experience had come to an end, and—as in a good short story—the end was where it ought to stop. To turn up this way was a mistake, an aesthetic mistake, on her part.

Her question, moreover, was distracting, although through no fault of her own. She wanted to ask him about some of her lines, she said. And immediately Jerome thought of Monsieur Blumberg, the elegant Frenchman, who had been fired from Hunter for improperly answering such a question. One of those bright thighed, bushy tailed girls from the Bronx had been doing her translation exercises, and had asked, "Can I show you my loins?" "Yes, of course, mademoiselle, but perhaps after class, eh?" poor Blumberg had quipped. And out on his ear.

Miss Vattlis—Daniele, she said her first name was—had no such accent. She sounded rather Southern, in fact. "Lahnes." But the connection was there, and suddenly there popped into Jerome's head the image of the two of them, upstairs in some unused room, playing some particularly literary version of dirty doctor, as he checked out her loins. Lahnes. Lines. Lions. Gare de Lyon (Guard your lion).

No, he didn't want to go into all that. He was bored with it. But the girl was so intense about it, having worked herself up to come back this way with the question, having overcome a certain amount of shyness to ask him to look at her poem again, that he could not tell her, no, go away, I really don't care any more. Beside, he owed it to her. The interest was, perhaps, usurious, but having borrowed the poem he would have to pay the interest. By taking some.

"Well, it's a little noisy here, isn't it?"

"Upstairs?" she asked, almost pleading. "In Professor Burton's study?"

And there again, the image popped. Like a pimple. It was not the poem at all but him that she wanted. It was one of Stone's stories brought to life. For all Jerome knew, the girl had tried Stone, not maybe actually going up to him but in her own mind trying to find some pretext to do so, failing, and then deciding to make her play for him. She was an attractive enough girl, although a little thick in the body, and oddly short waisted. She looked as though she were a perfectly reasonably shaped girl who had been hit on the head by a huge cartoon sledge hammer and flattened out a little. Dark hair. Slightly sallow complexion. But it was the shape of her body that was interesting. It was as if all that compression were like a spring, and, somehow, were waiting to be released. As, for instance, by a good screw. She'd be five or six inches taller afterwards, he was sure. Maybe a foot. Six feet five! A veritable Varoushka.

He was imagining it all, of course. No evidence, whatever. Except the poem. A nice, dirty little poem. But still, it was unlikely. It would be a hell of a thing to get suckered upstairs and find nothing there but the girl and the poem and literary discussion. A kind of intellectual Murphy game. A waste of time. A shame. A waste of shame? Is lust in action. And till action, lust/is something, something, something, something full of blame, and something something, cruel, not to trust . . .

"Professor Burton's study?" he asked.

"I'm sure he wouldn't mind."

"Or we could go outside."

"But it's raining."

"There are cars out there."

"You're kidding, of course."

"Maybe," he said.

"I'm . . . I'm sorry to have bothered you," she said.

Suddenly he didn't feel clever any more. Oh, sure, it had been a way of putting it to her, and of getting away from that damned poem. And the dialogue had moved merrily along, so that he had fallen into playing Cary Grant playing Jerome Carpenter. But she had pulled the rug out from under it all. That poor, dark squatty serious girl . . . What the hell did he know of what was going on inside her head? Nothing. Not a damned thing. And he had put her off. Well, that was okay, he guessed. But the disappointment she showed was painful, nevertheless. And . . . And, oh, hell.

"I'm sorry," he said. "It's just that this kind of kidding around is dangerous. As in your poem, I mean. You go a trifle too far, lose the balance of it, and it's all terrible."

"My poem?"

"About Leda. And sex and all. It's a risky game, that kind of fooling around."

"But you liked it."

"There were turns in it I liked. The angle was nice. But the poem wasn't trying for much more than to be cute, was it?"

"No, I guess not."

"And even that's okay. I mean, that's perfectly all right. But if you're going to fool with Leda, the interesting thing it seems to me would be the eagle."

"What eagle? I don't think there was an eagle."

"Oh, yes. Yeats didn't use it, but there was an eagle. Some goddess turned into an eagle. Aphrodite, I suppose. And the eagle chased after the swan so that Leda would feel sorry for the swan. It was all a setup."

"Are you sure?"

"No, but I think so. It's something like that, anyway. And if you did the whole episode from the point of view of the goddess rather bored by it all because after the first couple of times it's all the same . . . That'd be cute, maybe more than cute."

"I'll go look it up," she said. "Thank you."

And she left him, and left the room.

He watched her climbing the stairs towards Burton's study. An invitation? Had she changed her mind? If he followed her up there in five minutes, would he find her spread-eagled on Burton's desk, waiting for him? He doubted it. And it had been up to her to make it clear, if that's what she had meant. An expense of spirit and a waste of shame, you bet! She'd had him scrambling there, turning his proposition into an exemplum, and finding an argument about her poem into which that could fit. Balancing, balancing, like a schoolboy walking a fence, carrying books, showing off for some girl in pigtails and braces but those nice little bumpies under the blouse.

That was what had happened to Daniele Vattlis, he decided. Some clown, some monster-clown up on the fence had fallen, smashing her down like that Tom 'n' Jerry sledgehammer and squashing the body that way. And the grief of it she bore to this day. Grief and the obsession about huge weights. No wonder she leched for locomotives.

He made his way toward the bar to refill his drink. Mustn't let old Burton keep too many of those good premium bottles unopened and in reserve for his private tippling for the rest of the term. The budget intended that booze for us, he thought. It is my duty!

He looked around the room while he was waiting for a shot at the bar and saw Royle. He thought of going over to talk with him, but considered the way Royle was sitting there, talking to Marty, laughing, smiling with that odd sleepy-slow smile and wondered whether he ought to intrude. He knew that he could, knew that Royle liked him well enough, but felt, still, that there was a time and place for everything, even for friends.

It was possible, of course, that he was putting too much importance upon the appearance of that conversation— Royle's and Marty's—but he had no way of judging it, not having been there, really, himself. What did he know about these casual relationships that writers seemed always to have? Not a damned thing. It was almost an indictment, as if the party girl were a part of the apparatus, like a standard typewriter, and listings in *Readers' Guide to Periodical Literature, Books in Print, Contemporary American Authors, Who's Who,* and the *World Almanac's* list of Nobel Laureates. Winners of the Novel Prize—as old Brownsuit had believed it to be. Well, okay, so it was a little rube-like, and had hay dripping down from under its hat, but there was—heh! heh!—a grain of truth in all that chaff. It was one of the perks of the position. Not a mistress, which was too grand and old world to describe the relationship, *maitresse en titre,* and all that. But these casually acquired, casually lost moments that Stone celebrated. Well, Jerome thought, he had suggested one, and the response had been, "You're kidding."

His mind ranged back to Versailles. Sun King—it sounded like the name of a Chinese restaurant in Memphis or Chattanooga.

"You're Jerome Carpenter," a man said. The man had been ahead of him at the whiskey bottles, and had finished pouring himself a drink, and now, having turned, had made the announcement.

It was an odd way to start a conversation. Jerome thought of thanking the fellow for saving him the trouble of checking the name tapes in his socks. But he decided against it. Why come on at the guy? He looked pleasant enough, standing there with his drink, hair en brosse, button down shirt, rep tie, flesh-colored plastic glasses. He looked to be the Browning man of the English Department.

"Yes, that's right," Jerome said, a little embarrassed because he had waited a couple of beats too long.

"I'm Warren Harding."

Instantly it flashed across Jerome's mind that he was talking with a lunatic. Not even a normal, sane lunatic who decided he was Napoleon or Jesus Christ or Abraham Lincoln, but a lunatic lunatic. Warren Harding indeed. Why not Salmon P. Chase? But then Jerome constructed a plausible explanation, supposing a family with the same surname as the teapot dumdum, its pride in the election of the president of their name, its chagrin at his disgrace, its defiance in the face of that chagrin, and its

decision to name the flesh of its flesh Warren in the hope
that he might expunge the shame of the other. This was
to have been *the* Warren Harding. Or maybe it had been
a joke. Jerome resolved to take no notice, to venture no
remark, for surely they would all have been made before. (Or, on the other hand, if all this was wrong, and the
fellow really thought he was Warren G. Harding, it
would be safer to humor him. Maybe he'd even get oil
concessions out of the conversation!)

"I teach here," Harding said, and suddenly he was
like Charles Kinbote, the deposed king of Zembla, living
incognito in some small American college. It was only the
liquor that had muddled his wits so that he had given
his real name. Or he assumed the real name to confuse
everyone.

"English?"

"Yes."

"Browning?"

"No, Pope. What made you think it was Browning?"

"Just a guess. No reason, really." He was lying. He
couldn't tell the fellow, though, that he looked like a
Browning man, because that could be, in a way, insulting.
An interesting question, though, the physiognomical cor-
relatives of the various specialities in literature depart-
ments. Men who teach Old English wear white athletic
socks and have salt-and-pepper hair. They are, in fact,
born with white athletic socks and salt-and-pepper hair.

"And you, do you teach?" Harding asked.

"No, I write."

"I know. But I meant to earn a living."

"I write. Under another name. I write . . . bestsellers."

"Really?"

"No, I'm lying."

"I didn't mean it that way. I was just . . . surprised."

"Of course."

"You couldn't tell me what your nom de plume is, could you?"

Jerome realised that a great nom de plume for someone desperate enough would be just that—Norm de Plume. He was tempted to try it on Harding, hoping that he was one of those guys who read nothing but "the literature" he kept up with—studies of the writers of his period, and reviews of the studies. Maybe he's never heard of James Jones or Herman Wouk or Henry Sutton. There was a chance that Jerome could make up something—not so far out maybe as Norm de Plume—and get away with it. Sue Doe (née Moss)?

"No," he said, after what had seemed a decent period of temptation. "I'd better not."

"I understand."

Did Harding believe him? Or was Harding now humoring him, as he had been humoring Harding? Jerome rather hoped so. There was an irresistible appeal to the idea of a conversation as in a lunatic asylum where madness complimented—and complemented—madness. A literary situation, in which some soi-disant Napoleon could argue with an equally soi-disant God about Waterloo.

"Is it . . . Is it difficult?" Harding asked. "Writing bestsellers?"

"Not very. A kind of knack is what it takes. But it isn't very hard work. I'm just lucky, I guess."

"I should say. I imagine it's . . . uh, profitable?"

149

"Oh, very. About a half million a book."

"Really," Harding said, "that's remarkable."

He looked as though he had been kicked. He pretended to see someone across the room—or, so bad was the performance, it would be more accurate to say that he pretended to pretend—and, quickly excusing himself, fled Jerome's presence. Jerome smiled benignly, thinking of what Harding would have done if he'd told him the truth, and revealed the workings of Ariel Editorial Services. Vaporised into ectoplasm? Probably not. It was the same thing, after all, a jolt of reality. The source of the current didn't make much difference. Priss!

He poured himself the drink he had come for, turned around and found Professor Burton and Ed Hungerford in the space that he and Harding had just occupied. And this pleased Jerome inordinately. He was possessed for the moment of a certainty that if he would only turn around and back again, Burton and Hungerford would disappear and two others would be standing there, as if the space were like the front of one of those revolving display cases where you push a button and watch rack after rack of books, or hair-brushes, or cufflinks or human beings.

They exchanged greetings. Professor Burton explained that he and Ed Hungerford had been discussing the desirability of Rockville's taking on a writer in residence in some form or other. The explanation was an invitation for . . . For what?

For Jerome to join in the conversation, of course. But was it a conversation or an interview? It was entirely possible that Burton was seriously thinking of taking on a writer, and these remarks could be a very informal sounding out of prospects for the job. Or, just as easily, it could be that Burton, searching around for interesting conversational gambits with his visiting writers had found that the writer-in-residence was ideal because writers listened to him, played up to him, tried for the entirely non-existent job, and old Burton watched them writhe, impaled on the naked hook by the imaginary bait of their own greed.

"My idea," Hungerford said, "is that instead of just hiring one writer, Rockville might do better to have a program in which they got four or five writers to come out for a month or so, spread out over the year. That way there'd be variety, and you could get a kind of excitement out of it that you wouldn't have from a year-long appointment."

"An interesting idea, don't you think, Mr. Carpenter?" Burton asked.

"Oh, yes. I'm all for it. It's a way of spreading the patronage around. And it's good for the students, too. There are places that do it that way, I think."

"Big names, younger, less well-known writers, poets, playwrights, novelists . . . You could vary it all kinds of ways," Hungerford suggested, pushing hard.

It was something about the inclination of his head, the forward thrust of his neck that gave him away, even more than the casual reference to "younger, less well-known writers" he had tucked into the sentence. But that was clearly his pitch. Come on, Burton, do it this way. It makes sense. And as a reward for my having told you about it, you could throw me one of your little bones, invite me to come and be a writer in residence for you, even if only for a month. Come on, please, please . . .

He was being hard on Hungerford, he knew. It was his own miserable, clamoring ambition he was attributing to Hungerford and then so studiously disdaining. On the other hand, he could not convince himself that the psychic carom shot was not accurate, and that Hungerford wasn't, in fact, making his pitch. Good afternoon, madam, I'm working my way through life selling magazine subscriptions, Cloverine salve, greeting cards, seeds, poems, and I'm earning big dollars and swell prizes . . . That eager, freckled boyish face on the backs of comic books that turned into a cigar chomping caricature of Willy Loman was echt Amerika, but there was a touch of it in the poet, too. In everyone.

Even assuming the most attractive of the possibilities, then—that Burton was seriously considering, honestly considering hiring himself a writer to hang around at Rockville—Jerome was not in the mood to stand in line for the plum—hell, the wrinkled prune—of Burton's bounty. He was too happy, too ebullient. And too wise-ass, for that matter. He could hardly resist the temptation to tell Burton that he already had a writer in residence, and that Mr. Harding, his doughty Pope scholar, was a writer of pornographic novels, under a pseudonym, of course, and a man of considerable talent in a (ho ho) hard genre. The pseudonym? T. Pott Daume or Warren Pease.

They were looking at him, expecting some comment. Had he been asked a question? He wasn't sure. But certainly he could crank up something to say.

"And it would be good for the writers, too," he said, trying by the tone and the timing to suggest that he had been thinking deeply all this time. "I mean, a month or so would be about as much as any writer could take of hanging around here, I should think. Here, or any college."

"I don't understand," Burton said.

"An English Department is a nice place to visit, but I wouldn't want to live there."

Burton laughed. Hungerford looked pained. Jerome smiled, raised his glass in a kind of toast, drained what was left in it, and said, "Excuse me, but I've got to go and change my colostomy bag." He walked away, satisfied. If nothing else, he had made Hungerford look good. A good deed of a kind.

He glanced across the room again, saw Royle, and saw that Royle was alone. Marty was off somewhere, getting a drink, in the bathroom, talking with someone else. It didn't matter. There was no question now of his intruding upon Royle. He started over. But Agnes Hartshorne stopped him.

"I liked your poems," she said. "I liked them a lot."

It was impossible not to stop to answer her. Had anyone else commented about the poems, praised them, even if only out of politeness? Had anyone else even acknowledged them? He didn't think so.

"Thank you," he said. "And I liked your story. Marvelous! Where did you find that bit about peacocks spreading their tails in the presence of poison? That's a great idea."

"I don't remember," she said.

"Careless of you, isn't it?"

"Me? Careless?" she asked, laughing. "You're the careless one. You really did lose those poems, didn't you?"

"Yes, I really did."

"I'm sorry, then, about making a joke of it at dinner."

"That's all right. It is a joke, I suppose."

"Did you lose . . . many?"

"No, not many. I have some of them out at magazines, and they'll either be printed or returned sooner or later. And the others—five or six, maybe—I have drafts somewhere of most of them."

"Still, the idea of it is frightening."

"It's not the greatest loss that Western civilization has suffered. I imagine we'll all survive."

"I'm sure we will. But it's kind of difficult not to imagine it happening to me. There's the same kind of dull pang in the stomach as when I see one of those photographs of automobile wrecks. I always put myself into the mess of glass and metal. Don't you?"

"I suppose we all do."

"Well, there you are. I am sorry about the poems, but it's more than sorrow. Pure fear, actually."

"Foolishness."

"I imagine so."

Jerome was about to say something else, was about to think up something else to say, for Aggie Hartshorne was indeed "okay" as Royle had said she was. Jerome liked her. But the patterns of the words, the trigger of "fear" and his reply of "foolishness," the versicle and responsus, put him in mind of his poem. Involuntarily, he put his hand to his chest where the envelope lay in his jacket

pocket and felt it, as if it were a wound and he were trying to determine how bad it was.

"Are you all right?" Aggie asked.

Had it been that obvious? Had he really looked as
though he were in pain? He did hope so. The Romantic
Agony, and other impressive titles came to mind. The
Wound and the Bow.

He excused himself and went off toward the bathroom,
half hoping that Professor Burton was watching, was
noticing, and was wondering whether there was in fact a
colostomy bag to change.

The neatness of it all was seductive. And yet, and
yet . . . He had more important things to attend to. He
went into the bathroom, put the lid down on the toilet,
sat down like Enderby, and withdrew the paper from
his pocket. He read the quatrain and the fragment:

> *Over the fear, the foolishness brays, the jay*
> *should be still, the whole grove be like a church,*
> *grave as the ceremonious beast of prey*
> *that crouches down before the lamb of March.*
> *. . . sound of the heart's beating,*
> *the blood's pulse in the vein, the vain . . .*

He was not pleased. It was possible, of course, that the
poem was perfectly good, and that his mood at the moment would not have admitted the excellence of "Lyci-
das" had that been scrawled on the paper before him.
But the artificiality of *the ceremonious beast of prey*, and
the contrivance of *the lamb of March* displeased him entirely. He read it again, and decided that the point of the

poem might well be that the foolishness of the jays or whatever was perfectly appropriate, and that the quality of those peasants in the Breughel paintings was exactly what he wanted to point out, to praise. *Brays* was wrong, too. Shit!

> *Over the fear, the foolishness of a jay*
> *spatters/defiles/unsettles the grove as children in a church.*
> *The carnivore is grave before his prey*
> *but woodpeckers rattle up in the trees in search*
> *of grubs. Acorns bounce on the ground the way*
> *they always do. The blood's pulse in the throat*
> *of the victim is scarcely noticed . . .*

That was rather better. He crossed out *spatters,* and then *defiles.* The first was wrong. Nice, but wrong. And the second was too strong. Children don't defile churches, but merely bother the celebrants. Then he crossed out *is scarcely noticed* and substituted *commands attention. They don't obey.*

> *The blood's pulse in the throat*
> *of the victim commands attention. They don't obey*
> *The hunter* something something

In the throat was the tickling phrase. It sounded like in-troit. He goes in. The beginning of the mass. Jerome knew this not from any experience with masses, but from having studied *Ulysses.* It was on the second page, after that huge S that took up the whole first page. *Introibo ad altare dei.* (Why was it *altare* and not *altarem?* "Surprise,

Sine, Abe de ex-pro! Come in! [*sub-prae-sine-ab-e-de-ex-pro-cum-in*] were the prepositions which took the ablative. *Ad* ought to be followed by an accusative. *Altarem?* But what the hell! Those Catholics knew what they were doing, Jerome supposed.) *In the throat* and *introit* were nice together, though, and less clunky than that damned lamb of March—spring lamb. *The hunter knows his introit by rote.*

So, an octave. All done, maybe. And all he needed now was six lines in favor of woodpeckers, jays, acorns, interruptions, foolishness, nonsense and stuff, and he'd have perhaps a passable sonnet. You don't have a pulse in a vein, anyway.

In order to maintain the proprieties, he lifted the lid and flushed the toilet. He put the poem back into his pocket and washed his hands and face, that last part of the charade being, in fact, rather refreshing and even practical. He was rather warm. No windows in here. There was an exhaust fan in the ceiling that worked when the light was turned on. He wondered whether Burton had done it himself. Look on my cellar bathroom, ye mighty, and dismay . . .

He dried his hands and face on one of the paper guest towels and opened the door, returning to the party.

"Jeromo! Been looking all the hell over for you!" It was Royle.

"Where would I have been?"

"Didn't know. That's why I was looking," Royle answered, and laughed.

Jerome looked at him, couldn't understand the hilarity of it, looked to Marty who was grinning as if it were the biggest joke in the world, manufactured the best smile he could, and said, "Well, uh, here I am."

He thought of telling them that he'd been in the bath-room writing a poem, but that seemed silly. Except in novels, who goes to the bathroom to write poems? A time and a place for everything, eh? No, he couldn't tell John that. And as he realised this he felt a pang, a thickness of tongue and fingertips. It was a moment of *déjà vu*. Oh, of course, it was just what he had felt that morning, on the plane, with Brownsuit. He hadn't been able to tell him, either.

Royle had led Marty across the lawn and out to the row of parked cars hunkering like beasts out there along the curb. Lowell had seen cars as fish, hadn't he? Odd's fish. Even's beasts. Fish, flesh or fowl. Anyway, foul. For there, in the dark, doing the dark deed, he had expected to find Jerome. But there had been an empty car, and then another empty car. Not merely empty, but mock-ingly, flauntingly, tauntingly empty, for the long stealthy creep, the painstaking silence in the rain and the dark, the bated breath and the noise of the blood's pounding on that little artery in the eardrum all served to build and heighten tension and expectation which the emptiness of the green Polara had not satisfied or relieved but only mocked. He had been about to give up, to admit defeat—or was it victory and vindication? Anyway, he had been about to return to the house and the whiskey, but Marty's being with him made that difficult. He had brought her along to see the mating of the tufted bandersnatch, and by God the old intrepid Indian guide was going to deliver the goods.

Without much hope, then, and really mostly out of stubbornness—which, for all he knew was what it took to be a number one Indian guide—he had crept up on car after car, Buick, Pontiac, Mercury . . . And there they had been, in the Mercury. He had always thought of Mercuries as not quite respectable cars, driven by foremen in abattoirs, caddie-masters, pin-ball machine dealers, deputy sheriffs. All sorts of low types. Of course, it would be a Mercury. A Merc, as the used-car ads called the breed, as if it were manufactured by the pharmaceutical company.

But it was not Jerome in there, hulking away in sleazy silhouette, but Stone. Of course. Who else could be the hero of a Stone short story but Stone himself? Trouble with the stories, as a matter of fact, was right there.

Beside him, Marty had stared like a doe, wide-eyed, calm, really like some kind of animal observing a curiosity down at the salt lick. And he had been presuming to guide her? Put that in your piece pipe and smoke it, Chingachgook! You're up against Bambi, and at best you'll come out of it looking foolish.

"Who is she?" Marty asked, not voicing the words, or even aspirating them, but only forming them clearly with her soft, mobile lips. The eyebrows were raised just sufficiently to indicate interrogation, but not shock or even surprise. Royle shrugged. Marty indicated with an inclination of her head that they might do better to go around the car and look in the window on the other side. He followed her. It was like being in combat, jumping into a foxhole and finding a sergeant there. A relief, for he could take charge, make decisions, lead. All you had to do was follow. If you were lucky enough to be a private, that is. And he had been lucky, lucky enough, anyway, to live through it. But the reflexes were still there, and he followed her around to the other side of the car.

He was glad to be with her, if for no other reason than that he knew she wasn't inside the car with Stone. But who was, then? That girl Jerome had been talking to? All hot to go, and then the bedroom barracuda had struck? Was that how it had been? Or was it Elaine Dinsmore? The bigger barracuda striking at the smaller one? Slowly, ever so slowly, he raised his head above the door panel and looked in, but it was impossible to make out anything more than shapes. Stone's face was visible enough, but hers was down in the shadows, among the pennies, gum wrappers, old Kleenexes, Sunny Dollars and mangled road maps that fall down into that crack between the back and the seat. Dangerous to go rooting around in there. You can cut your hand on one of the springs.

He had touched Marty's arm and indicated to her, with the same movement of the head that she had used, that they should leave. There hadn't been all that much to see, anyway. He had felt good about having found something to justify his being outside in the first place, something other than Jerome, that was. But the idea of it had been better than the thing itself. As so often happens in Life and Art.

They left the car, scurrying in a quiet crouch like kindergarten children imitating animals—wallabies? pottos?

giant anteaters?—until they were far enough away from the Merc to stand up.

"Shall we go in?" Marty asked.

"Sure."

"Or do you want to . . ." She nodded toward one of the cars.

"No, no thanks. Not . . . not now." He chucked her under the chin, as a way of thanking her for the suggestion. Or as a way of dismissing the suggestion as childish. Or both. Anyway, she smiled, which was all she could do. And they went back into the house.

He regretted having turned her down, and, at the same time, regretted the regretting. Both feelings, while contradictory, were legitimate. He had declined her invitation because of Stone's presence out there in the car, Stone's grossness, Stone's unattractiveness. It could have been, he supposed, a way of parodying Stone, a way of mimicking him, and the fun and games with Marty would have been all the more fun and more like a game for their playing off against Stone's style. But he was not up to that, was not himself sufficiently light and gay to make the contrast with Stone. And he knew it. Hell, if he wanted to probe into that cesspool, he could come up with all kinds of rich refuse. The whole thing with Marty and with all the Marties was a substitute for writing, a proof of another kind of potency. You didn't need to be a Viennese head doctor to figure that out. All you had to do was read the papers—as when the *Journal-American* on the evening before the signing of the Treaty of Versailles ran the headline, "WILSON'S PEN IS READY" but ran the second and third words too close together. Rare item now, in libraries. It had run only in the early edition.

So, if he couldn't write with it, he could dip it and pretend. The old balls-point. And with all that riding on his riding, he would rather walk back, into the house, enjoying in a subdued way Marty's complaisance, her patience, her willingness. And yet, regret. (Nice sound, that.) And a fine sadness, thinking of her high squeal and her legs up, damned near around his neck!

And he had gone out to prevent Jerome from making a dreadful mistake, eh? Pretty fucking funny! He opened the door and they went inside, where, in the warmth and the shelter, he realised that he was soaking wet. Marty too. Jesus, but she'd put up with anything!

And then it occurred to him that the twist, the kicker, the topper on it all was that when they went downstairs everyone would suppose, seeing them all wet from the rain, that they had been out there screwing. He began to chuckle. It was just too much! It was all too much. Or, no, it was what it always was, the ordinary, ridiculous world. But his mood, his mind, his metabolism were all ganging up, exaggerating, amplifying, distorting. The only trouble with being crazy was that it got in the way of one's thinking. How's that for news from Vienna?

Or, as they were always saying in funny farms, maybe everybody else is crazy. In Russia that was even plausible. Dissenters were put away there and declared to be nuts. And here? Why not? There was something so damned appealing, so vulnerable, so pure about Marty. It was the same feeling he got when he listened to a soprano singing Mozart. Even the arias that were supposed to be gay produced in Royle an exalted sadness. *Die sanfte Turtel-taube girret und klagt ihr Leid.* Ah, well.

Downstairs, the party looked to be about the same as it had been when they had left. There were new configurations, of course, but the same hubbub, the same smoke in the air, drifting upwards in sinuous, rather Moorish looking clouds. Royle looked for glances, for knowing looks, found none, decided that people were deliberately refraining from expressing the obvious, and looked for Jerome. Where the hell was he? Well, he could ask; that's what he could do. To hell with civilization! Obviousness was meant to be expressed. That's why it was obvious! Obviously!

"Have you any idea where Jerome Carpenter's got to?" he asked Professor Burton, who was, after all, the host.

Burton leaned forward, looked as though he were actually going to cup his hand, got the hand up to about chest height, changed his mind, dropped it, leaned even closer, and whispered in Royle's ear, "He's in the bathroom."

Well, the old boy was tappy! Ze most tseviehr caze ovv toilet dtrainingk I hoff ever zeen!

"Did you know?" Burton asked.

Royle looked at him more or less alarmed. Did he know that Jerome went to the bathroom? Was that what Burton wanted to know? Could he tell the old boy? The Pope goes to the bathroom! Queen Elizabeth pees. Doris Day shits! Everybody . . .

"About his colostomy?"

"His what?"

"Poor lad. It's some sort of operation they do where the bowel empties into a sack outside the body."

"Jerome?"

"Yes, he's gone to empty the bag."

"Is that what he told you?"

"Yes, it . . . slipped out, I think."

"I see." The information, not the bag.

"It's very interesting, actually. That may be where his poetry comes from."

"From the bag?"

"From the trauma! From the psychological trauma."

"I'd never thought of that," Royle said, very pleased with himself for not laughing, for not smiling, not betraying by the movement of the most trivial facial muscle anything but the most intense interest.

"He's been in there rather a long time," Burton said, still whispering. "Do you suppose he's all right?"

"Oh, I expect so," Royle answered in a whisper. "One grows accustomed to these things."

Burton nodded gravely. Royle tried to imagine what Burton was imagining—Jerome, fussing with some kind of plastic bag and deodorant powder. No, it was too silly. But the other idea, the notion that Jerome's *poems* came from the colostomy bag, that was appealing. Or, no it had to be revised. The poems were shit, like money or damned near anything else. Or, better yet, the poems were a result of the shit in the bowl, and Jerome read the markings in the bowl the way gypsies read tea-leaves. Dean Swift and his Electric Toilet had never come up with anything much better than that. Turteltaube? No, no, Wolfgang, the bird you've got in mind is the Stoolpigeon. He tried to think of what that might be in German.

"I'll wait a while and then maybe ask if he's okay," Royle said to Burton.

"I'd be grateful to you," Burton answered, still in a whisper.

Royle nodded. He'd wait a while, all right. Didn't want to intrude on the creative act. Catharsis. Ars/arse. *Ars* is the arse's catharsis.

But then Jerome opened the door of the bathroom and emerged.

"Jeromo! Been looking all the hell over for you," Royle said.

"Where would I have been?"

"Didn't know. That's why I was looking," Royle answered and laughed.

CHAPTER 5

Rubber. Or some kind of plastic. Royle could accept the fact that his body was turning—had mostly turned—into some strange composition. It was even interesting to perceive the subtle differences in density, specific gravity, porousness, texture. Fun, as it was fun to try on a new sports jacket or a new pair of shoes. Or boots that made the feet seem heavy and awkward but also indefatigable and invulnerable. But what concerned him was that with this chemical change he had noticed, sitting in the car, there arose the possibility of further and more drastic changes. How did this new substance of which he was now made react to heat, to light, to stress? Possibly it would melt as plastic toys do when they roll under radiators, losing color and turning into pastel puddles of gunk. And, hissing off the radiator, as vapor from the melting ice in the wooly nap of children's drying mittens, would be all that was left of him—his mind.

Silly, of course, that idea of the intellectual as a mind

on a stalk. He could feel, with all definite certainty, that his mind was fluid. Ideas arose from his head as the ghostliness of dry-ice evaporations arising directly from the solid chunks. Rimbaud had known about such things. The change from solids directly to gas, the changes of vowel sounds to colors. Immediate. Not through the liquid did the dry ice go, nor through the intelligence did the tonality pass. Ergo, the body was not only part of the mind, but the mind was part of the body. It was luminously clear, and also clear that St. Paul had never understood this. Of course! Eureka, as the vacuum cleaner salesman exclaimed! That was what had fucked up all of western civilization. Right there. "At that point in time!"—as those fools in Washington were always saying, not content to destroy the country but insisting on ruining the language as well. St. Paul had made a mistake, a miscalculation as in arithmetic, and we had all been screwed up by that. He had been the engineer, and there had been this mistake, and the two pieces of the bridge would not meet, could not connect, pointed off in different directions, and there was no longer any way to get from body to mind. But he was onto it, had an inkling of how to imagine it, how to solve the conundrum, correct the error . . . And would have no time, either, for even as he was beginning to understand this critical mystery, even as he had the entire cure for the ills of western civ. right there, in his mind, materializing (as the gas must somehow materialize into the dry ice), his body was melting, the features starting to blur, and sag and run, the shoulders were sloping, the chest caving in, ass spreading out on the leatherette seat, ankles swelling up. He could feel it all.

That cheap chemical into which his flesh had turned was beginning to liquefy.

He laughed aloud at the irony of it, the cheap and vulgar irony that understanding and death should blossom in a man at the same instant—like pumpkin blossoms, the male and female of which open, presumably, at the same time.

"What is it? What's funny? John?" Marty asked.

"Everything. Everything is funny."

"I don't understand you," she whispered.

"That's funny, too," he said, and started to laugh again, even as the body from which laughter came was disintegrating. And the idea of the liquefying body making the liquid noise of the laughter struck him as impossibly funny, and fed the laughter. It took a great deal of exertion of will power to stop. But he did.

He was sitting in the back seat of Hungerford's car with Marty and Jerome. In the front, next to Hungerford, Sam Stone and Elaine Dinsmore were squeezed together. The two groups were almost as separate as they would have been in one of those old fashioned limousines with the window between the front and back seats. There was the noise of talk and laughter from up front but it was indistinct. Or, anyway, Royle could not distinguish what they were saying. In the back, Marty and Jerome were discussing him, his laughter, his condition. They were concerned about him, beginning to be afraid for him. And it was out of affection and consideration for them that he had stopped the laughter, smothering the peals until they sputtered, twitched, bubbled and died. No point, after all, in terrifying them. Hell, they'd be startled enough when they got to the Collegiate Arms and discovered, as the car door opened and the little overhead light went on, that he had melted. They would turn to look at him and see this nasty glob on the seat, with the vapor of his mind rising from it like morning fog coming off a pond. Give them a little turn, that would.

But then what? Would he persist as that vapor? Would his intelligence continue, suffusing the world, or suffused by it? Surely he would not continue as a separate entity. But why not? Why not continue as one of those invisible men outlined in ectoplasm in the comics or by the special-effects men in the movies. He could become a special effect—a not unenviable prospect. He would retain scale and shape, but lose only his opacity. Maybe he could learn to walk through walls! He could not dismiss the idea only on the grounds of its cheapness and vulgarity. Nobody, after all, has ever vouched for God's taste. For all we know, heaven is tacky and hideous!

An amusing problem, that. There were no theological arguments he could think of that had been put forth about divine taste. Ruskin's? But that was mostly foolishness. Royle explored the idea that the aesthetic impalatability did not affect the odds against the possibility of invisible men. It was an appealing notion. All those poor hacks in the Hollywood studios had never realized the theological implications of their work.

("You gotta unnerstan' the theological implications, Harry," the screenwriter shouts, thrusting cigar forward to emphasize all the stressed syllables and dropping cigar ash on his custom tailored, white-on-white shirt.

"The what?" Harry asks, practically wetting his pants under his desk. "You're out of your helmet!"

And Royle, the invisible man—the *real* one—hears it all, learns everything that passes through his body, absorbing it and the understanding of it in an instant.)

Well, if that was what the future held for him after melting and vaporizing, he would accept it, and gladly. But what if, having learned everything, he found that he could no longer write. He hadn't anyway for six months. And the fingers had been solid enough to grasp the pencil. But the mind had been solid, too. Opaque. Impermeable. Now that he was liquefying, the mind would open up, but the fingers would fall off.

He was tempted to laugh again, but restrained himself out of consideration for Marty and Jerome. Consideration and an unwillingness to mislead them. They would think he was drunk, or dotty—but he had never been more lucid in his life. But it was difficult to keep from laughing, because it was all too funny. What if he was not lucid? What if he was not melting at all, but only thought he was, because of the liquor, because of all the liquor, or fatigue, or the incipient mania, or a combination of not one but a variety of several metaphysically proven ingredients? But even that would prove his point, prove the same thing, the reversibility of mind and body, for wasn't his physical presence solidifying itself even as he imagined it to be doing, and through his own imagining? That wasn't quite right! He furrowed his newly resolidifying brow and tried to remember what he had been thinking of before, what the great illumination had been. He remembered that there had been an answer to some terrible error of St. Paul, and he had had it, had understood it, and understood, too, all of its awful and wonderful implications. But he could no longer remember the error, nor the correction. It was Gertrude Stein's deathbed words, all over again: "What is the answer? What was the question?" His mind, now, was turning solid, opaque, inert. He couldn't feel it. There are, he recalled, no nerves in the brain. But he could imagine it. And it was all going pulpy.

He could not let it happen. He had to get a grip on himself. What? There was some formula, some order, some sense to all this, if only he could remember it. Hands, face, teeth, hair, fingernails. His mind ranged over old lists. The chart his mother had put up in the bathroom for him years and years before so he would know what he had to do getting ready for school. Latin, French, English, history, algebra. He shook his head. Those old cables were still there, cluttering up his head, as old houses are cluttered up in their empty walls by unused telephone wires as the successive occupants put in and take out their extensions in different rooms. Composition of place, exercise of understanding, exercise of will. It was the formula for the meditation according to St. Francis de Sales—but not wholly useless. Composition of place! That was, at least, a beginning. He was in a car, in Hungerford's car, on the way to the hotel. Where they were all going . . . to play anagrams. Yes, he remembered now. Silly idea, but not unpleasant. Some foolish thing that had happened to Carpenter on the plane. And he had said he was a professional anagrams player, and they had all taken that up, and had all resolved to meet and make his claim good, by playing anagrams. Well, why not? The only trouble was that Royle's mind was not right for it, not up to it. Or beyond it. He would soar over the letters and not be able to move them around. Anagram?

Anna Graham! Or, better yet, the rich joke that Tolstoy had in mind. That whole novel, with all those pages of writing, was a practical joke, a way of making good the pun—for she was, as soon as she ran off with Vronsky, no longer Karenin, but ana-Karenin! He started to laugh again, noticed that both Jerome and Marty were leaning forward, thought of explaining that this time it was different and that this laughter was all right, but changed his mind. It would be too difficult.

"No, no," he said, nevertheless, "it's all right. I'm okay."

It would be splendid, deliciously funny and splendid, if in this odd mood he just sat down at the board and played and creamed them all. Whipping those letters around like an old Mississippi riverboat gambler manipulating the cards. It was conceivable although unlikely that his precise combination of alcohol, fatigue, and mental state might produce the absolute, ideal anagrams player. Surely it was not a game that required setting up exercises, diet, no smoking, no drinking, no women, and all that dreary puritanical regimen. It was not democratic, but like Ping-Pong, and either one had the knack or one didn't. Practice did not avail. Nor training, nor effort. And, even more aristocratic than Ping-Pong, for a certain disdain for one's own body and mind, and even abuse of them could prove helpful. Well, then, it was his game. Or, no, it was Jerome's. Jerome had claimed it. But the two of them together, could be a team, like those Australian women midgets that worked in tag teams in wrestling. Or were they domestic women midgets working in Australian tag teams? In any event, he was ready to join the league.

A moment of practical concern: could he do anagrams?

He picked the last word that had come to mind—league. Well, there was nothing to do with it, but you could turn eagle into it if you got the free *u*. And if not, you could write I.O.U.—with more truth than ever before in the history of Mississippi riverboat gambling.

He closed his eyes and pretended to sleep to gather himself together for the big game.

Jerome had not meant for them actually to play the game. It had not even been his suggestion, really, but Royle's. Suggestion? Well, anyway, joke—but the joke had been couched in the form of a suggestion which the others had taken seriously—or humorously enough to follow. All Jerome had meant to do was to embroider a little bit upon the distressing fact of his loss of those poems to Brownsuit, a loss that seemed to engage the sympathies, and even to fascinate Agnes. It was she who had reverted to that painful subject, and, as an anodyne, Jerome had tried to turn it all into a pleasantry, working up the whole absurd encounter with Brownsuit, milking it shamelessly for laughs. And the business about his being a professional anagrams player had caught Royle's fancy. It was almost as if Royle had stolen his words as one does in the game. And then Hungerford had stolen them from Royle, turning the mock proposal into a real one. Hungerford, that odd, shy, unknowable fellow (who, Jerome now suspected, made his living hustling pool, or working as a shill in a gambling casino somewhere, or as a promoter of cockfights) had really wanted to play. His earnestness had been unmistakable, and had turned the joke into a challenge which no one else had been able to ignore. The complexity of the situation was interesting, even if the situation itself was uncomfortable. No one really believed that the game would be any relevant test of skill, but for that very reason it would have been awkward if anyone had declined to play. The very refusal to take part in the game would have given it the precise importance that everyone was so carefully trying to avoid . . . out of concern for the feelings of the losers, and out of the more or less immediate concern that quite plausibly one could turn out oneself to be among the losers.

The assent, the enthusiasm, the decision to leave Burton's and go back to the hotel for the big game were all too quick, too cheerful, too abrupt. And from the brightness and bustle of the shambly party, there was a sudden change to the darkness and the nervousness of anticipation of the automobiles—Hungerford's, in which Jerome was riding with Stone, Elaine Dinsmore and John and Marty, and, just behind them, some instructor and his wife who had Agnes with them, and who were stopping off at the instructor's house to pick up the anagrams tiles.

Royle's peculiar behavior, his intermittent silences and bursts of inexplicable laughter concerned Jerome, then, because he felt in part responsible for this whole stupid business of going to play the game. He knew that he could have argued himself out of that responsibility, but he felt, nevertheless, like the lemming who starts telling swimming stories just before the cry of "To the beach!" and the start of the suicidal migration.

Still, he tried to convince himself that it was only a

game, was not serious, could not possibly have any of those dire effects that he vaguely but persistently imagined. And was it not possible that Hungerford's eagerness, Stone's humorlessness, Royle's present oddness, his own apprehensiveness, had nothing whatever to do with the game? They could perfectly well be the reactions of each one of them to the tensions of the reading and the sudden relaxation afterwards. A case of the literary bends. And in that case, the game might be a good thing, serving to distract them all, or, to keep to the metaphor, to provide that healthy pressure that would dissolve those bubbles of—what was it? nitrogen?—in the blood.

The car pulled into the parking lot behind the Collegiate Arms, and the six of them scrambled out. Stone was carrying a bottle of whiskey, or not merely carrying it, but brandishing it.

"Where'd you get that?" Hungerford asked.

"From Burton. I stole it."

"But that's awful!" La Dinsmore said, perhaps even meaning it. No, she couldn't, Jerome told himself. But, yes, she could, he answered, depressed.

"From each according to his ability," Stone intoned. "And to each according to his need. Comes the revolution, schnapps will flow like blood in the streets of Vladivostock! The expropriators must be expropriated."

And then, for no apparent reason, he began to sing:

Avanti, populo,
Avanti, populo,
Baniero rosso,
Baniero rosso . . .

The singing stopped, and, in a new tone and on a new

tack, he said, in quite reasonable tones, "One could even make a case for this liberation as a virtuous act."

"Could one?" Hungerford asked, cheerfully.

"Yes, indeed, one could," Stone returned, and then, after a moment's thought added, "but how much better a case if it *were* a case."

It was not so much the volume nor even the resonance of his baritone voice, but his silhouette, the chunky body outlined by the lights of the lobby as he stood on the portico of the hotel. That roundness of shoulder and paunch, and the point of his beard—he had turned his head to deliver the line—combined with the whiskey bottle he held by the neck to make him look . . . Mephistophelean? Or, if possible, even worse than that. Like Stromboli. Only children, Jerome decided, have any understanding of menace, are familiar with almost groundless terror, see bears and bugbears in nursery shadows, which apparitions prepare us for all eschatology, theology, metaphysics, everything. And Stone, so close to the source of all our deepest visions of the world, a banal, Disney-like vision, was all the more convincing. Even the peculiarly Victorian locution—"Yes, indeed, one could!"—fitted in, for children's books tend to be Victorian.

"And in his pants pocket," Royle whispered into Jerome's ear, "he has three or four dozen ice cubes."

"And he has maraschino cherries," Jerome answered, "hanging by their stems from his garters."

"An alcoholic Robin Hood!" Royle suggested. "He steals from the drunk to give to the sober. Or is it the other way around?"

"He steals from the wretches to give to the pure?"

"I'll drink to that," Royle said. "With Stone's bottle, yet."

The elevator, set now to work automatically, brought them up to Stone's room. Jerome wondered how that bellman, that mental writer, was doing. Composing himself for the next day's flights of purest fancy—purest in that they were never committed to vulgar or common print.

In Stone's room they set to work preparing. Stone called down for glasses, ice and soda, but was told that ice and soda could be got from the utility room from machines.

"Well, then, the glasses, how about them?" he asked.

He listened, snorted, hung up, and announced that they would all have to go and round up bathroom glasses if they wanted to drink. An expedition was organized. Hungerford and Jerome stayed behind to move furniture, clearing the middle of the room to make a place for the game, an area in which they could all sprawl on the rug and, like swimmers in an aquacade, make the petals of a flower, the pistil of which would be the tiles, the letters, the words. Pistils? The pollen! Which they would mix up to make their hybrids, their multifloras and floribundas, even richer and more luxuriant.

After ten minutes or so of confusion, of looking for the bottle opener which was not in the bathroom after all but on the wall of the closet, and of arranging drinks and ash trays, and of passing around the top of the anagrams box so that everyone who needed to could look at the rules, Dan Tyler—the instructor who owned the set— poured the tiles onto the rug. They all helped turn the tiles face down, during which activity Ed Hungerford announced in what was, for him, a rather brash tone, "You've seen Paul Newman play pool! You've seen Steve McQueen play poker. Now, for the last word in chills, thrills and excitement, see Ed Hungerford play anagrams."

"You're good at this?" Royle asked.

"Oh, yes."

"Of course, Carpenter here is a pro, you know," Royle said. And then, after a pause, "But it's Newark Fats you've got to watch out for."

"What do you mean, 'Fats?'" Stone asked. "In the middle ages this was a girdle of Venus, and was considered to be extremely attractive."

"It was a compliment," Royle explained. "Minnesota Fats was the man, numero uno, the champ. He beat Newman. Didn't you see the movie?"

"A compliment? Some compliment!" Stone muttered.

"We learn to take what we can get, friend."

Jerome looked around the room, uncomfortable without being able to explain his discomfort to himself. Badinage! Nothing wrong with that, was there? But then, why wasn't there such a thing as Goodinage? Or, as in French, if there were *plaisantries*, then there ought to be *un-plaisantries* as well. So that one could make a distinction, could express it.

But maybe it was all in his mind. His, and not theirs. Maybe it was his own anxiety which he refused to admit to himself, and by transference, attributed to the others—that stupid fear of losing a word game to other writers. Which would be a kind of psychiatric anagrams game, in which people exchanged neuroses and built on them, making them more and more elaborate. His eyes focused on the sporting print with which the decorators had given a little cheer and individuality to Stone's room. It did not augur well. The print showed two men dueling with rapiers. Or foils. Hard to tell. His rapier wit was foiled by the duality.

Not so much soothed as distracted by these aimless exercises, he turned to the spread of wooden squares on the rug, and arranged himself between Agnes and John, lying on the floor on his side. He picked a tile—F. Not too bad. But Hungerford beat it with a B, and won the first turn. All the letters that had been turned up in the draw for that first turn were left in the middle of the circle, and Hungerford drew four more to make ten, and then drew his key letter, the letter around which he would have to build his word. T. And the letters in the middle were Y,B,N,R,L,S,H,E,A,A. Hungerford looked at the letters for a moment, turning his head this way and that so as to rearrange his vision of the tiles without actually touching them—which was, the rules had said—illegal. After an impressively brief examination he picked his letters out of the center and made BREAST.

"A soft touch," Stone said.

"You wouldn't allow BREASTY, would you?" Hungerford asked.

"You can chance it, but if it isn't in the dictionary and somebody challenges you, you lose your turn," Tyler's wife explained solemnly. Jerome had not caught her first name. She was a small, rather mousy little thing, but breasty, whether the word was allowable or not.

"I brought a dictionary," the instructor volunteered, also very earnest, sandy haired, somewhat jug-eared.

"I'll leave it this way, then," Hungerford said.

Jerome relaxed. BREASTY would have been difficult to do anything with, but BREAST could become BERATES, BAREST? No, there was no way of adding a letter. But BARONETS! There was still an N in the middle. Anyone who drew an E or an O could take it.

The play went to Stone, on Hungerford's left. He drew the O. Lucky, Jerome thought. But still, he had to see it. He had to be comfortable enough with the dance of the tiles to allow them to move. Could he manage it? Would he be any good? He studied the letters that were left in the middle, looked at Hungerford's BREAST and looked back at the center tiles. He hadn't seen it yet. Jerome figured that there was, perhaps, a hopeful sign in the length of time it was taking Stone to figure out so simple a problem. He looked around the circle of players. All poker faced, so that it was impossible to tell whether they were blind to it too, or just pretending to be so that Stone would not know from their expressions or attitudes that there was a move for him, a theft of a word.

He picked three letters out of the middle and made LOAN. Not a good move. The four letter word counted one point. Each additional letter counted an additional point. Had he taken Hungerford's word and made baronet, he'd have had four points, and a more difficult word to steal. But without even thinking about it, Jerome could see that with an E one could borrow his LOAN and leave him all ALONE without any points, any words at all. And it was curious to notice within himself the satisfaction that there were at least indications that Stone was only an indifferent player. Uncharitable, but what the hell! There it was, a kind of satisfaction, a deep, comfortable pleasure. He got up to make himself a drink from Stone's bottle of whiskey. Another anagram—Burton had organized the whiskey, which Stone had liberated—and which Jerome was now incorporating. It was all a loan!

Elaine Dinsmore drew a B with which she could do nothing. She looked at Hungerford's word, and at Stone's, then looked at the letters remaining in the center—H and Y—and threw her B in with them, passing. Jerome had not been able to see anything, either. So it was hard to tell anything about the quality of her play. She had not taken very long to decide that there was nothing she could do, and that suggested at least a minimal competence. But it was too early to tell yet.

Tyler drew an R, and turned immediately to Stone's LOAN.

"Loran?" he asked.

"Is it in the dictionary?" Stone asked.

"What difference does that make?" Royle asked. "If it isn't then it ought to be."

"It's an abbreviation for long range navigation," Stone said.

"It's a word."

"If it's in the dictionary, it's a word."

"I don't know about that. Which is to be the boss, as Tweedledum asked, us or the dictionary? We are the writers, the poets, maybe not the legislators of the world, but at least the lexicographers."

He was smiling and looking rather silly, as if he were

not really involved in the conversation at all, but only playing at it. Or perhaps not. Stone, though, was dead serious. He didn't want to lose his word. But the chances of his keeping it were so slim. He insisted that Tyler look the word up in the dictionary. Tyler did so, and found it. LOAN, then, became LORAN.

Mrs. Tyler said she didn't want to play, just to watch. Marty said the same thing. John took a tile—V. He looked at the two words that were available, and slowly, almost sleepily, reached out for Hungerford's BREAST, which he made into BRAVEST.

"Okay, maestro, it's your turn," he said, and relapsed into his sleepy, smiling silence.

Jerome turned up a T. Trolan, ratnol, torlan, lantor, antlor, lornat. There was no combination that made any sense, nothing he could see. And it was not only the competitiveness of the situation, although surely there was enough of that, but the pressure he felt was of another kind, a deep uneasiness about not being able to impose an order on the shimmer of the letters. It was as if he were in front of the cave and had to figure out the formula, the open sesame that would move the huge stone. But no matter how he shuffled and reshuffled the letters in his mind, there was no combination that would work. There was even less hope with BRAVEST. Reluctantly, he threw the letter in.

Hungerford drew an O, looked out at the tiles for a while, contemplating, studying them, his eyes slightly narrowed, and his finger touching his lower lip. He reached for Tyler's LORAN, the T Jerome had discarded, and, with his own O, made ORTOLAN.

"Very good," Royle said, "very good." It was not quite
an imitation of W. C. Fields' voice, but neither was it
Royle's own. But Jerome was not worrying about him
any more. He was, after all, leading. Or, no, he was tied
with Hungerford. So he couldn't be in such terrible
shape. All that oddness in the car, Jerome decided, must
have been the booze. But still Royle was able to function,
to concentrate. Jerome admired that, considered the
other possibility—that Royle was doing well without concentrating—decided that either way it was admirable,
and returned his attention to the game. What was there
one could do with an ORTOLAN? Eat it, he supposed. Or
it was better than that, or worse. They drowned them,
holding their heads in brandy glasses so that they would
drown in the spirits and—theoretically—absorb some of
the flavor of the brandy as they died. How decadent! But
then it was no worse than clubbing steers on the head.
But ORTOLAN. The T and the O and the N could make a—
TION ending. ORL—AT[I]ON? CORLATION? CORRELATION! It
would take a C, an E, an I and another R. It was unlikely.
But it would be splendid! The correlation of the ortolan.
It was a splendid title for something. He thought for a
moment of the poem in his pocket. Not that he was going
to whip it out of his pocket and work on it, or run off again
to the john to tinker with it, but the idea of ortolans . . .
Birds drowning in brandy. Better than jays if he could get
it to fit in. A little precious, but still intriguing. And the
combination of fear and foolishness was there all right, in
the bird's death in the snifter. Well, maybe another time,
another poem.

The play continued, as each of the writers struggled

with the randomness of the language, the affinities and antipathies of the letters for each other, the pure chance of the order in which the tiles appeared, and struggled, too, with each other. It was not just that moment of effort and its contradictory demands of concentration and free-floating scanning receptiveness which Jerome experienced at his turn, and which had made him think of the oriental hero trying to find the formula, but the mood of the game, of all the players, and of the competitiveness that they all shared. It was as if a coven of witches had assembled to have one of those contests in which each casts spells only to have the others try to break the spells or turn them into other, stronger, darker ones. Spells! The name itself went both ways, and even if it was only another quirk of language, it was to be taken seriously. What else do witches, anagrams players and poets have to work with?

Hungerford, actually, was doing well. Better than Jerome had supposed he would do. But that was another repetition of the same old lesson. The outward appearances, the personalities, the characters of the writers in the Theophrastian sense, had very little to do with their work, their talent, their worth. If these literary festivals were of any use at all, it was to demonstrate this obvious principle of literary criticism. The work, the work, only the work! Hungerford and Royle were sailing on, piling up tiles, points, words—and jealousy. Not from Jerome, who was enjoying the success of his friend, and Hungerford's, too, because it was so deliciously improbable and therefore right, but from Stone who writhed, who groaned, who disguised his fury in facetious table talk

and still, by the obviousness of that disguise, made the
fury all the more vivid and apparent. He had only one
word, one little word, a short, four-letter fluke, appropriate and amusing but still difficult to steal: HUFF. Agnes'
collection included DISMAL, FEISTY and the vulnerable
PEAR, which any could REAP or RAPE with a convenient
piece of S.

Next to her, the Tylers, both of them working together,
whispering, conferring, plodded on, doing respectably
well, but mitigating the effect of their accomplishment by
that awful togetherness. It was as if they were playing
together against a chess master, playing one of the fifty
simultaneous games of his exhibition. DEVICES they had,
and MAYHAP, which was pretty good. But because of
their collaboration, their play was not serious. But then,
Jerome wondered, what was serious about play. Certainly
Royle was not taking it seriously. He hardly seemed to
be paying attention. He accepted no suggestions from
Marty—not that she had offered any, or had had the nerve
to offer any, but still, he wouldn't have deigned, and
didn't need any anyway. Smiling vaguely, he would look
at the tiles, scratch the flange of his right nostril, and
then move, and he accumulated an impressive array of
transformations, transsubstantiations, transmogrifications
and creations: BLUBBER, WHEY, REMAINED [from RIME,
MIRED, MARINED] and SKIPS. The words themselves were
good words, but it was Royle's attitude, his amused, un-
involved, effortless competence that Jerome approved of
and delighted in.

His own performance was rather different, for he was
trying more than Royle was, but the letters had not fallen

fortunately for him. He was nevertheless satisfied, having stolen STILE from the Tylers and having made of it EPISTLE. It was not only the score, the four points that the new word was worth, but the style of the thing, the elegant unexpectedness of the combination. It was as if, in a losing evening of bridge, he had played a hand with weak cards and a low bid, but played perfectly, finessing (exactly the word!) and winning for a moment the acknowledgement of the others and that fine certainty on his own part of his own ability, at least in potential, that little bit of realization standing as an indication of the rest.

Considering the word, and trying to decide whether it could be stolen, whether anyone else could take it over by an even more dazzling display of legerdemain (for bookkeepers on the take, would it be ledgerdemain?) he played for a while with PILE-EST, with STEEPLI-- [STEE-PLING? "We were steepling the church when the end of the world came . . ."] but then, he considered the sound of the word, and hit upon something irrelevant to anagrams, but still interesting. He had been sidling up to the word, changing the vowel sounds around, as if working with a slant rhyme, when suddenly it was an epistle from an apostle. A tisket, a tasket? Epistle, Apostle, a green and yellow missal. The epistle to the Phillipinos. And he wondered if the masses in the vernacular worked, if the formulae in languages other than Latin had any effect at all. There are some things, he decided, that do not translate. Poems, anagrams, and . . . liturgies? Incantations? *Hocus pocus* cannot be rendered any other way. Wouldn't it be a disaster if all those priests were fooling themselves and the congregations they were trying so hard to oblige, missing the miracle, not turning the bread and the wine into anything at all. The flesh and the blood of the words are the letters, which cannot survive translation.

There were several passes, impossible tiles thrown into the hopper in the center. And then Hungerford drew an I. He looked around at the words on the floor and at the available letters. His glance came to rest on Elaine Dinsmore's one word. She had gone through the game and had either tried and despaired, or had never tried at all. Perhaps, Jerome thought, she had no interest in the game, or was more interested in Stone. Or possibly she thought it was unfeminine to appear to excel in such competitions. But she wrote poetry! Well, then, maybe she would have tried in the company of friends, but here, among strangers, was holding back. A not unattractive kind of diffidence. Or he could be less generous and assume that she had simply declined the risk that any commitment would have involved. At any rate, all she had in front of her was NUTS which was easy to steal, terribly easy [VAUNTS, AUNTS, STUNS] or, if it was her comment as well as her achievement, it was even easier to vulgarize it further, respelling the spell with a C. The Comedian as in the letter C. Old Stevens didn't know the half of it. Or St.-Jean Perse, either, with his C-marks.

But Hungerford, too intent on the game for such embroidery, took NUTS and made it UNITS. He did it with a display of exactly the right degree of regret—too much would have been sarcastic—and quite gracefully. Jerome immediately saw the progression that might come from that—UNITES, UNITIES, INSTITUTE . . . Perhaps even more.

From little nuts do mighty anagrams grow. But he also noticed Stone, scowling, more fiercely than ever now, and intent upon stealing the word, not so much to add to his own inadequate score, but to stop Hungerford. And Royle. His comments, his table talk had taken that turn during the last round or so, and the game itself was turning into something else, a thing of coalitions and ententes, political rather than simply—and purely?—individually competitive. The object now, if Stone's mood prevailed, was for the losers to unite somehow, to concentrate upon stealing Hungerford's and Royle's words, and to combine to bring them down to the general level. "Tear down Vanity," eh? But what would it tear down to? Or build into? Nativity! The Christian answer to . . . everything. Not that Jerome could say so. An anagram would not be a welcome kind of sermon for Stone, whatever its import. And besides, Stone wasn't Christian.

"We've got to get them," he was saying. "Every damned time, I think that this time it'll be my time, and that some nice, useful tile will turn up. But they all turn into Q just as I reach for them. It's a shell game!"

"That's a good game," Royle said, his eyes closed, or half-closed. It was hard for Jerome to tell. If there was a slit through which Royle could see, the view would be of a slice of ceiling.

"You play that too?"

"Any game that's going," Royle answered.

"I'll bet," Stone said, throwing his tile into the center.

"And you'll lose that, too," Royle answered, and whinnied, a country 'n' western laugh that mocked itself along with Stone.

La Dinsmore, the area of carpet in front of her now

entirely pristine, turned over a tile, looked at it as if she had never before seen the language of which this character was a part, looked around at the other words, and was about to throw her tile in.

"No, no! Think! We've got to stop these cartels, these superpowers . . ." Stone urged her.

"But I am thinking," she said.

Nevertheless, she held onto the tile, looked around at the words again (Jerome saw one—no two—possible moves for her) and then, shrugging her shoulders, she threw the tile in.

Tyler went next, made a word, albeit a small one, from the free letters in the middle, and turned to smile at his wife and to bask in her approval.

Stone had his own approval to add. "That's the way! That's a blow for . . ."

"The underdeveloped nations?" Royle suggested. "The undeserving poor?"

"Very funny!" Stone fumed.

"No, but a little bit. A little bit funny," Royle said, reasonably, contemplatively—he was already looking at the words, looking at his tile, thinking.

"I think I need a drink," Stone announced.

Later, Jerome realized that he had wondered about Stone's calling it out like that, like a little boy who broadcasts to the assembled company that he is going to the bathroom to make a wee-wee. To ask permission? To solicit praise for his control of his functions? Or, more simply, because he finds it interesting to himself and therefore assumes it will be interesting to the others, to the aunts and uncles, or the friends, the grown-ups. At any rate, he had wondered about Stone's announcement, not enough to consider it, but. . . . In the peripheral vision of his attention scan he had been aware of it, at least enough to be able to recall it afterwards, when reflecting upon what happened.

For Stone had got up, and had become dizzy. Perhaps he had. Perhaps all the blood had rushed away from his head and left him drained, staggering, reeling and falling. Or perhaps Stone had only remembered such an incident and was acting it out again, pretending to stagger, pretending to fall, in order to accomplish the purpose he had been scheming about for minutes and minutes before. He had staggered, had grabbed at Elaine Dinsmore—clever, if it had been intentional, making the gesture of the pass on the way down—missed, and collapsed on the floor, onto the tiles, the words, the accumulated ingenuity and intelligence that all of them had expended on the game, and turned it back into the primordial gibberish and babble from which it had come. He had, conceivably, made the announcement to establish the scenario in all their minds, pretending to fall, or, at an even further remove, pretending to pretend.

There was a moment of stunned silence. Which was, Jerome supposed, even worse than the babble of tiles. Silence. The unsaying of that first word that was in the beginning.

"Oh, shit!" Stone groaned, inertly lying there.

And then Royle began to laugh. It was like the laughter earlier in the car, Jerome thought, but richer, deeper, and louder. Or maybe it only seemed louder. Because it gushed up out of Royle's chest into the silence of the rest

of them. A capella, and solo! Hahahaha! Heeheehee!
Hoohoohoo! Worst of all, Jerome thought. Worse even
than the silence. Laughter. Maniacal laughter. Not with
a bang or a whimper, either, but with a giggle! A guffaw!
A robust chortle!

But then Hungerford took it up. He started laughing
too. And Stone, himself, still lying there, still awash in the
wreck of all the intricate verbiage, began to chuckle. And
then to laugh. And all of them, Jerome too, felt the giddi-
ness of the moment, the sublime nonsensicality of their
realization that they had, yes, been involved in the
damned game, but weren't any longer, were liberated
now, were free of it. The tension was gone, and the spell
—all the spells—were broken.

"For Christ's sake! Somebody help me up!" Stone
demanded.

"You really need it?" Royle asked, gasping between
the old laughter and a new wave of it.

"What's so damned funny, anyway?" Stone asked. He
was, of course, laughing himself.

"I don't know," Royle said. "Peri Bathos, or the Art of
Falling!" and relapsed into wordless laughter.

"Help me up, damn it!" he demanded again.

"Hungerford! Help him," Royle ordered.

Hungerford got up, went to grab Stone by the arm,
tried to raise him, but succeeded only in losing his own
balance and falling on top of Stone. The two of them lay
there in the middle of the floor, as if they, too, were tiles
some monster player had turned up, and of which he was
trying to make a word.

Slowly, ever so slowly, the new wave of laughter that

Hungerford's fall had occasioned spent itself. He got up, helped Stone up, and accepted one of the two glasses of whiskey that Agnes held out. Stone, accepting the other made a slight bow to her, and then another toward Hungerford. It was a graceful gesture, almost as graceful as her own, her finding the whiskey and the glasses, and making the drinks and having them there just at the right moment.

"Quorgzliff!" Stone said, by way of a toast. It was one of the random combinations of letters near his left foot.

"Lullid!" Hungerford returned, raising his glass.

They drank, and Tyler started to pick up the tiles and put them back into the red and yellow box.

"What time is it?" Elaine Dinsmore asked. She had just yawned, either out of fatigue, or possibly because of having just laughed so much. But Jerome felt that her question, and the answer it would elicit would bring it all to an end, the evening, or not so much the whole evening, which had very little to recommend it, as the moment, the present moment that they had achieved, or, literally, fallen into. It was a moment of harmony of the kind that hostesses work and hope for. He did not want to go to bed, not now.

"Food time!" Stone said. "It's time to eat."

And it was true. They were all hungry. It had been hours since dinner, and they had all been nervous then, picking at their food, or wolfing it down so that, somehow, it didn't count. Only food one tastes and enjoys counts, Jerome thought. And that dinner had not counted for much. What had he had? Ham? Yes, the Hawaiian pineapple slice garnished with the ham. He remembered, but only vaguely. He could not bring back the texture or the taste of it. It was as theoretical as the pictures of food in ladies' magazines.

"Yes," he said. "I'm starving." He was delighted to be echoing others, and more delighted to have the sentiment further echoed. Yes, they would all like to eat. But where? No, the hotel didn't have room service. After all, when Stone had called down for the ice, remember? And no, there was no place near by. Gloom and apprehension. But there had to be someplace. Where truck drivers ate. Or a Chinese restaurant. Chinese restaurants are open very late, always. Well, then, someplace where Chinese truck drivers eat. They could, at the very worst, just get into a car—or, all right, two cars—and cruise around. There had to be someplace where you could get something to eat at two in the morning! That was the great thing about New York City. You can go out and buy vegetables at two in the morning. But who wants vegetables? All right, fruit. Mangoes. Pomegranates. Passion fruit. Papayas.

The conversation swirled around, and they swirled out of the room, and into the elevator, and down, through the lobby, into the night air, where the coolness gave a new and interesting timbre to the talk, as if a musical phrase were being played through an electronic reverberator. The rain had stopped and the air was clear, peculiarly crystalline. It was, Jerome imagined, nature's compensation to these people who lived so far from the coast and the sea—that clarity of the air so that one had the feeling of being able to see around a branch or a trunk of a tree. The light bent, and the sounds of their discussion of food and eating shone. It was pleasant to try to unfocus the hearing and attend not to the sense of the speech but to the blurred music of it, the sibilants and the aspirants and the richness of the vowels.

They got into cars—Hungerford's and Tyler's—and drove off the campus and onto a highway. Tyler was in front, and the agreement had been that either car, finding a likely place to stop would beep twice to the other. The call of one mechanical moose to another. But for all of the prearranged business with the horns, it was mostly up to Tyler to find a place. Hungerford had nearly all he could do to follow Tyler, keeping the old car up to Tyler's sprightly Volkswagen.

After a motel with a huge horse—two or three times life size—and a nut shop with a Planter's Peanut twice the size of the horse, the Volkswagen signalled a turn. It may have beeped as well, but the noise was not audible over the gasp of Hungerford's motor. Tyler pulled into the BOWL-A-RAMA 24 LANES 24 HOURS.

Yes, of course, what an obvious idea! All these bowling places have coffee shops! How do you know? Don't you bowl? No, of course not, it's not our class! Crap, they bowl at Vassar! Vassar's not our class! You mean, really, you've never gone bowling?

"Now this is a game!" Stone announced. "This is a game we can all play! We shall *all* be terrible at this, and therefore, democracy being what it is, we shall all enjoy it."

And so, by one of those brilliant strokes that depends more on luck than anything else, the game itself had dissolved and reformed itself. Instead of ANAGRAMS, it would be BOWLING. A delightful permutation!

"You've got to give Stone credit," Royle was saying. "Suggesting a game like bowling? Well, it takes balls!"

And the marvel of it was that they all laughed as if it had been the cleverest remark any of them had ever heard.

"Allez! Allez!" Stone commanded.

"See the Rolling Stone!"

"Alley oop!"

Royle was not keeping score. Even if he had wanted to, he didn't understand those slanted lines, those X-marks, or the way the score of one frame got carried over into the next, sometimes. But it was better, he thought, not to be involved in the scoring, the organization of the game, and to enjoy the discrete moments of the activity. There was nothing simpler in the world than the rolling of a ball down the alley and the moment of suspense during its progress until the crash at the end, the rout of the pins, and the Brobdingnagian labors of the AMF pin-spotter, humpfing up and down, clearing the fallen pins and returning the ball down that chute. It was pleasant to consider the logarithmic diminution of the suspense and the growth of certainty as the ball travelled toward the pins, whether true and on course, or not true, not aimed at that ideal place between the lead pin and the one behind it and to the left. And the body English, the kind of physical prayer that each bowler offered up was interesting, too. There were as many sects, apparently, as there were bodies, and each offered up his ritual writhing in a slightly different style, either imploring or commanding or even begging. And then, sometimes, after the boom and spatter of the pins, the thanksgiving or the triumph. Or the resignation or despair.

But even more than these pieces of the game, Royle enjoyed the place, the bright, subterranean light as of some brilliantly lighted cave. And the glossiness! It was wonderful to consider the artificial flowers, the benches covered in the hides of Naugas, the marbling of the bowling balls, so exuberantly nonsensical and useless. He didn't even mind having to get up every now and then, pick up the bowling ball himself and hurl it at the pins. It was a way of keeping his perceptions true, a way of understanding the muscular strain and release of the others as he watched them. And while he tried to do well, to knock down all the little wooden men at the end of the alley, it didn't make any difference, really. None of them was very good at it. It was even a point of pride not to be. Bowling, they had all agreed, was déclassé, and it was desirable to be inadequate as a bowler—the very inadequacy serving somehow to endorse one's fancied aristocratic credentials. To be good at tennis, or swimming was fine. It was even acceptable to be adept at Pitch 'n' Putt. But bowling? Oh, no! And Royle delighted in the imposture into which they had slipped in order to play the game. They had become, somehow, members of the Italo-Polish Hadassah Altar Ladies, or the workers on the swing shift of the Ice-Cream Truck Insulators' Union. And yet, beyond the psychological and mimetic adjustments they had all made, there was a legitimacy to the game. The feeling of triumph that one had after knocking down all ten of the pins was real. The mastery, the achieve of the thing! All there. And the delight.

Marty, somehow, was good at the game, though. The

concentration, the intensity with which she went at it showed on her face in the forehead and the way the brow furrowed, and around the mouth and the set of the lips. But it showed in other, more relevant ways, too. Her carefully measured stride up to the foul line, the balance and energy with which she released the ball, and the forward leaning with which she followed its progress all showed up in the clatter of the pins. Allowing for the disesteem of the sport, her skill was still pleasurable. Perhaps even more so because of that disesteem. There was no side to it, as there was none in the despised art forms —baton twirling, tap dancing, cheer leading. All that sublime kitsch! The trouble with poetry, Royle thought, is that it comes on so. Too many people read it for the wrong reasons. Even of those few that read it at all!

He closed his eyes, shutting out the weird fluorescent look of the place and listening to the satisfying rumble of the bowling balls on the wood. And the crash of pins. And the different rumble and cluck as the balls returned. He thought of himself as a bowler, not here in this alley, but in a different life, in which the bowling took the place of the poetry. And instead of the fellowships and the awards of the lit. biz., there were the gaudy trophies of bowling leagues. And those sublimely flashy bowling jackets with Manny's Meat Market blazoned across the back in embroidered and embellished script. And his name, in a smaller, matching script, across the front, and on the bowling ball bag. A simpler life. The same demands for excellence, for performance, for accomplishment, but so much simpler in the terms of its demands. It would not be difficult to learn the knack of scorekeeping, and then, by God, you could know where you were. And maybe, once or twice in your life, you could bowl that perfect game. Three hundred, wasn't it? Well, whatever it was. Thump. Roll. Clatter. Right out there where you could see it, where seeing was believing, as old Empiricles used to say. Thump. Roll. Clatter!

He looked up. Marty had made a strike, or a spare, or whatever. She had knocked down all the little pins. Fantastic. Royle clapped his hands. She smiled.

"Oh, God, it was all so wonderfully simple. The great thing about these games was their idiotic, perfect simplicity. Benjy, describing the golf game, was perfectly right. How did it start? "They were hitting. First one would hit and then the other would hit . . ." Must have been a relief to Faulkner to write sentences like that. They were rolling. First one would roll and then the other would roll. Roll or bowl a ball, a penny a pitch! There was just nothing you could do to it to mess it up. Ineluctible.

"Very aggressive game," Stone said.

"What?"

"Bowling. An aggressive game, don't you think?"

"What are you talking about?"

"Those pins. Knocking them down. You think of them as animate. It's a way of sublimating aggression. You're killing people, symbolically."

"Maybe you are."

"All of us. Or castrating. All those little wooden phalloi."

"Phalloi?"

"Or phalluses."

"Castrating them," Royle repeated, stupidly.

"Symbolically. Why else would it be important?"

"But it isn't. It isn't important."

"Then why do people do it?"

"It's . . . It's . . ." And Royle started to laugh, and tried to smother the laughter. And, surprisingly, he managed. "It's a game, you see. It's a game they play."

Simplicity. Beautiful, utter, supreme simplicity. Of course it would elude Stone. In fact, Royle decided, he might well be the only fellow in the place who had the least idea of what it was they were all doing. Despite the fact that he had no idea how to score. They were rolling. First one would roll and then the other would roll. And that was it! All there was. And there wasn't any more! It was an avoidance of meaning. Meaningless. Fun.

He closed his eyes again, shutting out Stone and his ersatz thinking, shutting out Tyler and his thoughtful appraisal of how to get those two pins on the split, shutting out the glare of the lights that bounced off the varnished wood, shutting out everything but that satisfying, stupid noise of the balls as they rolled down the alleys. He would be content, he decided, to spend an eternity here, just listening to the thunder. That was what Rip Van Winkle had done. He had developed this love of simple pleasure, and had beguiled away the twenty or thirty years—whatever it was.

Thump. Roll. Clatter. It was old Tyler. Old Danny the T. Dan T? Like the poem writer, Dante Allergy! Who also wrote about bowling. Which circle? The violent against something. Or, no, it was spendthrifts. And misers. Wittily thrown together.

He was not pleased to have remembered this. The simplicity he had found and had so much enjoyed was blurred, now, marked. It could come off, he knew, would wash away. A little booze will cleanse of us this thinking. But the trace of the stain would be there, always. It was Tyler's fault, for having such a stupid name. Dante, indeed! He would have to change it. Dantès. Or D'Anthès. Or maybe just Tyler.

They roused him, and he had to go and heft one of the big bowling balls, walk up to the foul line, and heave it down toward the forest of pins a million light years away, and then again. Heft. A nice word. A nice, old word. To heave the heft. To cleave the cleft. To weave the weft? Old runes. Like Dagobert, the Rune. These fragments I have shored against my runes? Well, Heironymo's mad again.

Royle felt tired, not so much from the exercise of having bowled another frame, but from the thinking, the pulsating of his brain. The alky hadn't helped. Would an Alky-Seltzer? Enough of these old bromides! He had felt better, eating, in the little restaurant of this unstately pleasure dome, but the coffee afterwards had been a mistake. All that good whiskey undone. His nice padding had fallen off the cells, and they were sparkling bright, crackling their way into a real padded cell. But the fatigue was a good sign, was it not? When this was over, when they tallied up the last count of felled pins and went back to the hotel, he might fall asleep. And wake up in the morning all right again. It happened that way, sometimes. Sleep. That cares for the raveled sleeves of nuts.

Perhaps, if he were to set himself some simple task,

like remembering the names of all the presidents, or . . .
Or arithmetic. What to occupy the mind with? The dance
of numbers! Simple doublings, which would eventually
get difficult enough to be demanding. Or prime numbers. One day, some kid would figure out the progression
of prime numbers while screwing, trying to keep from
coming too quickly. And how would that look in the
Boys' Book of Mathematical Geniuses, eh?

He started to count, slowly, hoping that the rhythm of
the counting would take over, would entrap his racing
mind, slowing it down like in those dreams where one
runs through pudding, through gum, through amber.
Counting. Like sheep. All we like sheep, have go-o-o-o-o-
o-one astray! No, not sheep. Too rich in associations. Rife.
Fraught. Bowling balls. He counted bowling balls. There
were lots of them.

Twice more he had to get up, and he did so cheerfully,
bowling rather well, and astounding the millions of fans
out there in televisionland by managing not only to knock
down pins, but also and at the same time to keep in his
mind the tally of bowling balls up to the greenish one
next to the mostly brownish one on the middle shelf near
the artificial elephant ear plant. What a gas! An elephant
ear plant growing out of an elephant foot vase. Seventy-
nine bowling balls. Nine pins. And one elephant ear plant!

He sat down again and counted, finishing the count,
and then checking it, because if you don't check, there
will be silly mistakes that will creep into the work, and
it will reflect itself in your grade, young man, it certainly
will, and the difference between A and a B can be a matter of nothing more than that extra few minutes you

spend looking over your paper at the end of the assign-
ment. A lot of truth in that! And a lot of horse shit, too.
Because if your uncle's accountant uses an adding machine, then what's the point of all this meticulousness?

"John, come on. It's time to go now."

He looked up. He knew he shouldn't go yet. Had to
check the tally. The difference between a good grade and
a less good grade. And here Marty was, ready to go on
back to the hotel. Well, he supposed that he'd have to go.
But it was with a feeling of sadness that he got up, leaving
behind the rigors of virtuous checking and rechecking.
And it was with another sadness that he took off those
harlequin bowling shoes and gave them back to the man
in the booth for him to put on the ultra-violet athlete's-
foot fungus killer. It was the only shred left of that gaudy
bowling suit with the nifty jacket, like jockey silks. But it
was cool and clear outside, and quieter. It was good to
be put into the car and have the wind rushing in from
the window on to his face. Sure it was good! What the
hell else was there but that? Wind rushing on your face.
If you can still feel that, there's something going for you,
life left. When the wind breaks over the mountain, Kate
Smith waits for you!

Inside. Upstairs. Good-nights in the hallway. And then
into the room, finally, to lie down. Would that it were
bedtime and all were well! What splendid directness in
that. How little artificed. He tried to remember where
it was from, but couldn't. Or the other version, more elaborate, less successful: Christ, that my love were in my
arms, and I in my bed again. Not right. The craving for

bed should be unalloyed with anything else. Keep sex out of it. And religion.

But Marty was taking off her clothes. Royle was sitting on the bed, thinking about undoing his shoes, and trying to get up the energy to do that, to get them off. He was also examining, as one examines a swollen, pus-filled infection, the feeling that was there inside him of distaste . . . Or, no, it wasn't that, quite. But, like Bartelby the Scrivener, I would prefer not to. I would prefer to get these shoes off, and with no further interference or preparation simply keel over on the bed, clothes and all, and sleep. But she was taking her clothes off.

"I think I'll take a shower," she said.

"Why not?"

He considered this, as she went off to the bathroom and started the hiss of water from the showerhead. After all, she had been bowling. She was, in the immortal words of Leonard Bernstein to Jacqueline Kennedy after a concert, "all sweated up." Nothing could be more natural for a nice, fastidious girl. But the TV commercials have had their impact, and it is there and must be faced. No soap and water, no deodorant, mouthwash, depilatory cream, hair spray or foot powder but was an invitation to intimacy. No fools, those admen. They'd taken all the curse off cleanliness, taken it away from Godliness and put it next to sex. And he knew, yes, knew, that she would come out of the shower the way the women did in those commercials, all hot to go! Or call him in, to dry her off with the stacks of fluffy towels.

He regretted that he had not turned into that plastic blob earlier in the evening. Or that he had stopped half-way, for somehow or other his soul had made it, had changed, had turned into some lifeless lump. Or it could be just the fatigue. He was so tired.

He got the shoes off, not bothering with the laces, but just prying one off with the toe of the other, and then the other one with the bare toe of the first. But it wouldn't go. No leverage. It hurt his toe. He had, after all, to bend down, thirty-seven miles, to where his feet were. And he managed to pull his tie off. And even get his jacket off. He dropped it on the floor beside the bed. And then, with a wonderful sweetness, with the incredible comfort that drowning men must feel when they finally give up and go under into the delicate turquoise of the water, the silence, the shimmering, he allowed himself to fall down onto the pillow. It was better than Ralph Bellamy, bringing health and strength to every part of his body. It was better than anything in the world. He could feel the fatigue as a chemical pouring out of his muscles and into his bloodstream. The ultimate drug.

But he did not fall asleep. He had not been trying to do so, had not been planning to do that or to do anything. He had not been planning at all, but when the hissing stopped, and when he knew that she was coming out of the shower in a moment or two or five, he realized that he would have no choice, would have to pretend to sleep. Because, for all intents and purposes—or at least for *her* intents and her purposes—he was asleep.

He lay there with closed eyes, and heard, clearly as blind men must, the light footfalls as she came out of the bathroom. He could imagine her, all pink and scrubbed and eager. And he could imagine, too, her moment of disappointment—or anger? or disgust?—as she stopped, saw him lying on the bed with his eyes closed and his breathing slow. And sighed. He felt sorry for her. It was a shame, in a way. She'd been looking forward to this all day. But then, it's a contingent universe. And this is what you get for screwing around with old, tired poets. Beat-up, half-drunk, half-mad guys. With this one.

She came over to the bed. Would she try to wake him? Would she roll him, shake him, slap him awake? Or would she kiss him, or—like in Laugh-In, blow in his ear? But, no, she merely covered him. There was a resignation and a solicitude in it that was quite lovely in its dignity and its unselfconsciousness. She would be, he was glad to see, a real woman one day. She was well on the way. She would be, perhaps, an excellent woman.

Like Jill. Not quite, maybe. But near. And then, as he was beginning to drift off, as he felt the grip of the ex-ternal world relax its clutch upon him, and because, in those last few moments of limbo-land it didn't make any difference, he allowed her to become Jill, imagined him-self in some room in some hotel, not here, or anywhere in particular, with Jill covering him up, with her blanket and with her love. And, through his closed lids, he saw the redness of his blood turn to black as she turned out the light. He heard her get into the other bed. Her. It could be either one. Whichever he wanted. The key tile was in his head. Oh, what a game that would be.

It was as if, as if . . .

He was asleep.

CHAPTER 6

It was raining again by morning. There was no daybreak, nothing so definite as that, but only a fading of the darkness as by too many washings. And Jerome awoke in that same negative way, as by a fading of sleep. He lay there in bed for a while and gradually came to realize that he was conscious, that he could direct his mind, concentrate it, more or less, upon those questions that presented themselves. For instance, he was curious to know what time it was. His body was on New York time. It was an hour earlier here. But he could not tell whether he had slept into mid-morning or was up in the pre-dawn light. The window told him nothing. His watch was across the room at the desk-cum-dresser-cum-vanity-cum-luggage rack. The unit.

He remembered the business before him. He had to get up and dress, pack and be ready to leave. They were going to Frenion, a hundred and ten miles south. And there was to be another reading, and another party, another

evening. He remembered the night before. It had been
all right. Pleasant, in unexpected ways. And disappointing, too. The reading had been so small a part of it, merely
the occasion for the rest, an excuse for the horsing around.
Well, what the hell had he expected? A religious experience? It was only people, and it was only . . . Art? Too
imposing a word. Still, everything else should have been
an anti-climax. And it hadn't been. The reading, the
party, the games had all proceeded at the same level,
more or less interesting, more or less amusing, but all in
scale, continuous. And even so, in the blanched light of
the morning, a little furry tongued and sandy-eyed, Jerome thought back on the past evening as . . . As what?
Well, he did not think that the coming day and night
would be so good. But maybe it would all look better
after a cup of coffee. He got out of bed and busied himself with water rites—emptying out his own, running the
hotel's over him, and drinking that which had been
heated and passed through coffee grounds. In the hotel
dining room, Hungerford joined him. They discussed the
reading and their reactions to it. After a kind of diffident
twiddling of antennae, Jerome admitted that, while the
reading had gone well enough, he had been somehow
disappointed in it.

Hungerford laughed.

"All right, what's funny?" Jerome asked.

"You were disappointed? The implication is that you
expected something. Or that you expected something
good."

"I guess so. I guess I did."

"Why? From students? From teachers? From other writers? They are the enemy."

"They are the public. If we have one. Our audience."

"The enemy."

"Do you really think so?" Jerome asked.

"Yes."

"It isn't just that . . . Well, I mean, I understand that public appearances make you—uh, well—nervous?"

"Yes. They do. But I figure that my body is trying to tell me something."

"Then why do you do it? Why read at all?"

"For the money."

"For the hundred bucks, fifty bucks a reading?"

"What is it? Thirty minutes, maybe, for the two readings, total. That's two hundred dollars an hour."

"Just for the money?"

"No, I guess not." Hungerford carefully spread marmalade over the pitted lunar surface of his English muffin. He put the knife down, studied the muffin as if the answer might be somewhere in the flecks and strands or orange rind of the marmalade, and then said, "No, not just for the money. For the poems. One owes it to them."

He grinned, uncomfortable at having to say serious things so early in the morning. And he took a bite of the marmaladed muffin.

And Jerome thought, as he sat there, of the marmalade, and how real connoisseurs appreciate the bitterness of the condiment. The discomfiture of this *confiture*. Well, *chacum son* goo.

But still, there was a kind of rigorousness in Hungerford's answer, a dignity, even, that demanded some ad-

justment in Jerome's thinking. Here he had been worrying
about not enjoying it enough, not having a good enough
time, and he had been taking his emotional and artistic
temperature to see whether he was sick. But Hungerford had raised the question the other way round. He was
not suffering enough. He was not sufficiently miserable.
Did this mean that Jerome was a trivial person, missing the burden of the experience? Was he alone keeping
his head while all about him cried out in panic—because
he had failed to understand the problem? That was the
joke. Something like that. But was it true?

"I wonder," he said, "about these readings. The oral
tradition and all that."

"Crap! That's for epics. Lyric poems are private poems.
Yours are, aren't they? Mine are. Meant to be read. Several times. Worked at, to get the suption out. This reading
business . . . well, it's a fake."

"But you owe it to the poems."

Hungerford smiled. Or it was something between a
smile and a grimace. He was not unaware of the absurdity of his position, but there it was and he would maintain it. "For the poems. They deserve to be read. And if
I have to do this, if I have to go around like a medicine
show, then I'll do it."

"Even though they're all . . . what did you call them?
The enemy?"

"Sure they are. Collectively. But one or two, here or
there, could be . . . well, readers!" He shook his head.

Jerome sipped his coffee. He was glad to have had the
discussion with Hungerford. He would not pursue it,
would not press it any further, for clearly it was an un-

comfortable subject. But he was not sorry to have gone into it at least this far. Hungerford was no longer a figure of fun, a puker into Steinways, a joke. Or no, that was not exactly correct. Allowing him all the dignity of discomfort and even anguish, allowing him the honorable commitment to his work, he was still ridiculous. And the thing was to keep that in mind, to fix on the ridiculous, to maintain it above Hungerford and above them all, like a battle pennant! And as slogan, in fake Gothic script on a scroll: Over the fear, the foolishness! If it was good enough for Royle, it was good enough for anyone.

But how could he tell Hungerford that? How could he urge upon him the saving foolishness, the horsing around, the wearing of the fool's motley, for protective coloration? Like the stripes of zebras.

It could not be done directly. He could not say to Hungerford, "Look here, my dear fellow, what you must do is behave like an ass! For your own sanity. And for the good of your poems as well!" It would not sound right, would sound only as though he, Jerome, were behaving badly. No, the thing was to enmesh Hungerford in some practical joke, to win him over as a collaborator, through whatever blandishments, or appeals, or pressures, so that he found no other choice but to relax, poke fun, make merry. They should all proceed to Frenion as the members of the old *Sociétés Joyeuses* with their own *Prince des Sots, Mère-Folie, Abbé de Malgouverne*. The whole mad troupe. And why not? What was the dignity of a poet, anyway? Poets, back in the old days, were kept around like dwarfs, like idiots, as entertaining grotesques. The way to appear at Frenion was on a huge steam calliope, rented from Hertz. They could all be naked, painted blue and green, flinging handfuls of feathers and squirting aerosol cans of shaving cream or F.D.S. as they came. Well, maybe something a little less Ken Kesey-ish. But something.

Jerome finished his breakfast. Hungerford was still drinking coffee.

"Well, cheer up," Jerome said. "It could be worse. You could be one of *them.* One of the enemy."

"Yeah, that'd be worse," Hungerford said. And then, a fraction later, he nodded his head as if, during that slight interval, he had been considering the idea and had decided that he could accept it, that he agreed.

"If you'll excuse me, I have to pack. And I'm the world's slowest, and probably the world's worst packer."

Hungerford nodded again. Excusing Jerome? Or continuing in his exploration of the previous question and assent?

Upstairs, Jerome sat down at the desk part of the unit, took out his paper and revised:

> *Over the fear, the foolishness of a jay*
> *unsettles the grove as children in a church.*
> *The carnivore is grave before his prey,*
> *but woodpeckers rattle up the trees in search*
> *of grubs.*

No, it was wrong. Still wrong. Flabby and foolish. *Over the fear, the foolishness* . . . and then leave the phrase hanging. It's good enough. Let it proclaim itself. Let it stand as a kind of epigraph, almost. Or the moral, but up front. And the rest would be an exemplum. Take out *of*. It starts, then, with *a jay* . . . but the *children* in the second line? One child. One jay, one child.

> *Over the fear, the foolishness—a jay*
> *behaving badly, as a child in church,*
> *while the big cat crouches down before his*
> *prey.*

And then, by accident, by the deletion of *grove* the scene had changed. *Big cat?* It was out in the savannah, somewhere, the wavy grass. And *the trees* were merely a small clump. Okay, but now what? The yammering birds, and down there some big cat going at some victim. A toilet flushed in the room above Jerome. He was annoyed, he wanted there to be quiet so he could think, and then he realized that he wanted there to be quiet in the poem.

> *Hush! But the woodpeckers rattle the trees in search*
> *of grubs, bounce acorns on the ground, the way*
> *they always do. That blood's pulse in the throat*
> *of the victim commands attention. They don't obey.*

But then what? The *hunter* and the *introit?* They seemed forced now. A reach. And he wanted the yammering back. Because the way it would go was clear, was suddenly clear. All that propriety was wrong, was no damned good. At least the sounds of the birds and the acorns, and the rest of it kept the poor victim distracted, occupied, kept feeding data into the nerves and into the brain, so the poor thing knew that it was still alive. There were,

in those irrelevant noises, relevant affirmations! But of
course! The sestet would go down, would identify with
the victim, would notice, take in, hear, and then, maybe,
go blank, like the end of the *Dialogues des Carmelites*,
dwindling down from the chorus to the one voice, and
then the silence. Yeah, yeah, yeah.

That one note. *Note/throat*. Jesus! As bad as June/
moon. But there was a title? And a *succès d'estime*. And
Otto Preminger had bought it! Go with it! Back to the
bird, *the bird* something, something something *note*.

>   *A green bird trills upon his something note.*

Okay, but what? *His only note? His (zip) one note?*
Johnny One-Note? Idiotic. Yes, *idiotic!* You see, there
was something in those pots after all, Dr. Curie!

>   *A green bird trills upon his idiot note,*
>   *as if nothing at all were happening.* . . . .

Right. And then, into the business from the victim's POV.
The craving for these senseless sounds, the thirst for
them, and the suggestion that they are precious because
they are a part of life. Because they *are* life.

Pfui! But still, with the right concreteness, with the
right kind of attack and tact, he might bring it off. It could
be done, perhaps.

He tucked the poem—two papers now, dog-eared together—into his pocket. And hurriedly he began throwing
things into his suitcase.

He felt good. The poem, he thought, would make it,

would finish itself. And it would be all right. Whether it would be merely good, or very good, or even first rate, he could not tell. And it was not really his concern. It did not do to worry about such questions. That kind of worry could tighten you up, make it difficult to write at all. Let the others make such decisions. The point was to do it, and to feel it happening. And to enjoy it. Because it was enjoyable.

Yes, Hungerford was wrong. It was not agony, nor pain, nor suffering, nor any of that crap. It was not broody and solemn and pompous and dull, but fun. Gorgeous! When that damned green bird trills upon his idiot note, that's it. That's all there is. The bird is the note, warbling itself out into the wind.

He paused, to test *it* again. In the bathroom, picking up his shaving gear, cleaning that room out and bringing all the stuff together in one place, he stopped. Why *idiot* note? Was there any sense to that at all? The word had popped into his head, and he had caught it and kept it. But did he really want it? Idiot. A private person, originally. Yes, he was sure of that, etymologically, and therefore it was different from stupid or moronic. Yes, all right, *idiot*. Because the bird isn't singing to anything or anyone, or about anything, but just singing, privately, idiotically. Purely. Falala!

He picked up the styptic pencil and the plastic toothbrush container over which his hand had paused during the instant of his critical assay (impossible to tell the duration of the process but it felt like an instant) and carried them into the bedroom.

There was a knock at the door.

"Come in."

The doorknob rattled, but nothing happened. Of course. Because the door was locked. He put down the toothbrush and the styptic pencil and called out, "Sorry, I'm coming!" What the hell was he thinking of? Who was he expecting who could walk through doors? Mr. Ectoplasm?

He opened the door to find John Royle, smiling, standing out in the hallway.

"Hi, come on in."

"You had breakfast yet?" Royle asked.

"Yes."

"Good. I wanted to talk to you. To ask you a favor."

"Sure. Anything."

"It's about Marty. Or Jill, really. It's about both of them."

"Anything I can do," Jerome said, but he was worried. He didn't know exactly what it was that worried him. But he was aware of having to keep his voice the way it had been before, of keeping his expression just the same as it had been without letting it freeze into a histrionic mask.

"I'd like you to . . . well, sort of take Marty over. Be her escort, I guess. At Frenion."

"Sure. Will she . . . Does she know?"

"I'll tell her. She'll do whatever I tell her. It's mostly for appearances, you see."

"Of course."

"I mean, Jill knows, but there's no reason for everyone else to know. I think that'd hurt her."

"I see."

"It wouldn't be much of a burden."

"No, no. No trouble at all. As I said, anything at all. You know that."

"Yes. I know. That's why . . . Well, that's why I asked. You."

Jerome tried to think of something else to say, some helpful comment, some words that would reassure, comfort, help . . . both of them. But he could not. And Royle, too, was silent. They looked at each other, smiling, grinning actually, and both of them wanting to say something.

"Well, I better go down and get some coffee," Royle said. "And tell her."

The door closed and the spring bolt snapped. But Jerome continued to stare at it as if there had to be something more. A door opens, a man comes in, and suddenly you are a character in a bedroom farce! What kind of thing is that? The lights would have to go out, and stage hands would have to come on from the wings somewhere, grunting under their heavy burdens as they took away the door, the wall, the entire hotel, and left in place of all they had removed . . . a ship's prow? A ruined castle of the Gothic revival style? A small glade in the country with a *trompe l'oeil* brook that actually appeared to flow and from which, at a certain point in the next scene one of the players would actually extract a live fish? Or perhaps the door would merely open again, and someone else would come in, strike a pose, and start singing in Italian, in which Jerome would reply, plotting vengeance on the wicked Duke.

But that kind of retreat into grotesque exaggeration

was not going to be useful. What he would have to do would be to settle down, take several deep breaths and consider, calmly and reasonably, what would be involved in playing at being Marty's escort. Not so very much, after all. No more, certainly, than in Royle's playing at not being her escort. Or in Jill's playing at not knowing, not noticing what was going on. There was a poignance to it that was only intensified by its elaborate staginess, by its sedulous echoes of all the first acts of all those silly plays. For real people to be enmeshed in those coils of plot was outrageous. But then it so often turned out that way. Those hack dramatists were not, after all, so far off the mark of truth as he had always supposed.

For whether he was willing or not, whether he liked the idea or not, it did occur to him that Royle was being very cavalier about all this. Not cavalier about him, but about Marty. What was it that he'd said? "She'll do what I tell her." Well, yes, to a certain extent. But she was not a latah, and could, without very much trying, influence the development of the comedy. How would she feel about all this? Hurt? Angry? Amused? Any of these feelings, if they were strong enough, would work for the scenario that was building itself in the back of Jerome's head. Skipping all the contortions of the exposition, there was the second act curtain he could imagine—of himself and Marty, by that impressively realistic river, playing at being lovers, carrying on in witty dialogue about how this, too, was what they had agreed to do for Royle's sake, and doing it, all of it, naked and entwined. Where does the imposture stop, or become the reality? She was not an unattractive girl.

Not that he seriously intended to make Marty. But the possibility of its happening had been raised. In his own mind, and, presumably, in Marty's too. And in Royle's? He couldn't be sure. What was there that had been so strained, so difficult about their conversation? Royle's fear of imposing, or his embarrassment about Jill. Or maybe he hadn't been uncomfortable or embarrassed at all, but just sleepy or hung over, and therefore taciturn. Still, these things happen so easily.

When he had been younger, an undergraduate and after, it had been perfectly straightforward, a pursuit of girls whose fears for their reputation or whose fear of pregnancy were obstacles in the ancient course. But it had all changed. The time, the age, or maybe just Jerome's age. He was older now, and these things happened without much effort. Women made their moves, too. One could be pursued. There were so many richer possibilities for those farceurs than he had imagined. Sally.

He had gone to Sally—to Mrs. Wertham—to tutor her in Latin! Of all silly things! But she wanted to do something now that the children were in school, and teaching would be convenient because the vacations would coincide, and she needed the Master's. And being a little bit of a snob, she didn't want an education Master's, but a real one, and therefore needed the language competence. French, German or Latin. Pick one. And she was worried about her French and had no German. And the medieval Latin was a notorious snap. And therefore a trek through the jungles and poems in Helen Waddell's little green book.

So he had come to teach her Latin. And, like Francesca

and Paolo, they had reached the time when they read no more that day. Simple? No, simpler. Because Mr. Wertham, slaving away downtown in upper echelon executiveland, came home drained, tired, and, more often than not, impotent. And Mrs. Wertham had asked Dr. Rosen what to do, what pills there were, what elixirs. He had stroked his moustache and suggested a lover. Rx: One lover, as needed. Squiggle Rosen, MD.

Sally had even told Jerome about it later on. So there would be no pretense, no possibility of confusion. Just friendship, and some nice, simple, healthy fucking. A dandy arrangement.

Until Sally got pregnant, that is. By whom, God only knew. Certainly Sally didn't. For the angel came unto her, and said, "Laugh not, but, Jesus! you have conceived." And she went to Dr. Rosen, who stroked his moustache and declined to perform an abortion because . . . . Well, he never actually said why. Maybe he thought it was funny. Maybe he was a playwright too, a mental writer like the elevator man, and he wanted to see how it would—ho ho!—come out! Sally had taken her husband on a cruise, and got him to get it up a couple of times. And then she had broken off the relationship with Jerome, because, as she had explained a month ago, now that he was possibly the father of her child (possibly!) it would be somehow improper to have him hanging around. Well, human kind can bear only so much reality.

("Who said that, panel? A hand. Ah, Mr. Carpenter. 'T. S. Oleo, in Margarine in the Cathedral.' Very good!")

No, not very good. Very bad. But what could be learned from it all? Nothing? Was it even relevant? Jerome had thought of it, or had found it flashing across his mind, like the red light on the phone in one of those hotels with that kind of message system. And it seemed to fit with his discomfort about Royle and his little old favor that he wanted. It wasn't the favor, nor the complicity that it required, but the genre itself, and his gnawing suspicion that it was, for some reason, his natural genre. This playing at roles, this fooling around, was getting to be a natural and authentic condition. Sooner or later one could get to a point where it would be inauthentic to affect authenticity.

He wondered for a moment whether it would be worth while to save up such illuminations and try for a long, or anyway medium length didactic poem. Three Trios. Or Two Duets. The nearly flat line, the poetry relatively bare of imagery. The flirting with the gravity of the thought like an acrobatic clown, risking always the lunge into prose. Perhaps. Later, maybe. In the forties. When the lyric rush is supposed to burn itself out and you wind up imitating yourself or preaching. Like Wordsworth. A fine future.

He felt tired. Silly to feel so tired so early in the morning. And with so long to go, yet. All the way to Frenion, and all those hours to get through. And in the rain. He returned to the suitcase. If he could just get through that, just get all the junk in there, it would be a start. Off to Frenion! And party with Marty! Ho ho! He knew now, though, what had bothered him, what had worried him when Royle had asked him to do that small, simple favor. He was worried that somehow he could screw it up, mess it up, not play it exactly right, and then be responsible—or, just as bad almost, feel responsible—for God knows what disaster. For Jill? For Marty? For Royle? He didn't even know enough to be able to guess.

He wrapped his laundry from the day before into the shirt he had worn, making the previous day's shirt into a sack, and he stuffed the sack into the suitcase, flattening it as much as he could. Then he closed the suitcase. He looked around the room once more to make certain that he had not left anything. It seemed bare enough. Enough and more than enough. It would be impossible to tell that he had ever been in the room. That anyone had ever been here. As the astronauts had said at their press conference, "Yes, we look up at the moon now, but it's hard to believe that we were actually there. It seems just as far away as ever." So much for experience. It isn't worth the expense. It doesn't help.

He picked up the weight of the suitcase and went downstairs to the lobby to check out and to wait for the cars that would be going to Frenion. All over again. As if Rockville had never happened. Or, as if having happened, some huge gear had slipped, and it all had to be gone through again. *Jamais vu*. Or would it be *déjà vu*?

It was silly. The rain was coming down in sheets which the windshield wipers could not even fray let alone cut through. And the three cars made their cautious way along the long, flat highway, the *flaablap* of the wipers syncopating off against the *clubup clubup* of the wheels as they crossed the sections of concrete. All this noise and risk and adventure for a bunch of writers to get from one college to another to read their bits and snatches. It was a parody of the great American entrepreneurs with their salesmen, their area representatives, their lawyers and lobbyists, criss-crossing the land to make deals, build, conglomerate, amalgamate, spin off . . . Whatever they did. But they took it seriously, and so, therefore, every-one else took it, and them, seriously. But a bunch of writers! Itinerant fruit pickers in the groves of Academe. The budding grove. The darling buds. Mayday!

The effort of it was what amused Royle. To go at all was foolish, but to go this way, to have Hungerford's tire blow out, and to have to stop, try to get the car back onto the hard shoulder, in all that rain . . . It was abstract, surrealist, dadaist. It was crazy! Stone, and Carpenter and Hungerford and Royle, all pushing, while Agnes sat in the car and turned the steering wheel this way and that. It was all very funny. They were all soaked, which was okay. Nobody would melt. But they had slipped, too, and were covered with mud. They would make quite an ap-pearance at the reading. And on television! Yes, that would be the best part. Four muddy bums show up at the studio to be interviewed, and the station manager would worry. And they would explain that they were the poets and the novelists. It would be a gas! (Into the show-ers with you, friends!) Not that Royle minded. It would be perfectly appropriate for the disreputability of art to be affirmed this way. Even if only accidentally. Covered with mud yelling at each other about how to move the Volkswagen. And finally Hungerford had gone off to walk the two or three miles to the service station to get the tow truck to help them. And they'd changed the tire in about a minute and a half. With brio and panache (wasn't *panache* the word for tow-truck in French?). And they'd got back into the cars, and had driven off again, exhausted, wet, cold, muddy. Gorgeous! Songs of the earth they would sing. Covered with it. Wallowing in it.

He had thought of the way they would appear on television when they had got that great take from the waitress in the diner where they'd stopped for coffee. It was as if creatures from the enchanted swamp had risen up, and all swathed in graveclothes, had stopped in at the diner for a cup of coffee and an order of muffins before going on to spread plague, war, fire and flood through the town. That, too. Let the reader beware!

Feeling better, after the coffee, though. And feeling better today, generally. He had beaten it. Or had stood it off. For a while, anyway. He felt in control of himself, more or less. As much as he ever did. As much as was normal. And he would get through the weekend. Not that he took any credit for the temporary victory over the black dog. Not at all. But as those sailors said, when they'd rowed all the way across the Atlantic, "We didn't defeat it. It spared us. It let us go." Right. But as the mouse knows, it's better in the hole than in the cat's jaws. Even if only for a while.

Feeling better, and feeling even pretty good. Marty had been reasonable and even friendly at breakfast when he had told her that he was turning her over to Jerome. And Jill would be fine. Jill was always fine. And he could get through the reading. He was even looking forward to it, showing off on his home turf. It would bother Justis Corda. Corda always hated it when Royle got up to shine, restoring the balance between literature and criticism. Doing it. The scales of Justis!

Ahead, through the trees and the telephone poles, there was a dull gleam of wet light off the top of the bell tower. *"Venimmo al piè d'una torre al da sezzo."* Royle surveyed the sky, looking for some sign that the rain was letting up. A blue patch. A rainbow, even. Such five-and-dime manifestations, cheap and gaudy. And so often timed to coincide with arrivals and departures or great moments. Ludicrous. Lude Icarus. Loved to lick his licorice.

"What do we do now?"

Royle looked around, startled. It was Jerome. Asking a reasonable question.

"About our clothes," Jerome went on. "What do we do?"

"Why, nothing. I'd thought I'd decided that. I guess I forgot to tell anyone. But I did decide. That it would be fine to appear on the television show looking like this. A bunch of bums."

Jerome laughed politely. And then with some conviction. And told Royle about his idea of making a grand entrance on a calliope, with the feathers and the shave foam. For Hungerford's benefit.

"Well, it's something to play with. We've got to do something on that show. We could squirt shave cream."

"Or turn into werewolves."

"Or pumpkins."

"Or turn into each other."

"But Hungerford would never do it," Royle said.

"So much the better. I mean, if I were to say that I

were Hungerford. And you were to agree with me. Either he's got to insist that he's Hungerford and look like a lunatic, or he can be somebody else and appear to be sane. The thing is to accept his reticence. Use it. Play on it."

"Psychological judo, eh?" Royle suggested. "Right! Judo Iscariot! But it'll do him. I mean, what if Judas hadn't betrayed Christ? The Romans wouldn't have got him, and he'd have died in his bed at the age of fifty-seven, a kindly old carpenter with a lot of good ideas. Right?"

"The pieces of silver had nothing to do with it?"

"An agent is entitled to a commission."

They laughed. Even Marty smiled. And she had been pretty damned quiet. Not that he could blame her. What the hell! It was a long, wet, soggy trip. And they had been up late the night before. And . . . But he knew it wasn't any of that. Not that there was anything he could do about it. He didn't even feel guilty. Sorry for her, a little, because it was not the kind of time she had looked forward to. But that is not an uncommon experience in life.

She drove well. Hell, maybe that was all it was. In all this rain, she had to concentrate on the road. On following Hungerford. And on making sure that Stone and Dinsmore, in the rented car, were still behind her. Concentration and fatigue. There were so many perfectly ordinary explanations. None of which was really satisfactory. Because the jokes were funny. And funny jokes deserve laughter.

"What's the matter?" he asked her. "You're not laughing."

It was unlikely, but then it could work, he thought. Maybe there was some simple explanation. Tight shoes. In an ideal universe, one could ask such a question and get an answer.

"Nothing. It's just . . . foolishness," she answered.

He had to work very hard at not smiling. So that was it! She was disappointed in his not taking himself as seriously as she took him. "But the fool attains wisdom by persisting in his folly."

"You just made that up."

"No, dear. Blake." He thought it was Blake. It sounded, anyway, as though it could be. Ought to be.

"Mmm hmm."

Was she turning him off? Or just turning? Clickick clickick. The turn indicator lit and darkened. She was turning off. They were there. Alumnae House. A great, rambling mock Tudor pile. But it was better than Rockville's Collegiate Arms. Royle looked at his watch. It was a quarter past twelve. And they didn't have to be at the TV station until three. Or, to be safe, a quarter of. Time to unpack, to eat, and to get over there. Plenty of time.

"Well, are we going to do it?" Jerome asked.

"Do it? Do what?"

"Exchange identities."

What was he talking about? The deal with Marty? Or, no, he had already agreed to that. The television thing. That Jerome would be Hungerford.

"On the television show," Jerome said, making himself clearer.

"Oh, that. Sure. Yes, let's do it." He grinned. With relief, partly. The other arrangement was okay. Unquestioned. Oh, and he ought to call Jill. Let her know that he was back. And would be home soon. And was okay.

They all got out of the cars and went inside to check in. Royle stood there to make sure that there hadn't been any screw ups. There hadn't been. Brief conference, like that of football players in a huddle. Arrangements for lunch and meeting here at two. Fine fine fine fine. Good.

He crossed the lobby to the phone booth to call Jill. Feeling good. Ludicrous, lude Icarus. Lou Dicarus? Reed Diculus. Abe Serd. Ceil Lee. Dumb.

Whatever qualms he might have had were calmed, quashed, crushed, smashed by the posh floss of the lobby. Lobby? It was an entrance arcade, a gross ingress, a hall-lucination. It was the work of an interior decorator of monumental tastelessness. Huge walls of draperies, mir-rors, plastics, tweeds, laminates, plashing fountains. Pol-ish provincial regency. With a few accents of moderne. The planters along the railing of the nameless blond-wood looked merely expensive. All that beaten copper, with the artificial plants in them, and the red flowers. Royle could squint his lids together and let his eyes go out of focus and still it all looked terrible. Tasteless. The planters looked like coffins full of flames. For damned midgets. The communicasters, as they called themselves, the tastemakers and the pace setters, the men of the media worked here, came in and out of these doors, walked through this preposterousness and . . . And what? Accepted it? Tolerated it? Blotted it out? Or, worst of all, perhaps they liked it, took some kind of grotesque assurance from its obviousness, its expensiveness, its expensive valuelessness, which was like their own, but tangible, physical, and therefore real! None of them deserved a real name, an honest answer, a true syllable, nor did the improbable agglomeration of viewers out there, the ones who put up with them. Or who took the same reassurance from their phoniness, their gleaming smiles, their sincere haberdashery as the television people took from this dreadful building, this indecorous decor.

The name of the program was The Long View—because Betty Long was the hostess. A mind at work, there. You could tell that right away. Playing on language. There had been many long, executive meetings about it, with those terrific brainstorming sessions, as they considered All A-Long, or Wide and Long, or The Long Trail. Or Long Suit? Or Longitude? Probably nothing that remote. And they had wadded up a lot of paper, and smoked a lot of cigarettes, and sent out for a lot of sandwiches and black coffee. Just like in the movies, which was where most of them picked up their executive style, anyway. And they had come up with this.

The chief shaker and mover of this executive team, the executive producer, a chunky, sandy colored fellow, who either wore collars a half size too small or had developed the non-objective tic of craning his neck every so often as a kind of punctuation to what he said, was welcoming them, offering coffee to anyone who wanted it, providing them with mimeographed releases to sign, and tactfully suggesting that anyone who wanted to wash his hands ought to do so. It wouldn't do to go on the august program with dirty hands. Of course not. Clean hands, clean hearts. Or was it warm hands, warm hearts? Or big hands, big pricks? Something like that.

They all stood there for a moment, like sheep, and then they allowed themselves to be herded into another, smaller lounge, all lilac and cocoa: Stone looking intense and even a trifle nervous, as though this meant anything; Hungerford also nervous, but that was reasonable (What if they didn't have a Steinway on the set? Could he puke into a Baldwin? A Knabe? A Yamaha? A tuba, even?); Jerome, feisty and full of beans, all ready for the big joke; Elaine Dinsmore, looking rather good with her hair slightly straggly from the rain; Agnes, competent and businesslike, composed, sensible. And himself. All spruced up now at Jill's insistence, with the brown tweed jacket, the charcoal slacks, the blue shirt for television, and the silk rep tie. Or maybe demi-rep?

What could they all say, what could they possibly say in the format, the discussion that was no discussion but a performance, broken up by commercials, moderated by Betty Long who would keep things moving not according to any logic or sense but rather in conformity with the suggestions of the director who would want a new face for his camera, and then another, and then another. And even without all this mechanical impediment, all she would want to know was what they all wanted to know —How does it feel? How does it feel to be a poet? How does it feel to have your husband assassinated? To win the Irish Sweepstake? To have your child rescued from kidnappers? To be alive? To be dying?

She entered, not quite in Loretta Young's old swirl of diaphanous junk, but damned near. Pert, perky, the not

very faded stewardess or cheerleader, she went around
the room introducing herself and getting the names. A
professional touch, that, for Royle was sure that she was
memorizing the names. She made it a point to use the
name in the next sentence ("Yes, well, John, it's good to
have you on the show . . .") making her guest feel important, known, comfortable, and also setting the name
in her own mental card file. One of those memory tricks.
Let me unlock the secrets of your mental powers! Let me
show you how to double, triple, quadruple your mind's
computerlike sorting device! And the eyes of Bruno You-
know staring out, obviously aflame with facts, names,
dates, numbers, brain power.

"Yes, well, Betty, it's good to be here on the show with
you . . ."

She looked at him, not quite hard enough to suggest
that she was puzzled or suspicious that he might be parodying her. It was more vague than that, an uncertainty,
as dogs have sometimes, when they see themselves in a
mirror. He liked to think that she was wondering whether
she had said that or he had. Yummy! A very philosophical
joke they would be playing, perhaps. And how does it *feel*
to be playing a philosophical joke?

Sorta tingly, kinda, in a way, like . . .

And really? He wasn't sure. He hadn't even gone so
far as to decide, definitely, that he was going to do it,
that they were going to go ahead. It would be up to
Jerome, mostly. And he would go along with the game if
Jerome started it. It didn't feel like anything so much as
a visit to the dentist. That slight nervousness at the base
of the stomach. Stagefright? Not really. But a heightened

awareness of the situation and of the surroundings. He could virtually feel the raspiness of the fiberglass draperies across the room, those long, lilac swaths down the cream colored walls. You could get a rash from that fiberglass stuff.

They were being herded again, out of the little lounge and into the big studio where it was cold, the air conditioning on and pumping in the cold air so that, later, when the lights came on, it would still be tolerable. There were areas in the studio—a kiddie-show corner, a weather forecaster's corner, the interview platform with the swivel chairs . . .

"Don't swivel!" the executive producer was saying, swivelling his neck again. "It makes the viewer at home feel seasick." Or see-sick. Everyone a philosopher, eh?

And down at the end of the studio, a huge window from which the men in the control room looked out and gave directions to the cameramen. The fish tank, Royle thought it was called. Or, certainly, it ought to be called that. Those fishy eyes, and fishy mouths opening and closing in the aquarium silence of that cubicle. Their fishy breath. (Could there be such a thing? Of dolphins, maybe.)

They sat, arranged by the executive producer, and another underling provided them with microphones that tied around the neck and glasses of water and ash trays. Miss Long was nowhere to be seen. Had she gone off to wash her hands? Or was it more deliberate than that? Conceivably, she wanted to keep the freshness of the interview for the camera and the microphones, as if people were like food, like coffee, and began to grow stale as soon as the vacuum pack was ruptured by that little key and the hiss of air. A shelf-life of mere minutes. Not Royle thought, an unattractive idea: the perishability of intellect.

Miss Long—Betty, she wanted them to call her—appeared again, glanced at her clip board with her notes, looked around like a teacher taking attendance, and sat down in her slightly larger chair at the head of the table. And . . . And nothing. She did not speak. She waited, like a Chatty Cathy doll, for someone to pull the string, to activate all this mechanism.

"Fifteen seconds," one of the assistants called out.

Royle looked at the monitors. The colors were not in agreement. One was too greenish, the other too pinkish. They showed the table and the microphone—a prop microphone that wasn't even plugged into anything—and the name of the show superimposed in rather Aubrey Beardsley looking letters. Very smart. It bothered him that he had not yet invented a name for the show better than the one they'd picked. Long . . . Long . . . The Long Spoon! It would sound a little like a cooking program, but so what? If she made a living by dining with the devil this way, let her be a little whimsical about it.

"Five, four, three . . ."

The last two numbers of the countdown were silent, done with the fingers. And then the pointing finger aimed at Betty Long, who smiled, dazzlingly brightly, and then, in a dazzling bright display of bathos, said, "Hi, there, and welcome to The Long View . . ."

It was difficult not to laugh, not to break up into a roar of whooping and guffawing. "Hi there," indeed. All this paraphernalia, all this technology, all this precision and

237

expertise building up to "Hi, there!" He looked around. Jerome was grinning like a cheerful banshee, about to wail to warn Miss Long of the death of her program, of her entire career. Hungerford was even smiling a little. A small, wry smile. Agnes looked pained.

But Stone looked absolutely philosophical. It was the beard, maybe. It showed up on the monitor as pure cerebration, oozing out of his head, and dribbling down his chin in hirsute complications! The faker. The fakir. The fucker.

". . . and I thought we might talk a little bit today about writing in America, and the problems that writers face these days. But, first, I want to tell you about a wonderful cheese spread that comes in an aerosol can and some of the clever things you can do with it for parties . . ."

No, no. Stop, right there. You've just said it. You've got it. The problems that writers face? It's that cheese spread. It's all the wonderful things you can do with it at parties. It's *you*! (Where was that from? "It's you . . ." He thought for a moment, casting around, and came up with Robert Penn Warren. He wasn't sure which poem. It could have been any one of a number of them. Those odd, second person poems. Which suddenly seemed right and appropriate, and maybe the only way to talk to a world that said, "Hi, there, let me tell you about writers and cheese spread and the anti-death spray on sale this week with a wonderful bonus . . .")

"I think what we ought to do is go around the table," Betty Long was saying. "You can all introduce yourselves and mention any books you want to plug . . ."

Royle glanced around and saw there was a piece of film on the monitor, where a pair of hands were spraying cheese flowers on little crackers. The studio microphones were off. But the Long smile was still on. And these were instructions. Wonderful instructions! The poor bitch was trying. Go ahead and plug your books. If it works for cheese spread, it'll work for poetry, right? But wonderful in another way, too. There was Jerome looking up at the ceiling and rubbing his face, obviously to hide the smile that was flowering like a cheddar rose on a melba round, for he too had seen the possibility, the perfect opening of which he would have to take advantage. Yes, well, all systems go.

Royle felt a slight pang of wistfulness that he hadn't thought of it first, that he couldn't in fairness introduce himself with some truly loony piece of nonsense. My name is Joel Kuperman and I'm six years old, and I can do any cube root there is. No, he would have to be John Royle so that he could vouch for Jerome's imposture. And then, hoho! when the real Ed Hungerford stood up, he would have to make something up, some other person to be. The supposititious Hungerford having already been established . . . Royle lingered over the word. It had popped into his head the night before, about James II's son. But how else could you use it? To describe the off-spring of a couple of homosexuals?

"My name is Elaine Dinsmore, and I'm the author of *Shock Treatment*."

"I'm John Royle," Royle said. "I'm on the faculty here at Frenion, in the English department. My latest book was *Into the Trees*."

He thought for a moment of plugging it as she had invited him to do, mentioning the National Book Award. But what the hell! It was three years ago. Nearly four. And it was a dumb award anyway. And immodest to mention. And, really, how many copies would he sell by mentioning it? Two? Five? At forty cents a copy? The spiritual expense was not worth the two dollars. "I guess that's about it," he said, smiling.

Next to him, Carpenter said, in a perfectly matter of fact way, wonderfully straight, entirely natural: "My name is Ed Hungerford. I make a living by speculating in frozen hog belly futures. I write poems to amuse myself and my friends. My book is called *Something for Nothing*, and it was published by the University of Missouri Press."

They were all staring at him. But of course they would be looking at him anyway. Even if he had given his real name. Nobody was laughing at least. Or maybe they just hadn't got that far. Maybe they were still trying to take it in, to figure it out. Hungerford was smiling.

But then Stone erupted, "No, no he isn't."

"I beg your pardon?" Miss Long said. This had not been programmed in her notes for the program.

"He's not Ed Hungerford!" Stone said.

"Sure he is!" Royle said.

"He's Jerome Carpenter." He pointed to Hungerford and said, "*He's* Hungerford."

Hungerford shook his head. "My name is Walter Savage Landor, and my book is called *Imaginary Conversations*."

"Who are *you*?" Betty Long asked of Stone. She was worried. Her program was being hijacked and forced to land in Havana! Her cheese dip was turning to gall—in an aerosol can. Her world was collapsing.

"I'm Sam Stone!" Stone said, displaying more than a soupçon of annoyance. A soupçon? A soupcan! A cauldronful! That he should be asked for his name. All that beard down the drain and of no use.

"The famous folksinger!" Jerome chimed in, picking up the outrage from Stone and turning it against him.

"I'm a novelist," Stone insisted. "And a writer of short stories. I . . ."

"And a famous liar," Hungerford added.

"Now, really," Betty Long interposed.

"What is reality?" Hungerford asked.

"Life is a fountain," Jerome suggested.

"Life is an aerosol can," Royle offered.

"Life is a metaphor," Agnes said. "My name is Agnes Hartshorne and I want to get in a plug for my book too. It's called *The History of Boredom.*"

"Perhaps Mr. Stone would sing for us?" Hungerford suggested. "Mrs. Landor and I have all his records and we play them often."

"What records? What the hell are you talking about?"

"Please, Mr. Stone, this is a family show."

"What?"

"Your language, sir."

"Oh, sorry."

"But do sing," Royle pleaded.

"No, I'm not in voice," he countered. "And I don't have my theorbo with me."

"What's a theorbo?" Betty Long asked. Right on top of things she was. One had to admire that.

"A kind of bass lute," Stone told her.

So, even he had come around. A rock, that Stone!

But there was nowhere to go from there. For all of the fooling around, the games and jokes, the nonsense, they were still bound by the logic and the rigors of their craft as surely as they were bound by their physical natures to inhale and to exhale, to pump the blood among the same intricate conduits, to blink their eyes. The reasonableness of the conversation was, Royle decided, the most outrageous part of the whole program. The contrariness of the stuff of the world, and its stupid resistance to variation, to whimsy, to magic, to foolishness was a kind of joke in itself. As if God were a very literal minded child who recited, "This is the church and this is the steeple/ Open the doors and see all the fingers . . ."

Stone discussed, in all apparent seriousness, the condition of folk-song writing, and the hope for it as a kind of popular poetry, a way for poets to revive the lost connections with their audiences. He cited his own—supposititious—efforts, and the other, real and rather more tiresome efforts of Rod McKuen. Jerome, as Ed Hungerford, talked about the suspicion that he felt for this, and that many other poets felt, too. He wondered whether all these readings, these poetry-with-jazz performances, these poems-as-folk-songs were legitimate, whether there was an oral tradition any more. And he suggested that there was an advantage in not having an audience which was not to be dismissed. "One is not tempted to pander," he said.

And Hungerford, as Walter S. Landor—for Christ's sake —agreed with . . . Himself?

And then, predictably, they talked about the writer in the university, and the writer in the world of crass commerce, and the disadvantages of both situations. And Landor volunteered that he knew a fellow who had the best of both worlds. The fellow was a poet, and a very good one, and he made a living by ghost-writing Masters' essays and doctoral dissertations for academic drudges, fooling them all.

And then there was another word about cheese spread. And then Betty Long mentioned the reading which would be held that night at the Langly Auditorium of Frenion College, at which all of these writers would be appearing, and promised that on tomorrow's show Antonia Sheil would be telling about the Animal Rescue League's work, and would be bringing several cats to show. And she signed off. Music. Credit crawler over silent shot of the guests pretending to talk. End of show.

A loudspeaker barked out into the studio, "Would you all keep your places, please."

What now? They were going to be scolded? They had been found out, and they were going to have their movie passes taken away. They would have to stand in the corner, over there in the fragment of the room for the kiddie show or write on the blackboard a hundred times, "I will not impersonate Walter Savage Landor."

But, no, it was better than that. The executive producer appeared, conferred with Betty Long, and announced that they would straighten out the tape . . . They would cut Miss Long's reprimand to Mr. Stone, but Mr. Stone would have to say, "Heck."

"What?" Stone asked.

"You don't mind, surely?" the executive producer said. "It's a very good show. Really, a first-rate show. And we'd like to run it, and maybe re-run it later on in the season. And it would be . . . better, if you could say 'Heck.'"

So Stone said "Heck."

"Again, please."

"Heck."

"Four or five times, please."

"Heck. Heck. Heck. Heck."

"Thank you. That ought to do it. We can just stick this in on the audio portion, and it will be impossible to tell."

"Sorry to put you to all that trouble," Stone said.

"Oh, that's quite all right. You'd be surprised how often it happens. We had to do all kinds of work a month ago to clean up the remarks of the lieutenant governor at the meeting of the Elementary Education Association."

Royle imagined the lieutenant governor, any lieutenant governor, telling the Elementary Education Association, "You've got to learn the ass off them fucking kids, or this country ain't going to be worth shit!" And they'd take out the bad words but leave the grammar.

Miss Long presented them each with a can of aerosol cheddar cheese spread. They all thanked her. Even Stone, who said, "Heck, it was a pleasure."

And out into the gray afternoon. Terrible weather. Or terrible adjustment. The brightness and contrast of the world need to be fixed. It was all blurry and out of focus. Gosh darn it!

Jerome sat in the car outside Alumnae House, waiting for John to come out again. Royle had dropped Agnes and Ed off to rest and freshen up. They would be coming by later on, for the drinks and dinner, for the reading, of course, and for the party, afterwards. But Jerome was going on ahead with Royle to the house. They could have an hour or two alone, to talk, to relax, to catch up on what had really been going on in each other's lives. The trouble with these damned readings was that they were all so scheduled, so busy, so organized that nothing had a chance to happen. Nothing important, anyway.

Jerome was looking forward with a mild sort of curiosity to seeing Royle's house. He had never been there, and he couldn't even imagine it. Not that he expected anything bizarre or peculiar. But the idea of a poet's house was . . . Well, he just didn't have one. Poems, he supposed, get written in trains, in Venetian pensions, in Pisan jails, in Parisian garrets. In New York City apartments, even. But in comfort, in a house out in the country, in prosperous farm land near a women's college? Well, why not?

Still, it seemed odd, somehow. Novelists, Jerome assumed, would have houses, would have comfortable establishments, overstuffed furniture, huge regency desks, heavy draperies. Even cork lined rooms. Any comfort for that long pull, the daily application, the persistence which required order and a certain routine. But poetry came in flashes. Anywhere. That was the fun of it. He could think of exceptions. Enough exceptions, really, to invalidate the whole conception. Emily Dickinson was a household type. And George Eliot wrote all over Europe. Still . . .

Royle came out, got into the car, and drove off. He

talked about the program, and how well it had gone for Hungerford. "I never saw him so loose."

"Too damned loose! All the bit about writing Masters' essays? He needed that?"

"Fair's fair. You'd taken him over. He took back a little from you. Nobody will believe it, anyway. Walter Savage Landor, indeed!"

"I guess."

Out through an orderly, residential section of town, and beyond that, to a fringe area of service stations, automobile graveyards, some sort of light industrial plant, and then country, with cows and barns and second growth timber. It was not idyllic. There were trailers on concrete blocks, and billboards with their gaudy messages about candidates for election and automobiles and pralines and pecan delight. But it was country, nevertheless. Royle never wrote about it much. Oh, here and there, there was an image that suggested he had not lived all his life in cities. But no rusticity. He didn't make a thing of it. Deliberately? Or maybe because he just never took much notice of where he was. The interior landscape could suffice.

The car turned off onto a black-top side road, and up a rise. Over and down, and up another, and off the black top to a dirt road.

"Muddy in the spring," Royle said.

It was perfectly nice. But it was no different from the sort of house a lawyer, or an insurance broker or a hardware store owner might have lived in. And that was what had been nagging at Jerome, really. The connection he was trying to make between the house and the work, between the ordinariness of the external circumstances and the extraordinary quality of what went on there. It was like battlefields one visits, expecting some special signs of the bloodshed, the agony, the bravery, and finding only grass and trees and markers from some historical society that make it all even less convincing than it might otherwise be. But this was different. This was still going on. This was present and active. And the connection had to be there. It wasn't just a transcending of the ordinariness. That was too easy. There had to be a connection. Between the commonplaces of life and the extravagance of poetry. Bishop's line: "A ceremony must be found to wed Desdemona to the huge Moor."

Inside, ordinary things. The Things of This World, as Dickie-bird Wilbur sings, in antiphon to that Byzantine budgie of the Yeats poem. Center hall with one of those big pier glasses. Dining room on the left, with a Sheraton table and a centerpiece of porcelain fruit. Light, papered walls with a cream colored chair rail. Silver on the sideboard. Or, allowing for the constraints of academic salaries, assume the table to be a copy, the silver maybe plate. Still, the effect was of tranquility and order. "Many a time I think to seek/One or the other out and speak/Of that old Georgian mansion, mix/Pictures of the mind, recall/That table and the talk of youth . . ." So, Yeats knew, too. But what was the rhyme for mix? He'd have to look it up.

Across the center hall, the living room. A piano, its lyre shaped music stand in bloom with those yellow covers from Schirmer's. Did Royle play? Music references in his poems?

"Do you play?" Jerome asked.

"The piano? Oh, no. Jill does."

Jill. Of course. The eye and the fingers and the order of the house were hers. And John moved through all this order like a comet, elliptical through the circularity of the solar system, moved through the living room to the tray table on which bottles of whiskey and gin were set out, along with mixers, a crystal pitcher of water, and a teak ice bucket. Jerome watched and felt . . . Envy? No, not really. Or anyway no more than enough to spice his pleasure in the goodness of Royle's life. That he should have such a room to cross, and that there should be that table there, all laid out . . .

Beyond the living room, an enclosed sun porch, with rattan furniture, paper flowers, and toys, carefully stored under the rattan love seat to be out of the way. A three-dimensional tic-tac-toe set, an Etch-a-Sketch, board games, and a basketball.

"Scotch?"

"Thanks."

"Soda?"

"Just a splash."

"Right."

On the wall, a Baskin etching of a bird. A dead bird? Possibly dead. At any rate, very sick. And a Chagall lithograph. A fire laid in the fireplace, ready to be lit. Ah, the order of it! It was almost depressing that there should be so much yet for him to find. Got to pull the socks up, one of these days. Settle in somewhere.

"John? Is that you?"

"Yes, we're in here," he called.

And Jill appeared. John introduced Jerome. Jill welcomed him. John made her a drink. They sat down.

She was a handsome woman, dark haired, green eyed, and rather more voluptuous than the standard academic wife for whom the Marimekko she wore had been designed. And tall. And graceful. But mostly Jerome was fascinated by her legs. They were splendid legs, not the caricatures of the Vargas girls or of Billy Rose's long-stemmed American beauties, but more . . . intelligent. That was the word. And curiously, in order to justify such an improbable adjective, in order to rationalize it, he constructed on the instant a theory. Intelligence was not a matter that could be read, necessarily, in the face or the eyes. But in the legs. The graceful definition of the shin bones, and the delicacy of the flare from that leading edge of bone to the fullness of the calf muscles all proclaimed some corresponding mental abilities. Acuity of intellect and perception in that leading edge, and the ability to generalize, to feel, in that modulated muscular swell. Stupid women have legs like Bechstein pianos. Bitchy, waspy, strident women have skinny legs.

Was it true? Jerome wondered, but he did not particularly care. Or, rather, he would admit its truth for the moment. Yes, intelligent legs, intelligently held in an oblique manner, the ankles crossed in easy propriety. The legs seemed to resonate with her conversation, with that trace of Boston in the vowel sounds. Jerome thought of the gag about how Boston ladies don't get their hats anywhere, but say defiantly, "We have our hats." How much better to be able to say, without uttering a word, "We have our legs." And then he remembered that George

Meredith hung a whole chapter on some woman's comment about some fellow: "He has a leg!" For the first time, that chapter made sense. He promised himself that he would go back and finish *The Egoist.*

But later. Now he would delight in the convenience with which he could cast his eyes downward, as if staring at the rug, or perhaps in a kind of diffidence, but all the while looking at the legs.

"Absurd that we've never met before," they said.

"Yes, isn't it," Jerome answered.

"Like each other," John said. "That's an order."

"Of course, dear," the legs said, mock-meek.

"I shouldn't think there would be much difficulty," Jerome said, to play the game. He looked up at her face, wondering whether there would be any difficulty. The friendship between himself and John had established itself years before, almost as a parody of those literary friendships that biographers adore. They met only rarely and briefly at odd campuses, and out of the way hotels in provincial cities. They corresponded a great deal, exchanging those letters that the biographers treasure. And now all this was getting translated into the world of tables and chairs and arrangements of porcelain fruit. Into Jill's world, the real world. For all he knew, she disapproved of him. Not personally but as an example of that shiftlessness against which she had to contend in order to achieve this delightful order. Maybe not even consciously, but instinctively—which would be worse.

Or, no, it was just the ordinary awkwardness of the imbalance of their meeting, of the new acquaintance and the old friendship. Or not even that. Or it was just his own awkwardness, for she sat there, perfectly at ease, rather crisp and composed, with only one strand of hair curling down on her forehead, the counterpart of that deliberate error Persian carpetweavers put into their work to avoid the curse of perfection, the jealousy of the gods.

"How did the reading go yesterday?" Jill asked.

"All right."

"Fine," John said. And he started to tell, amusingly, easily, about Jerome's loss of his briefcase, his translation from the Hawaiian, his 'theft' of a poem . . . And the conversation was established. Her smiles, her laughter, her comments were right, were natural and right. It was impossible to be wholly ill at ease with someone who could dismiss Stone with the grand simplicity of a wave of the hand, and then, "Of course, he's an ass!"

"He's a good writer." Royle insisted.

"I didn't say he wasn't. He's still an ass."

"Well . . . Yes." Royle agreed.

"But he's harmless enough," Jerome said.

"Is he?" Jill asked. "I can't think of anyone I'd trust less."

"Perhaps," Royle said.

Closing the subject? Or opening it for discussion? It was impossible to tell from his tone, and, in the event, impossible to tell at all, for the telephone rang. Royle went to answer it. Jill took over and continued the conversation, leading Jerome through a familiar quadrille of subjects—the weather, flowers that were in season, other places where other flowers bloomed, travel—but still with infinitesimal pauses between the sentences. Of course, it could have been Jerome's own impression, arising from his own peculiar situation. But if he was spacing his comments in such a way to allow time to listen to the laconic yesses and noes of Royle's conversation on the telephone, he had to admit that she was not making it difficult for him, which in turn led to the recognition of the possibility that she, too, in her very competent way, might be listening. And the fact that Royle's conversation gave away too little made it all the more suspicious. Jerome was convinced that it had to be Marty. But would she call at his house this way? He knew too much and too little. And Jill? He had no idea how much she knew, but as he looked at her, and heard her say, "I have always wanted to visit the Costa Smeralda, as much for the name as anything else," he could not help but think that she knew rather a good deal.

At last there was a clack of the receiver dropping down onto the cradle, and Royle returned to apologise for having to leave. Hungerford's car wouldn't start. He would have to go down to Alumnae House to fetch a carload of writers.

It was certainly plausible.

"You have time, yet, though," Jill said.

"I want to get a couple more bottles of bourbon."

She seemed about to say something, but she didn't. Royle left.

And now they would make conversation for half an hour eh? All right. It was a shame, really, Jerome thought, that there had to be such constraint. John's phone call, the conspiracy about his appearance of being Marty's escort, the peculiarity of the relationships anyway—his meeting his good friend's wife for the first time—all made it more and more difficult for them to talk in any sensible, any real way. But the forms must be observed. He cast around for something to say.

"I like your house."

"Thank you."

"It's . . . It's not quite what I expected."

"Oh?"

"It's all so comfortable and attractive. Not that I expected it not to be . . . But I didn't expect anything. It's sort of odd to find John's surroundings. From the poems, somehow, I got the notion of a kind of bareness. I guess if I'd thought about it, I'd have expected a lot of straight lines. Chrome sofas. Breuer chairs. Silly, I suppose. This is . . . nicer."

"You weren't all that wrong, actually."

"I don't understand."

"The study is like that. Very spare. That bareness. Would you like to see it?"

"Yes, thanks. Is it all right?"

"Why not? It's just a room. Out in the barn. The only luxury to it is the view. The house is on a rise, you know. And there is a view from the study of . . . well, on a clear day, twenty miles." She laughed. "If he ever looks out of the window, anyway, it's there."

She got up and led the way out through the kitchen, across what must once have been a kitchen garden, and to a renovated barn. It was still a barn, but it was heated now, and there was plumbing in it. And three of the stalls that had once held horses had been made into a study. Not by John, Jill explained, but by the previous owner, who had been a professor of history. John had just taken it over.

It was, as Jill had said, a bare room. No picture hung on the walls. The steel shelves held books that gave the only touch of life and color to the place with their dust jackets. The desk was entirely bare, with an old blotter on it, and three ball point pens arranged in an orderly row, exactly perpendicular to the bottom of the blotter. Not a knick-knack, not a curio.

"You see? It's very bare indeed," Jill said. "What made you think it would be?"

"I don't know. It's difficult to find reasonable reasons. But the house surprised me a little, somehow."

"I've offered to fix this up, to try to make it a little more comfortable. But John likes it this way. He's afraid that anything else in here will . . . Well, he says it will fight with him."

"Distract him?"

"Perhaps," she said. And then, with hardly a pause and in such a way that it seemed perfectly casual, perfectly natural, she asked, "How was he at Rockville? How did he seem?"

There was no special emphasis to it. And it did seem perfectly idle, a natural enough question to ask, because, after all, they were there, the two of them, in his room, in his place, in that bareness which, by its very lack of anything else to fight with or distract, was full of John Royle.

"He was fine," Jerome said. "Just fine. Very gay, really. Ebullient."

He told Jill about the anagrams game, and about the

bowling afterwards. And the drinking they had all done. It was easy and even something of a relief to tell her all this, because she had not asked about Marty, was not, apparently, concerned about that. But he was. And in his concentration on not discussing the girl, he told everything else. She listened quite intently, even gravely, and said, at the end of his series of anecdotes, comments and bright remarks, "I see."

Looking down at the floor, and with her brow not exactly furrowed but clouded, she said, "I see," a second time.

"Is there anything the matter?" Jerome asked.

"No. Oh, no," she said. She looked at the empty chair, a wooden chair that rocked and swivelled, something in the style of old railroad dispatchers' chairs, and she ran her fingertips along the worn wood of the back of it. "It's just that John has been rather depressed lately. The weather, perhaps. Or Frenion. It can get very dull and oppressive around here. I'm surprised to hear that he was so ebullient. But perhaps it was the change of scene."

She continued to run her finger over the rim of the chair, and then, deliberately withdrawing it, she said to Jerome, "Why don't you make yourself comfortable for a few minutes. I've got to scuttle back to the kitchen to check on one of my pots. I'll be back in a moment."

Jerome, left alone, tried to decipher the message. It was quite possible that there was no message at all, that she was merely going back to do what she said she had to do. But somehow, Jerome could not believe that it was a matter of pots and food. He was sure it had to do with John. But what had he said to concern her? Had she been bothered by the idea that John should be happy and ebullient away from this room, this house, this life? Jerome didn't think so. And it wasn't Marty. Jill had drawn out of him exactly what she had wanted. He assumed that. She could have drawn him out in any direction she had liked. She had been concerned with John, with his mood . . . His health? Was he all right?

Or perhaps it was nothing at all. He was like those FBI agents who followed around that communist leader— Jerome couldn't remember which communist leader. But he did recall having heard how the communist had borrowed old carbon papers from friends, crumpled them up, thrown them in his wastebasket, and then had left it to the FBI to retrieve them, send them down to Washington, and laboriously decipher all the layers of typing which were, of course, irrelevant and valueless. Served them right. And him too, now that he was partaking of that kind of suspicion.

On the other hand, John remembered how he had been concerned himself the night before. In the car especially, on the way from the party to the hotel. John had been chuckling for no reason at all. Was he all right? If Jerome could worry, then Jill could worry too.

In order to think, in order to concentrate his attention on the question of Royle and not on the fatigue of his calf muscles from standing, he sat down in the chair. It was Royle's chair. It was more comfortable than he had expected it to be. It hit right, in the small of the back, gave the right kind of support. He swivelled in it, rocked, and looked out of the window at the view, wondering even as he did so whether Royle ever noticed it, ever looked out, except perhaps to rest his eyes. "Scenic View," the signs proclaim on the Mohawk Trail up in New York, and the dutiful tourists get out and snap their Instamatics.

A slight squeak. He did it again, rocking backwards and swivelling to the left and, yes, there was a squeak in the mechanism of the chair. Annoying? Or something to do, a kind of auditory doodle in which one could vary the rhythms or the volume or both. All this view to view, and he sat here squeaking metal springs, making the noise of the mating call of mice in must. Was it possible? Certainly. And would Jill know such a thing? He wondered. Her concern had been real, sharp enough. She had left the room—to call the psychiatrist, the druggist, the chiropodist, the chiropractor? All of them?

He had no idea. And sitting in this chair, at this desk, in this room, he had no idea what went on in Royle's mind either. The typewriter on the stand next to the desk had no secrets, held no clues, told nothing. He had taken off the gray plastic cover and looked at the venerable Underwood office machine. Perfectly standard. No fancy academic trappings. No dagger key, no accent keys. There was a § which was pretty, but useless. For legal documents? A second hand machine, then.

And then, with considerable self consciousness because, after all, he had seen the scene in movies—not ony particular movie but that ur-flick left in the mind as a kind of residue of all the movies—the scene in which the pianist stops at an old upright in a warehouse somewhere, touches a key, another, and another, and then sits down to break into some impassioned Chopin thing and dissolve into the concert hall, his life retrieved, his woman back, and his music singing out all the hell over. Jerome took a blank piece of paper and put it into the machine. He did not even fool himself when he typed a row of

§§

Yes, it was an elegant kind of scroll-work. And casually arcane. Because he had no idea what the symbol meant or what its name was. But he wasn't fooling himself. He had not put the paper into the roller to see that symbol, but to type out his stanza, his octave, to see it in type-script where it would be less personal and cooler. Our own handwriting, and our own farts—opines Auden—are lovable. And the deodorizing transformation of the poem from holograph to typescript is the occasion for the second stage of critical judgment.

He pulled the rather soggy scraps of Collegiate Arms letter paper out of his pocket and copied:

> *Over the fear, the foolishness—a jay*
> *behaving badly, as a child in church,*
> *while the big cat crouches down before his prey . . .*
> *Hush! But the woodpeckers rattle the trees in search*
> *of grubs, bounce acorns on the ground, the way*
> *they always do. That blood's pulse in the throat*
> *of the victim commands attention. They don't obey.*
> *A green bird trills upon his idiot note*
>
> *as if nothing at all were happening*

There was a reassuring omen to the line of §§§s up over the page. *The foolishness* up there again, eh? Ride with it. As the girl in the urinalysis lab said, "Bottle your product!"

He took another sheet of paper and went on, in pen now. He would try for the end. But before he did, he forced himself to look up, to look out of the window. The view? It might just as well have been a brick wall. It was the other, the parley-view that was hinki-dinkier. By far.

In script, then, on the new sheet:

Exactly so!

But he crossed that out. Instead, he tried:

below
which is perfect, for those delicate ears still hear
the twittering of ordinariness, the eyes

No. no. *The ordinary twittering.* All right. Onwards!

the ordinary twittering, the eyes
flee to an unperturbed horizon where slow
clouds play at random shapes

Then what? *It's queer* was too weak. *Fear?* Too thumpy to go back to a key word from the first line that way. Too neat. *Dear? Spear?* Shit! The thing was to go back and change the rhyme from *hear* to . . . To *catch.* Better. The activeness of it.

which is perfect for those delicate ears still catch
at that ordinary twittering, the eyes
flee to an unperturbed horizon where slow
clouds play at random shapes.

259

And then what? *Watch? Much? Twitch? Snatch?* But
what would the last line be? A rhyme on *eyes.* Surprise?
Sure, the death as a surprise, with everything else distracting . . . *Distract?* With *tact.* So, the sestet:

> *as if nothing at all were happening below.*
> *But credit the bird [blank blank blank] with the tact*
> *to fill those delicate ears while the [something] eyes*
> *flee to an unperturbed horizon where slow*
> *clouds mimic random shapes, and distract*
> *so that death is an irrelevant surprise.*

Coming on better now. The second line?

> *But credit the bird-brained babbling with tact:*
> *It fills the delicate ears, while the still bright eyes . . .*

And so on. Those last three lines would stand. He turned
back to the typewriter and completed the typescript of
the first fair copy.

He was able to finish the typing, but not to get to reading the poem, because he heard approaching steps.
Royle's? No, a woman's. Jill's. But in any case, he did not
want to be discovered here, at Royle's desk, typing at
Royle's machine. There was something just a little bit
indecent about it, as if he were to be found peering curiously into the Royle's medicine chest. He was aware that
this was entirely irrational, that nobody could have any
possible objection to his working this way at Royle's
typewriter, but irrational or not, he felt odd about it, and,
in that last second before the door opened, he popped the
plastic cover over the typewriter. Not an instant too soon

—but still, curiously, plenty of time for him to consider the similarity between typewriter covers and birdcage covers and how, when one is tired of the warbling of the Underwood, one puts its cover on so that it will think night has come and shut up.

All this, of course, to no purpose, because the piece of paper and the pen were still on the desk. And Jill saw them and asked, "Oh, are you working?"

"Just making some notes," Jerome said. And he picked up the holograph sheet and folded it so that he could tuck it away in his jacket pocket.

"You're sure I'm not interrupting . . ."

"No, no. Of course not. Really."

"I had to call the drug store."

He had no idea, for the moment, what she was talking about. What was he supposed to say to that? Ask how the druggist was?

"For John," she went on. "What you told me about his . . . his mood. At Rockville. It's probably not serious, but he has these spells. Episodes, the doctor calls them. And after he's been down for a while and starts to be up— or, as you put it, 'Ebullient'—he sometimes needs a tranquilizer. I'm grateful to you for telling me."

Two thoughts occurred at once to Jerome. One was concern for John, and a new understanding of some of the odd behavior that had been so puzzling the night before. The other was a kind of guilt at having forgot all about it, having forgot even that Jill had bolted from the room. And those two thoughts proliferated and intertwined. He now thought of Jill's ordering of John's life not merely as a conceit or the external business of por-

celain center-pieces and comfortable rooms, but deeper
and more complete. And the admiration and the envy
he had felt before were increased. He looked at the
woman, apparently calm and collected, all dressed and
coifed and ready for her guests, and he felt a great
pang . . .

What the hell was John screwing around with Marty
for? What the hell was he doing, himself, pretending to
be Marty's escort? For Christ's sake! This woman was
keeping the poor son of a bitch's life together. Even
pharmacologically. And she was infinitely more attractive than Marty was. It was all . . . Well, no, he wasn't
angry. Sad? Not even that. But great feeling, of that in-
determinate kind that whatsername talks about when she
explains about the emotional aspects of music, the forms
of feeling. Langer? The sluice gates, through which any
feeling, or all feeling, can flow. And they were flowing.
Even physically. He could feel the blood pounding in his
chest, and the weight of his arms and legs, as if the feelings were substantial things, heavy.

"What else are friends for?" he asked at last.

"Exactly," she said, and smiled. Oh, God, a great smile.
And then it struck him that her reply was not just an
agreement with his general comment, but a profession on
her part, delightfully demure, of *their* friendship.

"Shall we go back to the house?" she asked.

He followed her across the yard and back in through
the kitchen. He was already in the living room when he
remembered his poem sitting there in Royle's typewriter.

Oh, well, he could get it later.

Besides, there were people arriving.

CHAPTER 7

"Of course, you know that story about Stanley Kunitz and the goose . . ."

"Yes, indeed!"

"Marvelous!"

The exchange, between Sam Stone and Professor Justis A. Corda, Chrmn. Dept. of Eng., was within earshot—but out of sight. The pure self-congratulatory foolishness of it amazed Jerome, but the parley of strategies was fascinating. First, there was the obvious name-dropping, and then the exchange of credentials as insiders, as familiars with the stories about the great and near-great . . . Finally, their pleasure was topped off by the maraschino cherry of likelihood that he, Jerome, would not know the story, and would have to ask. And then Stone, artful old operator that he was, would defer to Corda, and let him tell it, earning Corda's friendliness and gratitude, and still keeping the option to himself of correcting, of amending, of intruding himself into Corda's narrative.

But Jerome had crossed them; he had outsmarted them. He had nodded, smiled, and said, "Marvelous," which implied not only that he, too, knew the story of Stanley Kunitz and the goose, but that every gum-chewing sophomore and crew-cut freshman knew the story, too. In which case, of course, it was not worth knowing. He had diminished it to a knock-knock joke, a crack from last week's Laugh-In.

And about Mr. Kunitz? And the goose? Well, there were stories and stories. And Jerome could imagine whatever he liked. Or as many as he liked. Kunitz goosed by Roethke at a White House dinner, and hooting into Jackie Kennedy's ear . . . Kunitz goosing Louise Bogan . . . Kunitz shrieking while George Plimpton goosed Marianne Moore? It was a perfectly reasonable game. Or, more elaborately, there were any number of like openings that could be manufactured. He and Royle could say, across the dinner table, "You remember the story of William Jay Smith and the peeing contest . . ." and then both of them could decline to tell the story because, after all, it was at the dinner table. And let Corda and Stone sweat that one out!

It was a perfectly reasonable cocktail party, with the same talk, the same drinks, and mostly the same faces as at the party of the night before at Rockville. A slip in the gears of the time machine. A few more cogs like that and they'd be wearing pinafores and Eton suits and playing musical chairs. Jerome held his glass of Crown Royal, which he'd asked for because John drank it, and he wanted to be agreeable. He'd wanted to propitiate the spirit. Use the man's desk and typewriter, and drink his spirits! The Frenion biggies had come to meet the visiting biggies. And of course Corda and Stone were talking together, the chairman with the biggest name of the traveling show 'n' tell troupe. Jerome had observed the changes in his own responses to Corda. At first he had liked the guy, for after all he was soft-spoken, civilized, tweedy, and nicely gray-haired. He looked rather like Wilfred Hyde White, that English character actor. Except for the eye patch. And Jerome had liked him for that, too. The disability of having only the one eye was not serious enough to be off-putting. One didn't recoil from it. As the Hathaway shirt people had figured out. But it was serious enough so that one felt sympathetic, interested. And then, suddenly, Corda and Stone were talking and laughing, and twiddling antennae. Picking intellectual fleas or cerebral salt . . . Whatever it was that those monkeys are looking for in each other's fur. And Corda had begun to lose points on Jerome's Big Board. Bellies are softer today, the commodity speculators fear . . . He thought of Brownsuit.

Wanting to check himself out and to determine whether he was being entirely unreasonable, he had asked Jill what Corda was like.

"Hateful!" she said. And it was marvelous to see the way she said it, the smile on her face not changing a whit or a jot. From two feet away, had anybody been eavesdropping, it would have looked like "Delightful."

But even so, that judgment might not be entirely reliable, no matter how attractive the style of its pronouncement. Royle, after all, worked for the guy. And no man is a hero to his valet, or his department.

"Why?" he asked.

"Later," she said.

Fair enough. And the configurations of the party changed as some new arrivals fell into the living room like some blue pebbles in the end of the kaleidoscope, altering the patterns. Jerome found himself with Aggie, whom he asked for any information she might have about Stanley Kunitz and the goose . . . She had none, but she understood and even shared his reluctance to inquire of Stone. Corda, yes. But not Stone. And Jerome promised to find out later. To talk to Corda.

And he would have, yes, almost certainly he would have, if he had not met Jules Rijn, the crying Dutchman. Rijn had been standing against the wall, next to the bar, drinking studiously and looking for all the world like any background figure in a northern Renaissance painting. There is always some fat guy with a little Van Dyck in the shadows, way back in the left, for the composition or as a joke, as a portrait of the artist's father-in-law (careful inspection will reveal that the old codger's codpiece is unbuttoned). Rijn was buttoned up well enough, but he stood there, lurking, drinking, getting up his courage.

Or, no, it was beyond that. The courage was already there, or that desperation born of necessity that amounted to the same thing. He was probably picking his stratagem, trying to decide, like the big bull with the shoulders full of metal, whether to go for the bullfighter or the cape, pawing the earth, all rage and huge powerful ineptitude. And then the charge—not like in the bullring, but damned near, as Rijn moved out from the wall, crossed the carpeting, and approached Jerome.

"You remember me?"

"No," Jerome said, pleasantly enough. "Should I?"

"Should you? No, of course not. Of course you shouldn't. That's part of the deal, or at least I thought it was. But still, I mean, it was something of a shock to see you here, I mean, on this campus, in this room, talking to Corda and everything . . ."

"What are you talking about?"

"You're Jerome Carpenter, aren't you?"

"Yes, I am. And who are you?"

"Jules Rijn. You remember?"

"No."

"Run-on Couplets in the Eighteenth Century."

"You?"

"A client."

"Jesus."

"What do you think I was thinking? Triple Jesus!"

"I didn't remember. I honestly didn't."

"But I couldn't know that, could I? And even if you didn't remember now, you might have later. I've grown a beard since then, but you might have recognized me . . . And I was . . . I am, right this minute, scared shitless. I mean, I've got a wife. I've got a kid. I need this."

Jerome was perspiring. He felt the prickle of the spouting sweat glands, the rivulets running down the back of his neck, the sides of his body, the hollows at the base of his throat. The lips of the round face with the tawny beard continued to move, and the insistent pleading, the desperation, the plaintiveness continued to sound. *Planh.* It was a peculiar Provençal word that Pound had used, and, later, Dudley Fitts. Provenance from the Provençal. That popped into Jerome's head and he clutched at it. But this wounded animal's noise continued to sound at him.

". . . a real son of a bitch. And when I saw you talking to him, I just about dropped my load. I mean, you don't know what it's like here. It's crazy! Just absolutely crazy! Most of these bastards don't like teaching, don't like the kids, don't like themselves. There's the irony, eh? I mean, I'm the fraud, but they're frauds too. All these bastards. Oh, there are exceptions. Royle. A couple of the others. But even if I weren't a good teacher, the ethics of the thing . . . Hey, that's funny, me talking about ethics. To you. Right? But I mean, I paid the money, didn't I? And it's got to amortize itself out over a period of time. I've only been here two years . . . You can't blow the whistle on me, you just can't . . ."

"No, I wouldn't. I wasn't going to. I didn't remember you."

"The beard, I guess, huh? Do you like it? Kate made me grow it because . . . You'll laugh at this. Because I had a doctorate! She thought it would make me look more scholarly . . ."

Jerome didn't laugh. He only sweated. The poor bastard. The poor, dumb, vulnerable bastard. With that tawny beard wiggling up and down as the fellow's mouth moved, as he kept on trying to placate, to ingratiate, to wheedle and cajole. That doctoral beard.

". . . by the short hairs, man. I mean, I'm begging you!"

"Shut up, will you? I'm not going to say a word. Why would I?"

"I don't know why you would. But you could. You can. And that's the terrifying thing. That you can. You've got the power . . ."

"Well, I'm not going to use it. I'm not. Okay?"

"Okay."

Jules Rijn looked at him, forced a smile, one of the cinematic brave smiles of the guy who has just heard that his leg is about to be amputated, and then, not knowing what else to do, he stuck out his hand. Jerome shook it.

"Let me get you a drink, okay? What are you drinking?"

"Crown Royal."

"I'll get it."

He took Jerome's glass and went off to get the drink. Jerome felt relieved that he'd gone away and wondered whether, if he'd asked Jules to drive to New York City to fetch him a piece of cheesecake from Cake Masters, Jules wouldn't have said, "Okay, sure, right away," and marched out to his car.

But the poor bastard was right about one thing. "That's the terrifying thing," he had said, "that you can!" The power. It was awful to have such power over another guy's life. That Jerome had not tried for it, but had merely found it like a piece of fluff in his trousers pocket made no difference. Or made it worse.

He looked across the room at Justis Corda who was still talking with Sam Stone, flattering and being flattered. They were like two horses standing head to tail so they could co-operate in swishing away flies. And he tried to lay off some of that power on Corda. There was nothing Jerome could do himself but tell Corda about

Rijn and the bought dissertation. And if he did that, then Corda would do what? Respond instantly like a button that Jerome had pushed? Or hold it, tucked away in case of need, to be used in moments of departmental squabbles to ensure Rijn's absolute loyalty. But that latter possibility was even more distressing than the former. And Corda was, in Jill's word, 'hateful'.

The other possibility, and in fact the actuality, was that Jerome would not tell Corda anything, would not say a word. In which case he, Jerome, was exercising a kind of power not only over Rijn but over Corda as well. And that was more attractive. But still it was not what he had signed on for with Ariel. He didn't mind being a pirate or a crook, but he wanted it to be clean. Steal from the rich and give to the poor. Rob only banks, insurance companies, the government. Not this stealing of crumbs from the mouths of widows and orphans. Or the bearded *bouche* of Jules Rijn with his wife and his kid and his anal obsessive whimpering about being scared shitless and dropping his load. He wanted no part of it. Not even to know about it. Especially not that!

He mopped the beads of sweat off his forehead and neck and tucked the handkerchief back into his pocket. Better? Yes, he felt better. But there was Rijn, the abject object, bringing the Crown Royal back to his master.

"Thanks," Jerome said.

"Glad to do it. Glad to do it," Rijn said. "Ha ha! Glad to do anything I can!"

It was, Jerome supposed, a kind of joke, all the more funny because it was true. And more and more horrible, as Jerome savored it, along with the whiskey. Within reason, he could ask anything of this Rijn—and get it. More money? The loan of his wife? Jesus!

But the most painful part of it was that there was no reasonable avenue along which he could direct his resentment at having been put in such an awkward position. Dr. Lee, the proprietor of Ariel Editorial Services, Inc. was a mild mannered, almost Pickwickian creature who had launched his peculiar business venture partly out of necessity and partly as a way of getting back at the academic establishment by which he had been so badly used. A once respected member of the Mt. Holyoke history department, Lee had been fired when the Massachusetts police had broken up the big homosexual ring of which he was a minor baguette. Which was, of course, absurd. From whom could the Mt. Holyoke girls be safer than a queer? It was so sensible, so satisfactory an arrangement. But the cops had come, found the cache of pornographic books and pictures, tapped telephone lines, dropped *agents provocateurs* into the campus, and leaked it all to the lewd wiseacres of the local newspapers. And the administration had responded by firing all the implicated teachers. Irrational. Farcical. Dumb. And Lee had needed to earn a living somehow. As a reader for a publishing house in the text division? As an underpaid editor in a second rate encyclopedia sweatshop? The choices were narrow and all unattractive. And then, he had thought of Ariel. It was a way of getting back at them, at *them*, at the system, the big paranoids, THEM. But, as Dr. Lee mentioned, in that ersatz-British accent, "Paranoids sometimes have real enemies, dear boy!"

So, Ariel. The scholarly fifth column, burrowing from

within, getting even. "It can even be . . . One could think of it as a kind of good work," Lee explained to those disaffected or eccentric or rejected intellectuals from whom he recruited his workers. "It is a way of getting jobs for perfectly good second rate men who are, nevertheless, quite well qualified for positions at many of our third and fourth rate colleges and universities."

Jerome had drifted into it, doing his first Masters' essay because he needed the money, and staying because the hours were his own and the work was pleasant. And he liked Lee. And felt sorry for the poor bastards who slunk into the office to buy their essays and theses. He felt no more guilt than a forger of passports and visas in some grubby Balkan country who was helping his desperate countrymen to circumvent the officious heartlessness of the local U.S. consulate. What better for a poet and freelance intellectual to do?

But now, with Rijn beside him, it felt different.

"Anything at all. You name it," Rijn said.

"I don't suppose you could find out the story about Stanley Kunitz and the goose . . ."

"Stanley who?"

"Kunitz," Jerome said. But Rijn's vacant blue-eyed stare continued, as Jerome had feared it would. As he supposed he should have known it would. Before Rijn could ask, "Who's Kunitz?" Jerome shook his head.

"Forget it," Jerome said.

"No, no. I can run over to the library."

"It wouldn't be there."

"It wouldn't?" Rijn asked, hurt, shocked, disturbed to discover that there were pieces of information that were not in libraries.

"No."

"I could ask people . . ."

"I can do that, myself."

"Well, if anything else occurs to you that I can do, anything you need, anytime . . ."

"Right," Jerome said. "Excuse me, would you?"

He strode across the room, trying to look purposeful, or trying to look as though he had some purpose other than the real one, which was to escape this person. He had not meant to humiliate the guy. Stanley Hoo? The Chinese novelist! He had a recipe for goose, like Pekin Duck, but with a goose. He stumbled on it when he was translating Dickens' *Christmas Carol* into Cantonese. Stan Li Hoo! Master of Kung Foo, the ancient Oriental art of instantaneous death without any bodily contact whatever. Jerome had seen the ads for it in *The National Enquirer*. (Life with Kim Novak is Hell!)

"How're you doing?"

Jerome looked about, rather startled. It was Hungerford, good old Chuck. No, Ed! But a reasonable person. Someone with whom Jerome could talk.

"Okay."

"Are you sure? You look a little pale," Hungerford said.

"I'm all right," he said. He smiled. He opened his mouth and put his tongue out. "See?"

The idea that Hungerford should be concerned for his, for Jerome Carpenter's, health and stomach was too much. Besides, the spinet wasn't a Steinway anyway. And you don't heave into just any piano. That, and the impossibility of explaining to Hungerford the reason for his paleness, the nature of the shock he had undergone, struck him as being amusing. What a sketch! This guy I wrote a thesis for offered me his wife, but I settled for Stanley Kunitz, and he thought it was a Chinaman named Hoo. You couldn't say a thing like that, not even to Hungerford, without expecting to be locked up.

"What have you been up to?" he asked, changing the subject away from himself and his encounter.

"Oh, just messing around. I've been fiddling with Justis Corda's name. It's got to be an anagram. It feels like one."

"I'll work on it too, if you want. Sort of a rematch from last night?"

"Okay, you're on."

It was merely a game, a diversion, but Jerome welcomed it, and felt a disproportionate warmth for Hungerford for his having provided a way to get through the next few minutes. They were, Jerome realised, both out of place here, both of them feeling more comfortable and more themselves when manipulating letters and words than when they were in a room like this, manipulating—and being manipulated by—people. Corda, for instance, in all his tweedy power over Rijn, over Jerome himself, in a way, could be reduced to a jumble of letters. Let Sam Stone go and exchange stories with him, trying by that old drummer's trick to drum up trade one way or another—hoping to get Corda to order Stone's book for literature courses, to invite him to come back and lecture again, to line him up for Guggenheim grant letters of recommendation. Whatever. Hungerford had the right idea. They could exorcise his power . . . Nullify it. Turn him into . . .

Jerome grabbed a piece of paper from his pocket. The poem. On the back, he started. JUSTIS A. CORDA. *Adjusts?*

276

That left *croia*. No good. He was sitting on the sofa, fiddling with his pencil, engrossed in the problem, when
Corda spoke to him.

"Getting something ready for this evening?"

It was, of course, impossible to explain that, no, he was
working on an anagram of Justis A. Corda, hoping for
something ridiculous, or, even better, obscene. And, with
what he thought to be a rather deft sleight of hand, he
whipped the paper over, turning up the side on which
there was, in fact, a poem, and looked up.

"Yes, that's right," he said.

"Is this your own work, this time?"

"I beg your pardon?"

"Sam was telling me about your performance last night
at Rockville. With that student's poem . . ."

There was a moment, a rather enjoyable moment
actually, during which Jerome felt himself deciding
whether to be angry or not. It was an interesting physical
sensation, and really quite pleasant—because he felt in
control of it. It was very quick, but his mental and emotional machinery was working at an incredibly rapid rate.
Yes, there was provocation, and he had a right to be angry if he chose, but, on the other hand, after the business
with Rijn, and the deftness of turning the paper over,
there was no necessity to be annoyed. More in an effort
to prolong that nice balance of tranquil pique, he smiled,
and said in an affable, cordial tone, "Sam has a big mouth,
doesn't he?"

"Yes, I suppose he does," Corda said, oddly, with
affability.

"I gave the poem to the girl, you know."

"No, he didn't tell me that," Corda said.

"It wasn't good enough to steal."

"Oh? I must say, you seem very cavalier about it."

"What the hell, it's only poems."

"Poems are my field, young man," Corda said, rather more sternly than before.

"Your field? Poems are your . . . field?" Jerome looked at the man and then burst out laughing. A whole cluster of wise cracks blossomed in Jerome's head, none of them distinct enough to pluck, but all contributing to an effect, as an out of focus flush of color in a landscape. The notion of cultivating the field with horseshit was more distinct than the rest. And from the shit, the image of a Port-o-san toilet in the field, a W.C.–Field's.

He did not feel obliged to reduce any of these stray notions to actual discourse, but as they bubbled up and subsided, they added to the laughter, which, naturally, Corda assumed was directed at himself.

"Well, I shall leave you to your . . . uh . . . labors, then," Corda said, each word one of those crystal clear ice cubes.

What was there to say? Jerome settled for a precise "Thank you."

He looked down at the poem in his lap, pretending to examine it, because, after all, that's what he claimed to be doing. He read over the last few lines, the new ones:

> *It fills the delicate ears, while the still bright eyes*
> *flee to an unperturbed horizon where slow*
> *clouds mimic random shapes, and distract*
> *so that death is an irrelevant surprise.*

The penultimate line was defective, short a beat. It could be remedied by putting in a *they* before distract. But that would make it flabby. No, he wanted to do more with the random shapes. Very like a whale. Very like a water closet. Shakespeare, damn him, had been there before. But why not ride with that? Use it! He took the pencil— Royle's pencil, taken from the desk. He'd have to return it. Later, when he went to pick up the typescript of the poem. He took the pencil and wrote, *clouds mimic Hamlet's random shapes, distract.* There wanted to be a breath there. He put three dots at the end of the line, crossed out *so that* and inserted *The.* Right.

Funny to think that yesterday he had been pretending to crap so that he could write a poem, and today, he pretended to write poetry to cover up his working out of an anagram. It was, itself, a kind of anagram. He turned the paper over again and continued: DRASTIC? That left JUSAO.

"Got anything?" Hungerford asked.

"Not yet. You?"

"Not quite. It works out to Judas Iscariot, except that you need an extra I."

"Ah, but so does he."

"What?"

"He's only got one eye, right?"

Rijn, who was standing there, with a fresh drink for Jerome, started to laugh.

"That's wonderful. That's really terrific!" Rijn said. "Here, I freshened your drink for you. That's just great. Judas Iscariot, missing an eye. It couldn't happen to a nicer guy."

279

"I'll drink to that," Jerome said, and he took the glass from Rijn.

He put the poem, now perhaps completed, back into his pocket.

Jill announced that dinner was ready.

Royle was trying, was honestly trying, to discount for the pills. They were from a discount pharmacy and deserved to be discounted, didn't they? He could blame them for his feeling of discontent, of downishness. But what the hell. It wasn't anything so clearly irrational that there was a need for a pharmacological explanation. One could also be legitimately having a lousy time.

Jerome, for instance, with that showboat stuff of writing during a party. That was depressing. Either the kid was so nervous and insecure that he was forced to pretend to be writing—which was depressing—or he was actually writing, really working on some poem. And that was more depressing.

How long had it been, for that matter, since he, Royle, had been able to work anywhere at all? But that was only the pebble in his shoe, the annoying irritation he was concentrating on to avoid thinking about a broken leg. Because he had not enjoyed the party. And he counted on at least that kind of feeble minded pleasure. He had always liked the idea of many guests assembled around his groaning board, drinking his liquor, eating his food, and basking in the warmth of his hospitality and the comfort of his house. But he hadn't. Not this evening. The pills? Perhaps.

The way in which they worked was invidious. He had been at first only slightly subdued, and that he could attribute to the chemicals and their effect on his nervous system. But his feelings had been unimproved by Jerome and that business of his writing or pretending to write a poem, and his encounter with Corda. Royle had watched and overheard. Jerome had really put the old fool down. Good and proper. And ordinarily, Royle would have admired the style of it, the way in which Jerome had carried off the pretense of writing and used it, like a club, to bludgeon the addled pate of J. A. Corda. But somehow it had depressed him, made him worry, made him play stupid games. And he knew, even while playing these games, that they were stupid. They were like those walking races that kids have with strangers across the street of which the strangers are unaware . . .

Royle had sat quietly, had gone into dinner to eat, and had waited, not making conversation himself, not playing the host, not drawing anyone else out, but waiting for the others to talk with him, to come to him, to . . . Admit it! To praise him, praise the dinner, ask for more booze, more wine, more flesh, more blood! To tell him what a hell of a fine fellow he was, what a great host, what a great, warm, wonderful human being! And what a fine writer! (They could throw that in, too, and why not?) But nothing, nothing at all.

Be charitable, he told himself, arguing. Be generous. Admit at least the possibility that they sensed your mood, that they realized you were out of sorts, and that they were reluctant to intrude upon your . . . Delicate sensibilities. Shee-it!

Jill, of course, had been busy trying to cover up for him, occupied with seeing to it that everyone did get enough to eat and drink, did get attention, was properly engaged in conversation, was enjoying it all. And right she was, he supposed. Right? It was only a know-nothing chicksie-babe like Marty who would neglect the duties of a hostess to cater to the self-indulgent, foolish, childish moods of a bum like him! But that's what he would have liked! Not always, not all the time, but just once, this evening, when for no reason at all he felt the weight of all those yammering voices on his eardrums and the heat of all those bodies around him like furnaces. All those bodies, masticating and churning away, as the stomach acid ate a hole the size of a handkerchief in the aspic and the turkey and the moussaka and the roast beef and the carnage of barnyards and vineyards and Lord knows how much work and planning . . .

Jill's. Yes, Jill's, not his. But still, just once, was it too much to ask? Was a whole lifetime of so little worth that you couldn't cash it in, once, for an evening of outrageous, unreasonable pampering?

He sat on the platform, aware that he was slouching, aware that he must look like a sack of moldy potatoes no Irishman would have touched at the nadir of the famine . . . And not caring. Or, actually, taking a certain perverse pride in it. What the hell did he care how he looked? And what would anybody else care? He was not here to model Edwardian jackets and formal turtlenecks? He was here to read poems. And he would. Not even well, because it wasn't an elocution contest, either. They could hire Richard Burton, or Richard Boone, or

Pat Boone for all he cared. Let them show off their round tones and their white flashing teeth. Let them wring every drop of emotion and meaning out of the lines! He didn't have to do that. He'd put the goddam emotion and the goddam meaning into the lines. He'd made them. He didn't have to do another fucking thing!

Not out of principle and certainly not for the money. Corda had conned him into this, first asking Royle to introduce the other writers, and then changing his mind and deciding that he would introduce the writers but that Royle could read a few poems . . . For a fee? Why the reading of a few poems wouldn't be any more arduous than the writing and reading of the introductions, would it? And, after all, Corda had said, you are a writer in residence here. The compromise was that Corda would authorise fifty dollars from the department's funds for Royle's dinner party—which had cost a hundred and fifty? At least that. And with Jill doing most of the work! Some big generous offer, eh?

He was half tempted to get up and walk off the platform. But he didn't, because that would be to admit that Corda had won. It was better to remain on the platform, slouched in the chair, looking terrible, and making Corda look terrible. It was no skin off Royle's ass. Nobody cared, or even noticed much, he imagined, except Jill. And Marty. And for all he knew, Marty was enjoying it, was hoping he'd fart or wet his pants. Or puke, like Hungerford! After last night he could hardly blame her. And Jill, well, he could always claim it was the pills, the effect of the pills. What could she say to that? She'd given them to him herself, had insisted that he take them. Well, he'd show her how to play doctor! The pills could be his weapon too.

No, that was wrong. Unfair. There was a certain terrible pleasure in this kind of self-indulgent, self-pitying wallow. But there ought to be some bounds, some limits. He didn't want to go quite so far as actually to feel guilty. Concede Jill's good will, her support, her love. They were there, and real enough. But Marty? That was a more workable vein.

Not a bad title, that. The Workable Vein. He regretted that they were all up there on the platform and that there was no way for him to tell Jerome about the latest score in their running game. Or maybe it was even better than that. There was something appealingly beat-up and professional about it. Like that George Garrett phrase, "Buddy it's the only way/A poet can make a book." The Workable Vein. And there could be a piece in it with lots of variations on vein/vain/vane . . .

Royle smiled, shifted in his chair and sat up rather straighter. The slouch was emotionally appealing, or had been, but it was also uncomfortable. It had made him stiff in his left side. What could he have been thinking of?

Oh, yes. Of course. Marty. And that was funny, now, too, because he was not even able to be faithful and attentive to the poor dear when he was using her as an occasion for a really squashy session of self-scourging. Used the girl badly, he had. By not using her at all. He'd taken her along as a kind of ornament. Or as a souvenir, like one of those little turtles they used to sell with American flags or Golden Gate Bridges or Statues of Liberty on their backs. And they always died. You would find them, months later, under a radiator or behind a sofa, dessicated, pathetic, and with the gaudy emblem still there. Crazy! One could drum up sympathy, measurable in dols or whatever the measurements of pity were, for a god-damn turtle that had been dead for nearly forty years, but a girl, a human being, right here in the room, out in the audience, her eyes riveted not upon Agnes Hart-shorne at the lectern but upon you! And you can hardly pay attention. It bounces right off.

He supposed that he might have been able to feel worse, or to feel more accurately, if he had talked to Marty since they had all returned to Frenion. This way, all he had to respond to was what she ought to be think-ing and feeling—if she had any sense. And that was dan-gerous. And unreliable. You can't live that way. You can't even teach that way. You get way ahead of the class and they don't know what the hell you've been talking about. Silly. Marty was going to be at the party afterward, at Alumnae House. But she would be with Jerome, or she would appear to be with Jerome. Or, no, maybe she would really be with Jerome. That would be funny! That would be one of those nifty twists, all right. The kind of thing Sam Stone depended on. In Art and Life.

He looked over at Stone and felt . . . Well, not anger. Nothing that definite. But the old adrenals were trickling away, now, weren't they? Drop by drop, pouring into the blood-stream their chemical goodies that would argue with Jill's pills, and bringing anger and alertness and in-telligence—for a little while, at least. The funny thing was that he had thought of a Sam Stone story as good as any Sam Stone had ever written. The four characters would be the Royle figure, the Stone figure, the Carpenter figure, and the Marty-doll. And the Royle figure would be either about to lose the Marty or tired of her and ready to cut her loose (he could decide that later, come back to that one). And the question would be whether to try to throw her to the Jerome figure, or let her get snapped up by the Stone. That was, by God, an area that very few writers got into—the situation in which the current lover, in a state of benevolent satiety, lays out the girl's next love affair . . . Kind of sophisticated and wry . . . A little Colette-ish, but from a masculine point of view not intolerably so. Worth doing? He doubted it. But worth thinking about. Anyway, fun to think about. He looked at Stone again, smiling, and was delighted to see Stone return the smile. There are, he decided, some of those secret walking-races that you can really win!

By the time Corda called upon Royle to read, he was feeling pretty good. Good enough, anyway, to get up there, pick out some poems, and say them with some interest, some energy. His audience—and it was his, because this was his home ground and these were his students—was attentive, friendly. He could not fail entirely to react to that. He did well. And even while standing there at the end, listening to the applause, and every now and then bowing his head slightly, he could not help wondering who had the last laugh . . . Himself, the audience, or Justis A. Corda?

Another title, that. The Last Laugh. He'd mention this one to Jerome.

Again, a party. This time they were in a large room inspired by some English baronial hall, or, more precisely,

by some Hollywood set designer's rendition of a picture
of some actual room in an old abbey. The fireplace was
large enough to roast an ox. Or a Volkswagen. And covered with bunches of grapes and curlicues of vines with
stone tendrils grasping the stone. At the top of the arch
there was a shield, but it was blank. Was the coat of arms
to have been painted? Or had there been some endless
series of conferences which had produced no agreement
on what the carver should chisel, how many quarterings,
what fleurs de lis, rising suns, sunflowers, lions, yales? Or
had there been a precise drawing all ready for the work-
man who never showed up? Or had someone intended
this blank shield, deciding that the *tabula rasa* was as appropriate an emblem for a public room in an American
college as anything else?

Jerome considered these possibilities very carefully,
and further, considered whether to perform with them
for Marty, in order to amuse her, distract her a little bit.
Or, not for her sake, but for John's, in order to make the
charade more convincing. But he could not bring himself to begin. Not yet. Perhaps, he thought, stalling, after
a couple of drinks. Yes, then he would talk to her, try to
make her laugh . . . For now, it was enough to stand beside her and share with her the careful observation of the
details of the mantel, at the other end of which Royle
was talking with Hungerford, Jill, a couple of undergraduates, and another man, probably Frenion faculty. Curiously, Jerome felt himself to be all the more close
to Royle because of the distance between them, the
length of the huge mantel, the conspiracy. But, by the
same measure, Marty had to feel light years away. He sup-

posed that the only decent thing for him to do was to
talk to her. That was, after all, what Royle had meant
for him to do. For the sake of appearances, and for her
sake.

"Big mantel," he said, because it was such an absurd
way to begin. "Really big."

"Isn't it."

"Probably the biggest mantel in the whole college."

"I expect so."

He had meant to be funny, to impersonate . . . Well,
all the mindless conversations he supposed were being
carried on in the room. But her acceptance of this lunatic
nonsense as perfectly plausible talk only depressed him.
It stabbed him to the core. The poor broad! He could, he
understood, discuss any subject, no matter how dreary,
how amazingly tiresome, and she would go along with it,
chirping her noises of social assent, behaving herself, being pleasant.

"What it needs is model airplanes," he went on, driven
by her complaisance to further and further acts of intellectual atrocity.

"Model airplanes?"

"Yes, I used to build them. Did you?"

"No, I don't think so."

The furrow of the brow, the thoughtful pause, as if
she were trying to recall whether, in some inadvertent
moment, she had labored with struts and frets and
blueprints and glue and those little insignia . . .

"I didn't think you had."

"There are some girls who do."

"There are?"

"Oh, yes."

"Nice girls?"

She looked at him for a moment and then laughed.

Jerome considered carefully the quality of her laugh and the expression on her face as the smile lines subsided into the pose of obliging attentiveness that was as blank as the stone shield behind her and to the left. She had realized finally that he was joking. The polite thing, the expected thing, then, was for her to laugh. So she had laughed. He wondered what he could do that she would not go along with. Whip out a tuba and ask her to sing-along-in-Latin? Do bird calls?

What was she thinking about? Was she thinking at all? It was increasingly frustrating. And challenging.

"Have you known John long?" he asked.

"A while."

Ah, good! Reticence, at last. After miles and miles of a conversational terrain as flat and limitless as Nebraska, a small hummock.

"And you?" she asked. "Have you known him long?"

"Years. He got my book published for me."

"He likes to do that," she said.

An odd thing to say. Probably true, Jerome supposed, but still, from her it was odd. Sharper than he would have expected.

He waited for her to go on, but she didn't. She didn't say anything. She just looked at him, waiting for him to say something. But he couldn't think what it was, what she wanted him to say. Some comment on her comment? He tried to manufacture one. But somehow he knew that she was not waiting for him to say how nice it was of Royle to be helpful to young writers.

"Do you use pot ever?" she asked.

"On occasion. Not often, but on occasion."

"You want some?"

"Here?"

"Well, not right here in this room. But here. I have some. And I hate this party."

"Not here in this room, but here? What do you mean?"

"You've got a room upstairs, don't you?"

"Oh, sure."

"We could go up there."

And, just to make sure that he understood, she cocked her head slightly and looked at him in a sidelong way out of half-closed eyes.

The old "Come hither" stare, eh? Or, "Come, hither." Clearly, at any rate, an invitation. But at what rate? At the cost of Royle's friendship and—nearly as valuable— respect? But then, what the hell! Royle had asked him to entertain Marty. Let her make the instructions as specific as she would. Let her call the, *par exemple,* shots.

"What room are you in?" she asked, her hand fluttering up to adjust the fall of her hair over her left temple, and it seemed to Jerome that it was only by an act of will that she had kept it from lighting on some zipper or clasp somewhere. After all that vagueness, her new definiteness was amazing.

"Two oh eight," he returned, not satisfied with the way he had read the line. Because surely this all had to be made up, all had to come out of a rejected screenplay. Nobody talked like this! Nobody did such things.

"Give me a couple of minutes," she said, and then she left him staring at a cluster of those stone grapes that had been behind her. No, he would not permit himself the luxury of confirmation, would not move his head to watch her leave the room, or to watch Royle notice her leave the room. Not for anything. In case of fire, he would stare fixedly at those lapidary fruits, those crude schematizations of the glandular structure of her breasts (they were carved at about chest height). If necessary, he would turn to stone, himself, and they could arrange andirons and firetongs in his base, even, as those naughty girls would, arranging the poker so that the hook made an obscene suggestion.

That was his own scenario. What happened, though, was quite contrary. (Title: Contrarieties.) The stone fireplace at which he had been gazing with such fixity became itself unfixed, began to shimmer, seemed to be considering some Ovidian transmogrification into flesh. The result, no doubt, Maestro Houdini explains, of the unblinking gaze, an optical illusion merely. Look at it long enough, and it will turn past flesh to water. Victor Mature will ride his thirst crazed camel straight into it, knocking both himself and his backlot bactrian stone (ho! ho!) cold.

The rest of the room continued to function, to persist in its accustomed mode of being. Jerome permitted himself a glance at Royle, still with the same group, smoking a cigarette and drinking something. Talking. He was, poor soul, unaware of this little drama that was taking place, or was thinking of taking place. Also, he was unaware of the dismaying complexity of Jerome's position. The choices were clear enough. Either he could go upstairs where, even now, Marty was perhaps sitting on his bed, having lit her stick of Acapulco gold. He thought of the way her skin would be feeling, that odd, tingly feeling, and the way she might be stroking herself, the balls of her fingers tracing the musculature beneath while the skin sang on the calves, the thighs . . . Or he could not go. He could stay right here. Wait for her to get bored with waiting and either fall asleep or return to the party. But how would she return? In a furtive, sheepish way? Or furious? Which would be dangerous, because she would be also stoned. She could come down and cause all manner of unpleasantness, appearing, perhaps, quite nude, and accusing him—and Royle, and the world—of having no masculinity. Or, worse yet, she would appear to be perfectly normal, but would in the coming months turn Royle against Jerome, either by claiming to have been laid, or by . . . There were any number of things a mistress could do, as those wicked, glittering courts of the *dix-huitième* had so abundantly shown.

Perhaps, after all, he had better go up there. But that would be to betray Royle in order to maintain the appearance of loyalty. That was loony. Either way, it's your ass, buddy! Or hers! All those stupid pieces of folk wisdom popped into his head. Might as well be hanged for a sheep as a lamb. Or was it a sheep and a goat? Or a duck and a goose? (Oh, Stanley Kunitz, thou shouldst be living at this hour!)

Meanwhile, there she was, he supposed, up there in two-oh-eight, beginning to wonder where the hell he was, why he was taking so long. Beginning to wonder whether her own sense of time was still reliable. That was one of the things that marijuana did anyway, interfering with one's sense of time. And Marty would possibly lie there for hours, thinking that only minutes had gone by. A charming idea! But not without its sinister side, either. For all the time she was up there, he would be down here, toying with the idea, deciding, definitely and finally, not to go up, but then reviewing, reconsidering, appealing, making motions and counter motions. He would be acting out all that elaborate maneuvering of criminal lawyers, while he, himself, in death row was waiting to be marched off to . . . the arms of a waiting female of more than ordinary attractiveness. He felt like a beetle that thinks it is swimming, all the while it is being carried along by the pump and filter system to its certain end at the skimmer down at the end of the pool.

Unless, of course, he could contrive to think about something else, in the way that excessively speedy husbands are counselled to do square roots or conjugate irregular verbs while making love to their slower spouses . . . Something tiresome and just slightly disagreeable.

He looked around the room and saw Judas Iscariot, still with Stone, and he walked over to join the fight for the crumbs of crummy congratulations that served as conversation. It would be sufficiently irritating to listen to them, Jerome thought, but tolerable . . . And if it got too bad, he could take a certain private satisfaction in the idea that above their heads, on his bed, there was a girl stretched out like one of Doris Lessing's spider-women, all extremities leading in toward the furry center. (Which was, he suddenly understood, why Royle might have brought her along to Rockville, not for her own true self, or even for her golden hair, but for the idea, for the intellectual and emotional support of knowing that she was there—the way storekeepers frame their first silver certificate and hang it on the wall, no longer as currency but as an icon, an assurance that people have been willing to pay for the goods and the services of the shop.)

Stone was talking about the teaching of creative writing, saying, as Jerome gathered, all the correct, obvious things about how you couldn't teach people to write but writing courses were a good way to teach them to read. And Corda nodded and agreed, and said that he had always thought that the writing courses ought to be subsumed with the literature program, the sentence having no purpose except to use the word "subsumed." He was as deft with language as a Japanese wrestler. A second rater Japanese wrestler—a sub sumo?

Rijn came up to stand next to Jerome. Out of fear that Jerome was about to blow the gaff? Or out of pure hanger-on-ishness? Either way, it was distressing. And Jerome thought that maybe it was a sign, maybe God was trying to nudge him along the room, out of that doorway, up those stairs, and into the bed with Marty where he very possibly belonged.

"The question, though," Stone rolled on, gathering no moss, "is whether one can teach reading!"

"If we can't," the one eyed wrestler replied, "then we're all here under false pretenses."

"That's the only kind there is," Jerome said, unable to remain silent.

"I beg your pardon?"

"Is anyone ever anywhere under true pretenses? Doesn't pretense imply a certain degree of falsity?"

"I take your point," Corda said, in the way a small child might stick his thumb between his index and long fingers and announce quite solemnly, "I've got your nose."

"Surely we can make better readers," Rijn volunteered, getting into the act.

Or hire them, Jerome thought, but did not say. He would not say another word, would remain utterly still, would concentrate, instead, on the delicate shift from sexual excitement to anger that was going on upstairs, the glands carrying on the argument perhaps independently of the conscious thought process, now pouring out their fervor, now shutting off that honeyed flow . . .

"But can we? Do we make better readers when all is said and done?" Stone asked, furrowing his brow, waggling his beard, sounding downright philosophical.

The answer was obvious. We make any kind of readers we can get our hands on, unless they belong to our friends. Except that Stone makes no such exceptions, not wishing to spare his rod or leave any child unspoiled.

He was off, now, into a discussion of spontaneity versus critical sophistication . . .

As if it mattered. As if there were thousands and tens of thousands of real readers that the colleges were turning out. Sales of *The Double Agent* had been 682, which was depressing but not so depressing as the news from his publisher that 682 was not all that bad. Not bad at all for a first volume of poetry. Allen Tate's first book of poems, Jerome's editor had said, sold about seven hundred. But still, there were Stone and Corda discussing pedagogical strategy as if they were the generalissimos of vast armies of young readers, shaping and molding the sensibilities of a generation.

". . . the only sensible way of doing things," Stone was saying. And then he turned to Jerome and asked, "Don't you agree?"

Jerome, who had not been paying attention and had no idea what the only sensible way of doing things was, said, "No."

"But why not?"

"I just don't. Do I have to?"

"Yes, I think so."

"Well, I refuse."

"But on what grounds."

"I just refuse. Do I need grounds?"

"Of course you do! In any reasonable universe . . ."

"But it isn't. It isn't a reasonable universe at all."

"Then you can't have any sort of discussion whatever."

"Good. That would be just fine," Jerome said, smiling. And then, "Excuse me. I think I need to freshen my drink."

"Let me," Rijn said.

"No, you look like a renaissance poisoner. I'll do it myself."

He executed a rather military about face and strode off toward the bar that was set up along the wall opposite the fireplace. He felt rather smart, having maneuvered his way through an entirely non-objective conversation—it was as though he had found himself, suddenly, in a Basque railway station and, through sheer cleverness, had contrived a way of carrying on a conversation with the station master. Also, he felt good about not having thought about Marty for two or three minutes at a stretch. Vows of celibacy, he supposed, were like this and had their own peculiar aphrodisiacal effect. But they were not without their own rewards. For one thing, he felt a wonderful sense of power, of self-control, of mastery. He was ready for new tests, new challenges. Three girls upstairs waiting for him, or a hundred. All 682 of his readers, simmering in the juices of their desire!

Or, more reasonably, he could go over and join the Royles. To stand there and chat casually with John and with Jill would be an act of sublime showiness, of breathtaking insouciance. He got another drink and went to join them, smiling, feeling giddy, feeling like a skier on a long downhill run over the best kind of snow.

But suddenly a crevasse. A stone wall.

He still had fifteen feet to go to get to the Royles when he saw, in peripheral vision, the embodiment of his whole frame of mind, which is to say, Marty. Good God! She had given up her waiting. Patient Griselda would be patient no more. The balance had shifted and, with a great creak of bedsprings, desire was up and rage was down. And so was she. He stood still, waiting for her to come up to him and bop him with her purse, claw his eyes out, shriek like a shrill banshee . . . He would claim to have been caught up in a conversation. Stone and Corda would back him up. Rijn would vouch for him. (Even if he claimed to have been turned into a frog Rijn would swear to it, gribbitz, gribbitz, croa-a-ak! Brek-ek-ek-ek! Parabalu! Yale!)

But Marty did not approach Jerome at all. Or Royle. In the serene slow motion in which one watches automobile crashes, the fall of aerialists at circuses, the sinking of ships, and the collapse of buildings, Jerome saw Marty go up to Corda and Rijn and Stone, stand where he had stood, whisper something into Stone's ear, and then turn and leave the room.

No, it couldn't be happening. Not like that. It was too tawdry, too sordid. And too clever. What better way for her to get back at him and at Royle too than to do this and to do it in this way. Eleven, twelve, thirteen, fourteen . . . He noticed that he was counting, had been counting, as one keeps track of the chiming of a distant clock without actually noticing the beginning of the process. And at the count of thirty, Stone excused himself —Jerome, of course, seeing only a movement of the lips, but knowing, beyond any doubt, what Stone had to be saying. He watched Stone leave the room.

To go upstairs of course. But where? To Stone's room? Or to Jerome's own 208. Which would be safer, because who would think of looking for them there? And more precisely insulting too.

He felt annoyed with himself for having hesitated. What had he accomplished after all? Stone had not hesitated. Thirty breaths later and he was off and rutting, accepting as his due all the goodies of the world. Jerome tried to argue with himself. He was better than Stone, more intelligent, more honorable, more perceptive, more sensitive . . . And more of a damned fool. What could he say now to Royle? How could he explain this? With a thunder of hoofbeats, the Lone Rauncher had ridden off on his faithful Indian Friend, Pronto! (Those silver bullets were salversan, right?)

Feeling all of the reluctance of a schoolboy on his way to the principal's office for a reprimand, he resumed his progress toward his friend.

"Hey, how are you doing?" Royle asked, hearty and cheerful.

"Okay. Fine," Jerome lied.

"I'd begun to think you were avoiding us," Jill said. Her tone was, of course, perfectly pleasant. But it was clear that she knew and was announcing that she knew what had been going on.

"Oh, no. Not at all. I just got involved in a conversation."

"Yes, I saw," Jill said, bright as the jewelled scabbards of Ottoman daggers. "And what happened to her?"

"I don't know," Jerome said, trying to sound as casual and as bright as she. "I think she went off to talk to Sam Stone."

"Oh, really?"

"Well, that's okay," Royle said. "That happens."

Hungerford stood there smiling. And that was, after all, the most interesting thing—that a bright, perfectly reasonable person could stand there, listening to it all, hearing every word, and could not know what they were talking about. And if he did know, he would have reason enough to fill whole warehouses full of Steinways with a vomitus of pure bile!

"You can't win 'em all," Jerome said, not meaning anything in particular, but happy to find something to say that would fit into the conversation at all.

"You didn't lose much, friend," Royle said. He was not looking at Jerome, though, but at Jill, whose slight nod and bright smile were not merely triumphant (as Jerome would have expected) but grateful, which took the curse off it. Curse? Her expression was nothing less than a blessing. Of John. Of Jerome. For that matter, quite conceivably of Sam Stone!

It was too much. Jerome had to change the subject.

"A good reading," he said, looking at Hungerford. "You were fine." And then, looking at Royle, "And you were just splendid."

They thanked him and said something nice in return. And then it was his turn, but he couldn't quite think of what to say. It was outrageous that he should have to be searching for lines, foundering around in this conversation, trying to think up things to cover over the only real subject of the moment, Marty and Stone, upstairs, going at it . . . He thought of "Hills Like White Elephants," and how Hemingway had worked that situation for a whole short story. But he couldn't share that thought, couldn't allude to their own situation and what they were all so carefully not discussing.

And then there was that noise, like the noise of some kind of huge tropical bird. A baritone whooping crane, let loose here in Alumnae House? Jerome looked around to see Rijn, poor Rijn, the fetcher of drinks fetching his own drinks back up, retching, puking, not into any discreet piano, or into the beautiful pearwood rosette of a convenient lute, but right onto the rug (no trick in that) at Corda's feet. And, in fact, onto Corda's foot. Corda immediately sat down and mopped off his shoe with a couple of cocktail napkins. He had all the presence of mind of someone who has studied first aid and knows, in an emergency, how to sit down on the curb and put his head down between his legs to keep from fainting.

Rijn ran from the room, an optical, messily pied piper with all eyes following him. Shock. Sympathy. Suppressed amusement. And for Jerome, a touch of guilt, because he knew what fear had driven that poor faker, that rhinestone Jules back to the bar for more and more courage. He had screwed his courage to the chucking point! And a word of reassurance, a more emphatic word, a look, a gesture, might have saved him that humiliation.

Hungerford was grinning. Because Hungerford this time had not done it! And Royle was smiling too, but whether at this or at Jill's reaction to the business of Marty and Stone, or, for all Jerome could guess, at the business itself, it was impossible to say.

Slowly, like people coming out of their air raid shelters after an attack, the faculty members, the students, the faculty wives, the writers, the visitors, began to talk again. A janitor came, to cover the mess that Jules had left with that green sawdust stuff that only janitors have.

Corda, having finished his ministrations of mercy and comfort to his shoe, a scotch grain blucher, crossed the room, approaching . . . or perhaps simply getting away from the scene and scent of the peristaltic reversal.

"What happened to Rijn?" Royle asked.

"He threw up!" Corda said, curtly.

"Oh, is that what they call it?" Jerome said.

Corda bestowed upon Jerome a look of nothing less than utter hatred. "As a matter of fact, Mr. Rijn had just made the observation that my name would be an anagram of Judas Iscariot if I had another eye. I was not at all amused. He thought it was extraordinarily risible, and he started laughing. His laughter was not all that he brought up in the process, but also the attribution of the tasteless remark to you, sir, and then his dinner."

The attribution to Jerome? But that was crazy! Hungerford had thought of the anagram. Jerome had only made the crack about the extra eye, thinking of the Shakespeare line from one of the sonnets about something something blank whose eye I eyed . . . And Rijn had credited him with it? Out of revenge? Or out of gratitude? Either way, it was funny. Jerome started to laugh.

"And Frenion," Hungerford said, "is an anagram on inferno."

"It all fits!" Royle exclaimed.

"Good evening . . . uh . . . gentlemen," Corda said, the sarcasm as thick as honey. "Good evening Mrs. Royle."

He turned and marched out of the room.

"That wasn't very nice," Jill said. "But it was funny."

"Yes it was."

"In fact, this has been one of the funniest, one of the best evenings I can remember!"

"I'm glad you're enjoying it, dear," Royle said.

They laughed together. Jerome felt as if he had done something remarkably clever back there with Marty and Stone. He did not feel that it was either an intrusion or a presumption for him to join in their laughter.

"Let's get the hell out of here," Royle said. "Let's go back to the house."

It took nearly half an hour to pick out of the room those interesting or desirable or friendly enough to take back. Hartshorne, yes, but Dinsmore, no. Hungerford of course. A couple of students, mostly because they had cars and could drive Agnes and Ed and Jerome back to Alumnae House later. And it all had to be done in such a way as to keep the rest from noticing. The intricacies of the academic life!

They went back in four cars. Jerome rode with Jill.

"Quite an evening," he said, just in case she felt like talking about it.

"Wasn't it?"

"Corda was wonderful, sputtering like that."

"He hissed! It *was* wonderful. I've never seen him so furious. He hissed just like a goose."

"By the way," Jerome said, not with any particular hope, "do you know the story about Stanley Kunitz and the goose?"

"Mmm-hmmn."

"Would you mind telling me?"

He explained about how Stone and Corda had been talking and had referred to the story, but hadn't told it. And how he was damned if he was going to ask them to tell him.

Jill understood perfectly. And she told the story. She wasn't sure that it was true, suspected that it had been embroidered some as such stories always were, but she thought probably something like it might have happened. "Anyway, the Kunitzes decided they wanted a goose for Christmas. Just like in Dickens with Cratchett and Tiny Tim and the rest of it. And Stanley Kunitz found a goose farm out in New Jersey and went out to buy his goose. But they were live geese. And the farmer wouldn't kill the goose for him. So he decided to take it back to New York to get it butchered there. And on the way back, driving along the Garden State Parkway, or the Turnpike—I don't remember which, but it was some big road like that—the goose got loose in the back of the car and started flying around, and then it settled on Stanley Kunitz's head. It was facing backward, apparently, and he was trying to get it off his head, and he frightened it, and it . . . crapped all over his face. And his glasses!

"He pulled off the road, and cleaned himself off, and

went to tie the goose up again, but it got loose, I mean out of the car, and started running along the grass border of the road. And Kunitz ran after it, for maybe half a mile down the road until he caught it and wrung its neck. He killed it. With his bare hands! And the point of the story, I guess, is that he's a terribly gentle person, the last man in the world you'd think could do a thing like that."

"Did they eat the goose later?"

"I don't know. I never heard that part of it. I wonder."

"Well, I suppose we could ask."

"Ask whom? Corda? Stone?"

"Kunitz. We could call him up."

"It's eleven-thirty!"

"We could wait a couple of hours and then call."

"That's ridiculous."

"I suppose so," Jerome agreed. "And anyway, it's better not knowing some things. That way you can believe what you like."

"Is it?" Jill asked. "Yes, I suppose so."

There was a silence after that. And Jerome wasn't at all sure what Jill was talking about—Kunitz and the goose, or, beyond that, Marty and Stone, Marty and himself, Marty and Royle . . .

In the darkness and the quiet of the car's contemplative purr, the comment blossomed into the kind of generalization of a Thoreau paragraph, growing ever larger and more diaphanous, until at last it seemed to color all experience, as surely as the green goose turds that had once dripped down over the lenses of Stanley Kunitz's glasses.

"Well, here we are," Jill said.

It took a moment before Jerome understood that she meant they were home.

CHAPTER 8

It was very late. John had no idea what time it was, exactly, because he could not remember how far ahead he had pushed all the clocks. It would have been possible to find out the time, of course, either by turning on the radio and listening for a while to the alternating caterwaul and jabber of the late night disc jockey shows. Or, more simply, by picking up the phone and asking the operator. But he didn't care enough. The assault of the radio would have been too much. The phone would have been an effort. Besides, it was nice to be there, in the weird, aquarium light of the kitchen, alone with Jill, and knowing only that it was very late, but no particular time. To hell with time!

The business with the clocks had seemed quite clever at the time. Poor Aggie had drunk an awful lot, and had got to be sloppier than he had ever seen her. Babbling on that way about some dog of hers that had died! Inconsolable. And incoherent. She'd talked for a while about

what a terrific writer she was, and how unfair it was that
she wasn't famous and wasn't important. And then she'd
blubbered about that dog. And the rest of them had tried
to be sympathetic, but she had switched and talked about
her writing. And they'd agree with her that she was the
best there was, the heavyweight champion short story
writer of the English Speaking Peoples! And she'd bawled
that that wouldn't bring Patches back!

Patches! For God's sake.

And then she'd fallen asleep. It wasn't a deep sleep or
anything reliable, but a moment of psychological pause.
Hungerford had suggested the business with the clocks.
In a whisper, he had told Royle, "It wouldn't be very
difficult to push the hands of all the clocks forward a
couple of hours. She doesn't have a watch."

They had done it, not so much because Aggie was
really intolerable, but to see if they could get away with
it. They had pushed the hands forward two or three fast
turns around the dial. And then Hungerford had coughed
loudly. Aggie had started, had woken.

"You drifted off there, Aggie, old girl," John had said,
all amiability.

"Just for a moment."

"Oh, no . . . It's . . ." He'd stopped, looked at the
clock, and said, "twenty of four."

"Oh, good Lord!"

"Shall I take you back?" Hungerford had offered.

She had accepted, of course, apologising for the late-
ness of the hour, protesting that they should have
woken her, complaining that it hadn't seemed but a
minute . . .

They had forgiven her, assured her, and packed her off.

It had been shameless. And wonderful!

It was wonderful that they had brought it off, had managed to do it at all. And, now that it was done, it was wonderful to be alone with Jill. It was the last distillation of the whole weekend. It was finally and perfectly what the gathering back at the house was supposed to have been—a gathering to mark the passing of the literary festival from event into memory, to exchange memories, to laugh about it, grump about it, watch it disappear . . .

And partly they'd done all that. Aggie had babbled on some. Jerome had disappeared rather precipitately with Nan Whatsername . . . But Hungerford had been very funny. It had been all right.

"A hell of a weekend," he said.

"Wasn't it?" Jill answered.

"Stupid," he said, "but interesting."

"Oh?"

"At first I had a lousy time. And I worried about that. But then, this evening I guess, I realised that it was okay to be having a lousy time, that it was good to be having a lousy time . . ."

"You want some tea?" she asked. It was not an interruption, but an invitation to continue. They would sit at the table and drink tea, and talk. For as long as he liked. And she had to be tired, after all the work of making dinner . . .

"Yes, thanks."

He watched her fill the kettle and put it on the stove. She seemed to float around the kitchen, from cabinet to sink, from sink to stove, and from stove back to the table where he sat. No geisha ever performed a tea ceremony with such grace.

"You can learn something from having a lousy time," he said, continuing. "I don't know quite what. Not yet I don't. But I feel like I've learned something."

"About Marty?"

Not bitter? No.

"About all the Martys," he said, and inclined his head toward the study out in back where, presumably, Nan was filling in for Marty with a Jerome who was filling in for Royle, himself. "It doesn't signify."

"That's what you've always told me," she said. This time there was an edge, but of humor.

"I know. But I believe it now."

"When the Pope gets religious, the church is in trouble."

"Maybe. Maybe so."

"And what brought you to this vision? Hiccups?"

"Hiccups?"

"Wasn't it hiccups that made Pius XII see Jesus?"

"Oh, yes. No, not hiccups. It wasn't anything that dramatic. I was just thinking about what everybody got out of the weekend. What they wanted, and what they got. I mean, Stone got laid. Twice."

"Which was the other time?"

"Last night. At the Burtons'. I thought Jerome had gone outside with some girl and I went out to look for him. I can't think quite why. But I wanted in some vague way to tell him not to do it. Anyway, he wasn't out there at all. But Stone was. With some girl. In the back of a car. I couldn't see who it was with him. A pair of thighs."

"And Hungerford. What did he get?"

"He kept his dinner down. He got confidence."

"And Jerome?" she asked, inclining her head toward the study. "Is that what he got?"

"Oh, well . . . Sure. But he got more than that. He got Corda good and angry. Intentionally, maybe. Instinctively, perhaps. He got out, anyway. He's not going to join the Frenion faculty . . ."

"Had he wanted to?"

"He'd thought about it. He'd thought he wanted to. He wrote to me about it a while back."

"And you? What did you get?"

"I got . . . over it. I realized that I've outgrown it all. It all seemed so tiresome, so silly. What the hell do I need with any of it?"

"The chicks?"

"The instant admiration. They're like the groupies that go around laying the Doors and the Stones and the Clear and Present Danger, and groups like that."

"And you've outgrown that?"

"I think."

There was a low whistle that climbed in pitch and volume.

"That's either an editorial comment or the water's boiling," Jill said.

She got up to pour the boiling water from the kettle into the teapot.

"Not just that," Royle went on. "All of it. I mean, I was thinking of Aggie and how, if she were a man, she'd be laying everything in sight to make up for all those injuries. To make up for not having the money and the reputation and the rest of it . . . It's the only connection I could make between all that stuff and her dog."

"What connection?"

"The dog thought she was God."

"That's even better than Pope."

"If you're a believer, it is."

"And you're a believer?"

"Maybe. Or maybe I've just converted from one faith to another. Low church. Unitarianism, even. I just can't take all that seriously any more."

"All what?"

"Well, that, for instance . . ." He nodded again, toward Jerome and his intellectualized exhibition out in the study. "It's sad."

"He may be enjoying himself."

"Is that a suggestion?"

"Maybe," Jill said, "but not until after the tea."

"He's not enjoying himself. They've been out there too long. They're talking. That's the great pain of it. You've got to talk to them afterwards."

"Snookums had a boring time last night? Poor dear!"

"I didn't touch her!"

"You don't have to tell me that."

"I know. But it's true. I didn't touch her. I just . . . I just didn't feel like it."

"Let him who is without stones cast the first guilt . . ."

"Very good. Bitchy, but very good."

"Well, I don't want to be boring. To pain you with all this *talking* . . ."

"No pain. I can talk to you. I love talking to you. Sometimes I think the only thing that matters is that we can talk to each other."

"I could be snide about that . . ."

"I know. I'm doubled, redoubled and vulnerable as hell. But there it is. You know, 'intercourse'. Sexual intercourse is only a kind . . ."

"A nice kind."

"Sometimes," Royle said. "With us it is."

"Yes. I'll pour the tea."

She poured the tea from the pot into the pottery mugs, got the milk for herself and the sugar for John, and sat down again.

"To be a poet is to believe in words," Royle said. "Maybe to believe in them too much. But when we exchange words and understand each other . . . I love you for that." He smiled at her. "For other things too, but for that."

"What other things?" she asked. "Tell me. I like to hear."

"The way you make tea."

"That's an affectionate Uncle Belly."

The reference was to the name of a hamburger joint about ten miles south of Frenion. Jill had adopted it as an insult name.

"And you've got a great ass! Is that what you want me to say?"

"Only if it's true."

"It's true."

"If it were really true, it would be higher."

"Your ass would be higher?"

"On the list! Yes. It would be higher on the list than the way I make tea."

"You've got a very high ass. High cheek bones and a high ass."

"I do have nice cheek bones, don't I?"

He raised his teacup. His mug. "Hi, ass," he said.

He took the first sip of his tea. "You do make good tea."

"I wonder if they're waiting for us to go to bed," Jill said. "Wouldn't that be funny? She left her purse in here, and she must have decided that it would be too embarrassing to come in to get it."

"So they're going to come back when we're upstairs?"

"If we leave the doors open. Or they might just sneak around to the front of the house, drive off, and come back tomorrow morning to get the purse."

"Maybe."

"And so we could be keeping them up, prisoners of each other's conversations."

"Or they could have fallen asleep."

"I like my idea better," she said. "It's nastier."

"Heap good torture squaw! High-ass-watha."

"That's a boy's name."

"Nooky-komus?"

"That's better."

"Horny-haha?"

"Horny-haha?"

"Only so-so. Besides, can a woman be horny? Strictly speaking?"

"You tell me."

"Lustful, certainly, but horny? Doesn't that have to be male?"

"I suppose. Unless it has to do with the horns of a cuckold, maybe."

"Finish your tea!"

"I am. But there's no rush. Besides, I like to talk dirty."

"Poet!"

"Peasant!"

"You're making overtures, sir?"

"Yes, I guess I am," he said, and he finished the tea.

"Shall we lock up?" Jill asked. "Or should we leave the door open, so the poor thing doesn't have to come back tomorrow to get her damned purse."

"Should we make her suffer?"

"Well, I'd suffer too. I don't want to see her, either."

"Then we'll leave the door unlocked. I'll close up later."

"You won't want to move later."

"I might. I might be hungry."

"What a sybarite. Already thinking of your next pleasure."

"Is that bad?"

"No. I might be hungry myself."

He took her hand and led her upstairs, feeling great eagerness, great gaiety, and even a kind of smugness. For all of his breeziness, it still was true that sometimes, with the chicks, he was unable to perform. Old Horny would lie there, and sulk in a grotesque reversal of St. Augustine's notions about sex before and after the fall. Augie, the swinger, thought that before the fall erections had been a part of free will, but afterwards they became involuntary. Original notion about original sin. But, St. A., it also works the other way. Some shred of remorse, of conscience, of fine Old Testament guilt circulates in the blood, suffuses the corpus spongiosum (hic est corpus) and . . . the limp devotion of the recluse. (These are my rocks, Peter, and you're making a church out of them?) Royle lay on the bed, watching Jill get undressed, and wondering whether scrotal/sacerdotal had ever been used as a rhyme. It was too neat to use seriously, but it could nestle cozily in the middle of a limerick. About Graham Greene?

> *There once was a writer named Greene,*
> *who confused the profane and obscene.*
> *He went from the scrotal*
> *to pure sacerdotal . . .*

Clean? Too obvious. *Been?* Weak. *Keen? Manichean?* Yes!

"Are you composing?" Jill asked.

"What makes you think so?"

"Your lips are moving."

"Oh? Well, sort of. I was thinking of something."

"You want to work?"

"No. Let's play."

"Let's."

And for a while, all the words went away.

It was as if a man went into a gas station with a water pistol, one of those realistic looking little toys with which he intended to bluff the attendant into cooperation, but the attendant, terrified, had thrown himself to the floor, missed, had fallen into the grease pit, and had impaled

himself on a lug wrench and died. And now the poor
impostor with the thirty-nine cent squirt gun was being
sentenced for felony murder. What could he do but
laugh?

It was, Jerome thought, like that. Because he had not
intended this. Or—whining word—not really. He had
wanted to come out to Royle's study to retrieve the poem,
to retype it with the corrections he had made before the
reading. So? Why had he not merely excused himself and
come out? Was that so complicated? Was that difficult?
But, no, he had to muddy things up, confuse the issue by
inviting the girl to come out to see his new poem. And was
it not his intention, after all, to have her come out, read
the poem, look at him in amazed admiration, strip off her
clothes on the spot, fall down on the floor and beg the
great poet to favor her with a few jottings from his stylish
stylus? Yes, yes, but who could seriously suppose such a
thing would happen? All he had wanted was to entertain the possibility, the improbability, that she might respond in such a way.

She had chuckled at his invitation, as if in agreement
that it was the corniest thing in the world, surpassed only
by the knock of the travelling salesman at the farmer's
daughter's door and the invitations of lascivious enthu-
siasts of the art of the etching. And she was willing, he
supposed, to carry on the fiction, to play at it . . . But
what play! It was the new theater where, along with the
curtains, the dresses go up at the beginning of the scene
and, at the end, along with the curtain, the pants come
down.

That he did not know her name was only an accidental,

a further complication of the already extravagantly sharped key-signature. He had heard it, had been introduced to the girl, but her name had slipped his mind, excusing itself and rushing off to the study, perhaps, even before he had thought of going there himself. It was one syllable, but what? Buff, Foof, Kate, Kek, Gook, Gail, Lil, Nul, Syl, Sol, La, Ti, Do? And, after a certain degree of intimacy, it is impossible to say, casually, lifting a finger-tip from a very pink, very protuberant nipple, "I beg your pardon, but I seem to have forgotten your name, dear . . ."

Well, and let that be a lesson to you, he thought to himself. Because you never know what girl is going to surprise you and say, yes, she'd like to see the gazebo, the grape arbor, the attic, the septic tank, the pool pump. Or your poem out in Royle's study. And once you've got her out there, you can never even be sure that there will be a decent period of pretense during which she will examine the poem, discuss it with you, allow you to turn the conversation ever so deftly from art to life, from life to love, and then lunge . . . Nothing like that at all. She had not quite waited for him to close the door before she declared, "I fell in love with you at the reading, you know."

"Oh? Did you?" It was not one of the wittier replies in the tradition of lovemaking, but Jerome was too much in shock to worry about that. He had the weird feeling that somehow he was not tuned in right and that the video from one channel had crossed with the audio of another. There had to be somewhere in Frenion another couple who were entwined in one another's arms and who were saying the most commonplace things, the things that went with this room and this girl and this situation. But no, she went on.

"Yes," she said. "I just drank you in with my ears and my eyes. I . . . I knew this would happen."

"That's wonderful," Jerome said, thinking that it was nothing less than wonderful that he was listening to this and not hooting with manic glee. For, in some crazy way, so irrational as to be safely beyond any sensible doubt, he had the feeling that this was his reward, that this was the quiddity he was getting in exchange for all that static of the status quo he'd so assiduously—and acidulously— maintained with Marty. He had done the right thing back then, which is to say nothing at all. And it had come to nothing. But his intentions had been good. And therefore he deserved some reward, didn't he? Symmetry de- manded it. The idea of unity, the sense of endings, the notion of a coherent universe which lies at the bottom of all art—all nudged him with an insistence matched only by that of the girl, nameless as a wood nymph, who had materialized out of the audience, out of the furniture of Royle's living room, to bestow upon him his garland—not of myrtle or of laurel but of furze. The fuscous furze! Weep no more, lustful shepherds, weep no more! For now my oat proceeds. Hot damn!

She raised her arms, took the half step forward, and entwined them about Jerome, holding him for a moment before kissing him as if in some vaguely mythological representation adorning the ceiling of an eighteenth cen- tury French country house, or, for all Jerome knew, adorn- ing the inside of her cranium, painted in just that way with a *trompe l'oeil* cupola throwing rays of afternoon sunlight across some obscure corner of her brain. Fantastical? Of course, but so was this. Give fancy reign. For the rain it reigneth too damned much. He held the pose with her as if for a master of the Daguerrotype wrapped in his black cape and rapt in the contemplation of their inverted images on the ground glass. The muscles of his calves began to protest that the point had been made. And his intelligence—like a splinter liberal party glad of the chance to make its small voice heard—suggested that it might be well for him to make the next move himself. So he did, bending his head slightly, looking deep into her eyes—that would have to do for he could not remember her name and therefore could not murmur it passionately or accurately—and, at last, kissing her.

So, okay. Dissolve. Like in the movies into fuzzily photographed confluescences of streams, floating clouds that merge, and all the other quasi-symbolical paraphernalia of fashionable cinematography. Or the other way, literally, dissolve there with her. Stop, at least, this idiotic chattering as if you were a guide to the not very bright visitor taking the tour of your life. Acteon looks at Diana, just looks, and *verba animo desunt*, the words desert the soul. (Gorgeous phrase!) But here you are, clinched with this anonymous admirer, the self-appointed representative of all the admirers, the female counterpart, for God's sake, of Brownsuit! And all you can think of is that you, too, have been transmogrified into something as absurd as she, a kind of idealized version of the writer, a figure in the ads for Tabu, a five-and-dime knock-off of Byron. Or of Sam Stone, for that matter. Because it isn't you she's holding, and it's not your chest at all into which her breasts are grinding like the heads of ostriches into the tightly packed sand. It's talent. And not even your talent but the idea of talent. It is, your racing mind suggests, Platonic love, in which the imperious forms impose themselves upon the uncomprehending flux. In Japanese, Puritanicu Rabu, because there are no L's in Japanese and you can't have two consonants together . . . Is this what Talent is supposed to be thinking when it couples with Admiration?

It had been a long kiss. They came up for air, and then retired to the daybed. Jerome tried to undo the back of her blouse, but, no, she didn't want to get undressed. What? But, of course, she wanted to be able to flee if necessary. She was afraid of being discovered. Or perhaps it was just habit, the result of the years of dangling in the web of rules of proper schools for proper young ladies. She had learned the obvious lessons about not getting caught. And, after a while, it seemed only normal and natural to think of making love on golf courses, in trees, in automobiles, in back-stage store rooms, squash courts, rowboats, auditorium ticket booths, basement snack bars, on roofs, in library carrels, in the pipe cabinets of chapel organs, in greenhouses and terraria, in projection booths of the arts building, in the Memorial Belltower, where it was necessary to finish in fifteen minutes or risk deafness as the great bells boomed out the Westminster Chimes—anywhere except in a bed, in a bedroom. And always with the clothes on, in a state of disarray, but on. Nothing was really peeled but the eye. And the ear was as much cocked as anything.

The object in all this exercise of the imagination was breathing heavily, but she was as abstract as ever. And Jerome was having as much trouble fleshing this flesh as he had ever had in the fleshing of an idea. She remained as remote as ever, even after he unhooked the clasp of her brassiere because he expected to find anagogical—or at least analogical—breasts, with, say a lion and a lamb imbibing faith and understanding from each of the flowing Villa D'Este trick nipples. The more intimate, the more remote she became. He was afraid he was going to be a great disappointment to her.

But then, doubling back, he supposed he could think of someone else, and let her be as much of a role player in this roll as he was for her. And there, the dea ex machination, she appeared, like the muse of a poem. A Jill. Not *the* Jill, or not exactly Jill, because that was unspeakable, and to go from Marty to Jill would be ridiculous and incongruent—this was a reward for loyalty, remember? But a kind of a Jill. A serene creature of well appointed rooms who respected him, who cared for him, who loved him, and who just happened to have a bosom like Jill's, a belly like hers, a throat like hers. And legs. Oh, the legs.

It worked. He rose to the occasion, stood at attention, performed the entire manual of arms. And felt finally a closeness with this girl, this tousle of parts under a rumple of clothes beneath a jumble of identities. If Jerome could mate with the idea of domesticity and a fleeting thought of Jill, why could she, whatever her name was, not couple with the idea of talent and even the thought of some other guy? Why not suffer a sea change into something rich and strange?

Richer and stranger. And richer still because they were strangers.

"Oh, that's good, that's good, that's good . . ."

Her cry was the cry of the audience, of all audiences, of ideal audiences. And his reading was fine, was just fine, he could feel it, the control, the subtle inflections of the rhythms, the swing of the lines, the lilt of it, and underneath it all, a welling up of meaning. An act of creation.

They lay there on the daybed for a long time. He was not sure whether she was embarrassed now, or whether she had fallen asleep. He, himself, had not been able to think of anything to say, anything pleasant that would be at the same time true and yet not dreadfully diminishing to both of them. And he had begun to think that she might think he was asleep. Perhaps they were each faking it for the other, relying upon the other's considerateness, the other's tenderness. Or perhaps for a little while he actually drifted off into a doze. It was difficult to say.

At any rate, the scream snapped them to a sudden alertness. He was sure he had heard a scream. Could he have dreamed it?

But no, they heard it again.

He was glad they had not taken off their clothes. It took only a few seconds before they were put together enough to rush out of the study and run toward the house.

There had been, in fact, but one scream. As Jerome was to piece it all together, later, it seemed that Royle had gone down to the kitchen to make steak sandwiches to bring upstairs for a snack and to close up the house. Apparently, he and Jill had been laughing about something—Jerome was never able to find out what it was they had been laughing about, and, under the circumstances, could scarcely ask—and, as he returned to the bedroom, some further change upon the already established joke had set him to laughing again. And evidently it was the combination of the fatigue, the liquor, and the fit of laughter all together, and maybe just plain dumb bad luck too, that was the reason for the bit of steak getting caught that way in his throat. He had tried all the conventional treatments, lying on the bed with his head down, having Jill pound his back, drinking water. Nothing had worked. The bit of steak stuck there. Jill ran downstairs to get some water and some Adolph's Meat Tenderizer (bizarre, but, according to the doctor, exactly what they do in hospitals) and had called up to John to say she was coming. The first noise had been her calling. The second noise was the scream, for upon her return she discovered that John was unconscious.

Jerome got to the back door and found that it was locked. John had locked it himself, some moments before. It was to occur to Jerome, later, that the last thing John Royle had done was to lock him out. He would not make anything of this, but it was there to be noticed. To be noted. Finally, it comes to that. There are some things that are private, that cannot be shared.

Jerome and the girl went around the house to see if perhaps there were other doors that were unlocked. There weren't. And the peculiar feeling of nighttime stealth—

for the sake of the neighbors as much as anything else—
infected them, made them doubt not the scream, but
its meaning. What did Jerome know about Royle, after
all? How could he be sure that Royle was not a whips
and spurs enthusiast, a bondage boy, God knows what?
Or, for that matter, how could he be sure that the noise
they had heard was not a more or less normal cry of passion? To intrude by ringing the bell would be possibly
embarrassing. On the other hand, he did not feel easy
about simply leaving. Unable to decide what to do, they
stood there, just stood there . . .

Not that Jerome supposed there would have been
anything he could have done. Had he broken into the
house through a window and charged upstairs to the
master bedroom, he would have been of no use, of no
use at all. He might have got there three or four minutes
before the Emergency Squad with their resuscitators,
their oxygen, their drugs, and their competence. And
there was nothing they could do, either. Except to confirm
what Jill must have guessed anyway, that John Royle
was dead.

She must have guessed it, Jerome supposed, because
he knew, himself, had been convinced of it from the
moment out on the front lawn when he first spotted the
flashing red light of the Emergency Squad's truck. He
knew instantly that the truck was coming to this house,
and he knew, too, that Royle was dead. Jerome was no
ESPedant, had had only one experience of the kind before in his life, and had not taken that experience very
seriously. Who could? At camp, once, he had had a dream
about his cocker spaniel in which he saw the dog lying

on top of the garbage in the garbage can. And the following morning his parents had called him to tell him that the dog had died. It had never operated since, that mystical awareness. His grandmother, his father, his uncle had all expired without registering anything at all in his dream life, either before the fact or afterward. And the only reason that Jerome remembered the dream and the death of the dog now was that Aggie's sentimental blubbering had somehow brought it to mind, before. Oh, keep the dog far hence that's friend to men . . .

He told the girl to sit in her car and wait there. He would go in with the Emergency Squad, alone. She seemed just as happy to stay outside. And Jerome was happy not to have her with him.

"If you can get my purse out to me . . ." she said. "It's in the living room, I think."

"I'll try."

Jerome went inside with the Emergency Squad, followed them up the stairs, and stood in the hall, hovering, not quite in the bedroom, but still not very far away from the bed. He heard the chief of the squad tell Jill that John was dead, and the peculiar effort of the man to comfort Jill by telling her that two hundred and fifty people a year die this way, by choking on meat. "Mostly it's roast beef, but it happens with steak," he said and shook his head—as if it made any difference. It could have been Kung Foo!

Jill nodded. She was sitting in a chair, numb, her eyes blank. Jerome wanted to comfort her, wanted to say something . . . But what was there to say? What comfort was there?

He went downstairs, went to the living room, got the girl's purse, and brought it out to her.

"I got your purse," he said. "He's dead."

"Oh, God!"

"You better run on. I'll . . . I'll try to call you tomorrow."

She nodded, got into the car and drove off. It was only after she had driven away that Jerome realized he had missed his chance. He could have looked in her purse, inside in the living room. He could have found out what her name was. He was annoyed with himself for not having thought of it at the time. Had he not thought of it at all, that would have been fine, understandable, reasonable. Who could pay attention to such things at such a time? But here he was, paying attention to it now, when it did no good. Oh, well, it was all the work of Dame Fortune. She was being terribly precise, he thought. Reward for loyalty: one screw. Not two, you greedy bastard, or fifty. Or, maybe this was his punishment for thinking of Jill before. Or for not thinking of her now. She would need to have someone around, wouldn't she?

He went back inside. Up the steps, through the door, into the hall . . . And then he sat down at the bottom of the stairs, for only now, with the girl out of the way, only here on his way back into the house to do what he could for Jill did it hit him with the force of a blow so that he had to sit down to keep from falling down, that John was dead. He had been upstairs, had heard the man from the Emergency Squad say it, had seen the body himself . . . But he had not understood any of it. It had not sunk in. Now it was beginning to.

But only beginning. Because there were other matters to attend to. Jill, for instance, came downstairs with the men, and Jerome looked up, and said, "I've been sitting here . . . I had to sit down . . ." both of which fragments were of course true, but still, utterly misleading. He could have come downstairs and removed all the furniture from the living room to the unmarked van out in front. Furniture? He could have filched the very walls! Because he was Harry the Cat Burglar, or somebody like that—fantastically dexterous and agile. "I submit to you, gentlemen, that the entire testimony of the witness has been a tissue of lies . . ." learned counsel declaims in any British courtroom drama, making the double 's' an elegant sibilant, lethal in its hiss . . . Up in that league, eh? For he had darted from a deathbed to pick up a purse, had got the girl going, and returned right away to sit on the stairs, innocence incarnate . . .

It was like an Old English poem, "sit on the stairs, innocence incarnate . . ." And it was like a bedroom farce, too.

Jill had been talking to the Emergency Squad about the arrangements. Jerome gathered that the doctor would come by in a couple of hours, on the way to his early rounds at the hospital. The funeral people would come by shortly thereafter. Then, when they had left, she would go and get her two children, get them back from the neighbor where they were spending the night, and tell them . . .

Her voice caught. But she was not ready for that, had not scheduled that kind of thing until later. She swallowed and attacked the end of the sentence, changing the inflection so that it concluded with a downward, periodic lilt, " . . . and tell them."

"You'll be all right?" the Emergency Squad chief asked.

"Oh, yes . . . And Mr. Carpenter is here," she said.

"Well, good night, then. I'm sorry there wasn't anything we could do. But there was nothing you could have done, either. When a thing like this happens, and there's a doctor right there with a forceps . . . well, that's lucky. But otherwise . . . I mean, what I'm trying to say is that you mustn't feel guilty about it. These things just happen, that's all."

"Thank you."

He touched his cap in a salute and they left.

"You don't mind staying with me for a while, do you?" she asked Jerome. "I shouldn't like to be . . . all alone."

"Of course I don't mind."

"I'll . . . I'll make some tea."

"I'll do it," Jerome offered.

"No, it will be good for me to have something like that to do with my hands. I'll make tea and you'll sit with me. All right?"

"Fine."

They went out to the kitchen and Jerome sat and watched her make tea. He tried to think of things to say, but couldn't. What could there possibly be to say? But Jill talked while she worked, explaining how easy it was to make really good tea, and how she never understood about Americans being bad makers of tea as the English always claimed. "All you have to do is leave the tea bags in the water for a few minutes. If you take them out right away all you get is the color. But if you want the flavor and the body of the tea too, that takes longer. Three or four minutes. John always says . . . said, that I make really good tea."

Her slip and her correction hit Jerome in the chest. His heart pounded and his breath was shallow. That she should have to shift tenses like that . . . It was intolerable. But it was a linguistic matter. He was angry at himself for having responded to that, for having had to wait for a cue of language, for a word . . . What kind of over-specialised monster had he become? But still, it was better to be able to respond to that than not to be able to respond at all. What he wanted to do was to have the poise and confidence to go over and comfort her, take her hand, reassure her . . . But he couldn't do that. He didn't know her well enough. Silly!

So he listened as she went on, talking about England. Why England, Jerome wondered. Because it was far away? In distance and time. Because it had been happy for her there? Because it came to mind, was something to talk about? Probably.

She suggested that they could go out into the study.

"If you like," Jerome said. "Sure."

Of course she would want to go out there. She would want to be out of the house, out of the building in which John's body lay upstairs on the bed, and into another structure, separate but related, where he had done the work that was still alive. That Jerome should go with her, was, he thought, entirely proper. Let that be a lesson, he told himself. He had just been there, screwing some nameless girl . . . And now he found out it was as if he had been fucking in church. Okay, live with it, wise-ass. Swallow it down with the tea!

He was still thinking of the neatness of his having to go out there, and the outrageousness of its being him to sit with Jill out there in that room, and thinking too of walking carefully so as not to slosh the tea from the cup into the saucer as he followed Jill when he heard her say, "Oh dear! Oh, wonderful! Oh, Jerome, look!"

What? What could it be? A mistake? It had all been a dream, and there, sitting at the desk, John was sitting and working? No, not quite. But for Jill it was the next best thing. For there, under the grey plastic typewriter cover, she had found a poem.

Before Jerome could say anything, she told him, "He hadn't written a line in months. Not in months. And he was terribly down about it. But he was writing again. He'd been moving his lips this evening in that way he did sometimes when he was trying out a phrase or a line, and I knew he was working on something. I even asked him and he told me yes, he was. But I never supposed he'd got this far with it. I imagine it was to have been a surprise . . ."

"Yes, I imagine so."

What else could he have said? What, after all that, could he have told her? He had missed his chance. He had listened to her go through all that, knowing that he had missed his chance, that he should have spoken up at the first instant, and feeling each of her sentences bind the poem ever more firmly into the works of John Royle.

"It's good," she said. "Oh, I'm glad it's good. It's different from what he had been doing. A fresh start, a new direction . . . And so good!"

Now! Now it was irretrievable! Now it was hopeless! What son of a bitch could take the poem back now? Who could end that pleasure that she felt? Who would presume? He took the poem that she held out to him and pretended to read it. He didn't read it, but thought about it as he looked blankly at the words. He wished it were better. He realized suddenly that it would be judged, now, as a John Royle poem. And that would make it different. Give it a boost at the beginning, but give it a higher hurdle at the end, a more demanding standard up to which it would have to live. He wished it well.

And for himself? What the hell? Royle deserved it. Rental for the use of his study as a crib? Payment for the borrowing of Jill in his fantasyland fuck? Any of those things. A death offering. Yes, he'd like to think of it as that. But how selfish! And how irrelevant. What did he want from the poem anyway, or with the poem, or for it? That it should be read in some loony way in twenty years by a Brownsuit or by a Burton? What poet had ever dreamed of such an audience for his poem as he had now in Jill Royle? What poem had ever given anyone such pleasure, such comfort, such delight? And was that not the purpose of it all?

Let her have the piece. My piece I give unto you . . . Where was that from? One of the gospels, but which one? There was a Bible in the bookshelf, next to the desk, but Jerome could not go to look it up now. It would look peculiar, it would be misleading for him to go and read a Bible, as if in devout belief . . .

"Isn't it good!" she said. There was nothing interrogative about the sentence.

"Yes, it's good. It's . . . it's fine."

"You're not just saying so. You really think so, don't you?"

"I really think so."

"You know, John used to ask me always if I liked what he'd just written. And I'd tell him. And then he'd ask again, that way. 'You really think so? You're not just saying so?' And I would tell him that it was really good. Because he was, you know. He was a fine poet."

"I know."

"But he was never sure of it, himself. He was never sufficiently confident."

"He was never complacent."

"No."

"He was a good man," she said. And she finished her tea.

She went over to the daybed—ah, the daybed!—and stretched out. "You don't mind if I lie down, do you? It will be a long day tomorrow."

"No, I don't mind. By all means, lie down. Sleep if you can."

"I think I'll have this poem read at the funeral. Or . . . Or at the memorial service. I'm sure the college will have a memorial service at the chapel. They can read this. John would have liked that . . ."

Jerome did not answer. No answer was necessary. He drank his tea—and it was good tea. She made fine tea. Her steak was tough, maybe, but she made fine tea. Terrible idea!

She lay there on the daybed. He hoped she did not feel obliged to talk, to entertain him. He could read . . . He could look up that quotation in the Bible, that's what. And if she misinterpreted, too bad. Misinterpretation was one of the risks of life. He took the Bible from the bookcase and put it on the desk next to the typewriter, opened it and flipped pages. It sounded like a farewell, a sort of Last Supper remark. He tried the gospels in order, Matthew first, then Mark, then Luke. And, of course, it was in John. He read, "Peace I leave with you; my peace I give unto you; not as the world gives do I give to you. Let not your hearts be troubled, neither let them be afraid . . ."

It was eerie how well it worked with the homonym, with the "piece" pieced in for "peace." And the phrase after the semicolon was true enough. "Not as the world gives do I give to you . . ."

It was good to give any way at all. But fine to give this way. He was glad of the chance to have made her less uncomfortable, less unhappy.

Higher on the page, he saw another phrase; "He who does not love me does not keep my words; and the word which you hear is not mine but the Father's who sent me."

Jerome's words would be kept. And the attribution—whether to Royle or to divine inspiration and the Father—would not matter. He could live with either one.

Yes, she was asleep. Anyway, she was resting. He would rouse her a little before six. That's when the doctor would be coming. And the funeral people. Maybe he could hitch a ride back to Alumnae House with the doctor. Or with the hearse.

He checked his watch. He looked at Jill again. He wondered whether he could retype the poem, make those corrections now . . . Because if he didn't do it now, he'd never be able to do it at all. No, he didn't want to risk it. What if she woke up? Talk your way out of that, eh?

But he looked at the poem. He was surprised to find that the penultimate line was not defective, after all. It had been all right. He'd been rattled back then with Corda hovering over him, and that business about the anagrams game with his name. And the hubbub of a party was distracting. The poem was all right. He read it over.

Over the fear, the foolishness—a jay
behaving badly, as a child in church,
while the big cat crouches down before his prey . . .
Hush! But the woodpeckers rattle the trees in search
of grubs, bounce acorns on the ground the way
they always do. That blood's pulse in the throat
of the victim commands attention. They don't obey.
A green bird trills upon his idiot note
as if nothing at all were happening below.
But credit the bird-brained babbling with tact:
it fills the delicate ears, while the still bright eyes
flee to an unperturbed horizon where slow
clouds mimic random shapes and distract
so that death is an irrelevant surprise.